NOTHING BUT DUST

Sandrine Collette

NOTHING BUT DUST

*Translated from the French
by Alison Anderson*

Europa
editions

Europa Editions
214 West 29th Street
New York, N.Y. 10001
www.europaeditions.com
info@europaeditions.com

Copyright © by Editions Denoël, 2016
First Publication 2018 by Europa Editions

Translation by Alison Anderson
Original title: *Il reste la poussière*
Translation copyright © 2018 by Europa Editions

Library of Congress Cataloging in Publication Data is available
ISBN 978-1-60945-433-3

Collette, Sandrine
Nothing but Dust

Book design by Emanuele Ragnisco
www.mekkanografici.com

Cover photo SashaS/Fotolia

Prepress by Grafica Punto Print – Rome

Printed in the USA

To Jean-Michel,

joyful poet of the *bikkie*, of little rosés and the whisk broom,
tireless surveyor of the winding trails in the Morvan,
of Schopenhauer, and above all, maker of blue sky.

NOTHING BUT DUST

Because he was the youngest, his brothers had gotten into the habit of chasing him around the house on horseback when their mother wasn't watching. As soon as the twins had grown strong enough to grab him by the collar and lift him up at a gallop from astride their criollos, it became their favorite pastime. They tallied points for whoever managed to drag him to the corner of the barn, or beyond the old gray wooden outbuildings—then the dead tree, then the genista grove—before depositing him in the dust.

The little brother always saw them coming. He could hear their shouts, which they emphasized to frighten him; and the sound of the horses breaking into a gallop, the iron shoes striking the ground and coming nearer, causing his stomach to flutter, as if the earth were trembling beneath his feet; and of course the brothers, perched high in their saddles, thought it was funny, their shrill laughter drowning the clatter of hooves.

He froze, one arm in the air, his hand still holding the stick he'd been using to stir up waves in the drinking trough; never mind if the water was dirty. He stopped dead like a field mouse in the steppe, alerted too late by the rush of buzzards' wings overhead; he, too, with a panicked look in his eyes, praying that his ears and mind and instinct had deceived him; but then they always fell upon him with only a few strides, raptors swooping on their prey, leaning from their mad horses. Standing there in the middle of the rear courtyard, the little brother did not have time to reach the kitchen, where his mother was chopping, carving, rushing around: he'd barely learned to run when it all began. Once or twice he had tried to call out to her, he thought he could see her stern figure behind the windowpane, grinding meat or slicing vegetables, focused and angry as if she were slaughtering them, but she didn't hear him, didn't see him, even the day he managed to bang on the window before Mauro carried him off—or maybe it was because she was so uninterested in his fate that he preferred not to think about it. Truth is, the only thing she did do was give him a thrashing afterwards, shouting that she was fed up with him wetting his pants. And the brothers laughed as they looked on, and shrieked, *Bed wetter! Bed wetter!* while she obliged him to run bare-bottomed behind her to go get changed, tossing his soiled trousers into the laundry basket with a gesture of furious exasperation.

In his mind he already knew that he would never escape from their terrifying pursuit; but he tried, against all odds, until the very last moment, even in vain, even when he felt his brothers' fingers against his skin as they clutched his shirt collar. He waddled on his short little legs, desperately stuck where he was when he should have been jumping and leaping, and he whimpered in terror, which only made Mauro and Joaquin weep with laughter. In the beginning the twins, who were six years older, would join forces to harpoon him from on horseback, grabbing him by the shoulder from either side. It was only after they turned ten that they had the strength required to hunt him individually, and by then Steban, two years their junior, had joined in too, eager to have his turn at the sport.

Half strangled, his feet pedaling in the void, Rafael watched as the landscape rushed by at dizzying speed; he was being shaken like an old sack, deafened by the criollos' frenetic race. Already defeated, his eyes half-closed in fear, he could sense the grass and bushes hurtling by, the pebbled path a blur beneath his legs, which he lifted up to keep from being twisted or caught beneath the horses' bellies, and he quietly prayed that the brothers would not drop him. His cheeks were often sprayed with gravel, and he went home with bruises. His mother would berate him: *What the devil have you been playing at this time.*

One day he tripped as he was trying to escape, and his brothers missed him, because he was too low down. So he tried this again every time thereafter, sprawling his full length the moment they began the chase, scrambling to his feet now and again to make his way, between falls, back to the house. The horses would come to a sudden, almost squatting stop, pivot, and head back for him. Down he'd fall again. Sometimes he was struck by a hoof, but only out of awkwardness, because the criollos did their best to avoid him, reluctant to trample on the little form huddled beneath them—and the furious brothers would spur them back, kicking their flanks as they shouted insults, asshole, sissy, piece of shit, to be a man you have to be strong and stand up straight.

He was four years old.

The next season the twins had become more agile, and they scooped him up from the ground the way you pick up a ball, they arched against the girth of the saddle, which enabled them to lean down to him.

And the year after that, they fought over him during the chase. Whoever of the three of them managed to catch him would now have to fend off the attacks of the other two, making his horse dance from side to side, yanking at the bit, digging the spurs into its side to make it go faster. And if the little brother did not want to fall he would hold himself rigid, clinging to a leg or hanging from a strap, because the brothers needed both arms to fight among themselves. And as he heard them panting as they fought each other off, he swung against the horse's shoulder, his fingers slipping over its damp mane, until at the last minute he was seized by whichever brother had gained the upper hand. And then the chase resumed, over two yards or twenty, and it all started again. Steban regularly managed to outflank the twins before they realized it, and he'd nab the little brother from them over the last hundred yards; they were so unused to being surprised by the half-wit that it put them off their stride every time.

As the months went by the falls were ever harder. Joaquin had found a spiny thicket on the other side of the stream that he baptized *Rafael's house*—he even wrote it in clumsy letters on a wooden sign, placed at the edge, in a spot where he was sure his mother would never go, because otherwise she'd be bound to ask questions and make a fuss. But this far away they were safe, and with his brothers he crossed the stream at a gallop and cried, "Ready to drop the rat in its burrow?"

As for the little brother, he held his breath, not to swallow any water while they crossed the stream, and he curled up in a ball as they tossed him into the dense branches of the thicket. He would go home with a bloody nose, one eye half-closed, or his cheeks scraped by the thorns where he'd fallen. Sometimes he had to walk for an hour to get home, because his brothers took him further and further away. *You've got time*, they crowed, *you don't do any work!* So he sniveled the mixture of blood and snot, trying not to cry in front of them, and he watched them swing their horses round and set off again. He took the path back the way they'd brought him, through the pastures, along the green and orange fields shining in the sun in an expanse of dry grasses and fissured stone. An immense prairie—the steppe, said the mother with pride and a sort of resigned respect—and where it ended the *mesetas* began, with their rocky plateaus and paths of wind-burned scree. On these prairies of close-cropped grass, barbed-wire fences marked off the thousands of acres where the herds wandered tirelessly, searching for food and covering mile upon mile in order to survive. Moorland as far as the eye could see, arid and flat, so dry even the trees had deserted it, to be replaced, somehow, by a few scrawny thickets you'd think could not possibly survive with so little soil.

The forests kept their distance, far to the west beyond the plateaus, where altitude reclaims its rights, invisible from the plain. In the little brother's imagination, these were magical places, carpeted with grasses taller than a horse, vast expanses of inconceivable trees one's gaze could not contain, blocked at every instant by tree trunks and foliage. One day, when he was grown up, he would go and explore them. When he had his own horse. So he wiped his nose and eyes against his sleeve, leaving a damp brown streak on the dirty cloth. He tried to spit the way his brothers did, but most of the time his saliva dribbled down his chin and he had to wipe it again with his shirt, furious that he couldn't even manage this one simple thing. Joaquin had promised him he'd learn the day he got his first hair in his butt; every evening he inspected himself painstakingly, disappointed when he saw nothing coming. Often as he made his way home he would join his hands in front of his overalls in the hopes that someone or something would hear his prayers and make him into a solid, hairy fellow, who'd spend half his life on horseback and be able to spit farther than anyone. His gaze swept birdlike over the plateau, encompassing the plain, embracing the world. And the world came back to where it had begun, and it wore the face of the mother's lands.

Eight Years Later
THE MOTHER

E very morning the mother gazes out at this indigent
steppe as she opens the shutters, pausing in her gesture
the time it takes to locate the dogs sitting behind the
door, whimpering as they wait for their meal. A paltry domain,
worth less than its name written on a wooden sign; but it
belongs to her, and her alone, and the pride of owning these
vast lands goes some way toward consoling her for the desolate
vision of earth scorched by wind and drought. The mother
feels the tired pride swell in her guts, because not everyone can
say the same, out here, that they are landowners, and she has
forgotten that the domain came to her from her man, however
much of a bastard he might have been. There are evenings
when she reminds herself that she came from a family of
wretches with neither land nor fortune, and that everything
seemed to point to a future of working herself to the bone in
the service of others, and she grumbles and ruminates, finds a
thousand things wrong with the steppe she's been left with—
well, that was the least she was owed, after all the misery she
endured year after year. There is no room for gratitude in the
mother's life: what she has, she deserves. And no doubt she
would have deserved better, if only she'd happened upon a different man, but there too, she'd been unlucky, the man was the
way he was, as were these meager lands, where her livestock
have a hard time finding sustenance—cattle, sheep, and horses
alike. Every winter, sick with hunger, exhausted by the cold
winds, the weakest ones perish. And yet, to keep up their

resistance, she says, she never feeds the livestock fodder—but in fact, it's because the crops are inadequate.

Sometimes the mother does not know which way to turn, on her estancia, between the corn that will grow wherever the earth makes an effort, the hay that doesn't grow fast enough, and the animals that sell poorly. In San León they've been saying for years that people ought to stop raising cattle—if anyone still is. They're not worth it anymore. *And what else?* shouts the mother. *How long have we been bowing our heads?* But she has it in her blood, a sort of shameful defeat, with her family of farmhands and servants, and even on her husband's side, the grandfather had to capitulate when the cereal men and the bigwig stockbreeders moved into the pampas, driving people like them further into the hinterland. They withdrew once again when the railroad came. And yet the markets had never been better, at last Europe was accessible. The first refrigerated ship landed in 1876, and they'd been exporting Argentine beef to France ever since—one hundred and ten days, the passage, and when the ship arrived, there was red meat beneath a layer of fat as if it had been slaughtered only the day before, a proper miracle.

But naturally this was only a boon to those who could buy huge estates, and organize themselves in firms, and set up industrial farms and transport networks; indeed, the small-scale landowners are bound to disappear. Herds of tens of thousands of beasts and endless fields of crops have already driven them from the pampas, and in the plains of Patagonia where they have sought refuge, the cattle are thin and struggle to put on weight. If you want to survive out here, you have to accept your fate: only the sheep will make it. So they all turned to sheep. Nothing else, and they can't really complain, because wool has been in demand in recent years, with England scooping everything up for its industry, tens of thousands of tons. The mother spits on the ground. She produces wool, obviously, she has to, and it's not going too badly; but she would die sooner than she'd give up her Angus and her Shorthorns, or even the handful of Charolaises she paid top dollar for—even if it means eating every last one herself, if she doesn't find a buyer; if they prefer the pink, fatty meat the intensive farming gives, and which will snuff them out before the second generation. And those machines they're talking about, to replace the horses in the fields, she couldn't care less: they'll never survive the ordeal of the steppe. Does anyone listen to her, for Christ's sake? They'll never make it this far.

Obstinately clinging to her fierce convictions, she counts the pregnant heifers and with her sons she prepares the land, planning, plowing, mending fences as if nothing could ever change. She does not see why she should do things any other way. She doesn't know how to do anything else, she came to her father-in-law's house at the age of sixteen. For her, things are immutable.

And yet the years do go by, and change, and she ought to realize this, if for no other reason than watching her sons grow up. Sometimes she stops what she is doing for a moment to observe them, hard at work. Mauro is a full head taller than his twin, he's carrying beams, repairing the barn, he's unusually robust even though he did turn eighteen in the spring, it's as if all the family's strength poured into that one boy. Joaquin and Steban are holding the planks, driving in the nails and putting away the fodder, and freeing the trailer from the mud where it got stuck. The little brother is running all around, waving his arms and chattering like a magpie, as always. He puts his hands on a pitchfork or a hammer to help, pressing, driving in, cleaning. And while the mother had a devil of a time getting them to sit still on a chair long enough to teach them the rudiments of writing, now they know how to read and count, just so they don't get in a muddle when they go to the grocery store or the tobacconist's. Even though it took her years, where their learning was concerned the mother never gave up, wielding threats and slaps to wake them when they nodded off over their books or their figures—and watching how after every lesson they would scatter across the steppe, like birds kept too long in a cage.

And during all that time it took to ram something into their heads, the world was busy changing again, the world and her kids, even the youngest, Rafael, who is still skinny but has shot up like a bad seed, with his chestnut hair and fair skin. He must have gotten that from his father, from some extinct generation, whatever the gossips might say, wondering, as for sure they wondered, when they saw the infant the day he was baptized. But the mother has a clear conscience, she of all people knows damn well who allowed him to have his way with her, and plenty often. And when she looks at her last born, such a handsome boy, she can't help but feel a surge of pride, all the same, she's the one who made him, that little brother nobody wanted, who came too late, never mind, he has her smile, from when she used to smile; it makes her uneasy.

Of course in those early years, when he'd come home all beaten up nearly every day, it was the older boys getting their revenge. They wanted to go on being the three brothers, like when their father was alive. They would have left this fourth brother to be eaten alive on the plain if they weren't so afraid of her, the mother, the rage in her eyes, her ferocious thrashings. Of course she could have done more to protect him, but it is not in her nature to console. You don't make a boy if you cuddle him every time he gets a scratch. Let them sort it out amongst themselves: it had been the same for her, she had two brothers and, a very long time ago, a sister who died from a fever at the age of five. You have to have grit to live out here, it's a hardscrabble life. She'd been raised on thrashings, and so would her kids. So she never said a thing, even now that beatings have replaced the chases on horseback and

Rafael has taken to keeping to himself, like some undesirable beast in a herd, with his dozens of little scars on his cheeks and arms. To avoid his older brothers while they're rubbing down their horses in the stable at night, he carries on working outside. He joins them at the supper table, soundlessly, creeping in, catlike. The shadow of a bruise dusts his cheeks. Steban goes on eating without looking up, unspeaking, far away from them, as always. The twins snigger into their plates. Suddenly fall silent when the mother turns to them, looking furious, her hand ready to fly with a slap. She hates them when they're like this.

She hates them all the time, all of them. But that's life, too, she had no choice. Now that they're here. Sometimes she reckons she should have drowned them at birth, the way you do with kittens you don't want; but there it is, you'd have to do it right away. Afterwards it's too late. It's not that you get attached: it's just no longer the moment, that's all. Afterwards, they look at you. Their eyes are open. And the mother really did think about it, but she missed her chance. So on days when she cannot stand the sons anymore, she takes revenge just by thinking that she could have done it. They were within her grasp. All she had to do was drop them in the water. And they will never know just how much they owe her, even the simple good fortune of being alive. When she hears them sniggering at the table, she remembers how each one of them was born, her doubts, her temptations. She bites her tongue to keep from speaking—of course it would be such a relief, but she has to hold that card back for a special day, a real day of hatred, black and deep.

So she throws her plate to the little brother and shoots a nasty look at the twins, and merely shouts: "Are you goin' to leave him alone or what!"

Liars that they are, like the father who abandoned them

long ago, they nod their heads, swearing blind that they'll leave him alone.

The day after the father disappeared, Mauro and Joaquin led the grass-fed calves to the pastures in the Monte Alto; Steban fed the lambs, changed the rabbits' litter, he was unwell that morning, with bags under his eyes as if he'd partied all night long, at the age of four, now what.

"What's the matter with you?" the mother had said.

He'd shaken his head, not answering, scattering the dried grasses through the rabbit hutches, staring vacantly at the grass, and eventually the mother came over for a closer look. But there was nothing. She shook him by the shoulder.

"Well? Is it because your dad's gone?"

His child's gaze in hers. A questioning, immense. And something else, too, but she hadn't noticed, didn't want to know, something that looked like sorrow, and that was no business of hers, and even Steban himself, what did he really know about his father? Was he certain that his absence really deserved sorrow? Should she tell him? She waved her hand in annoyance. He was still staring at her and she was smart enough to know that he wouldn't let her go until she explained, but that had never been her strong point, words, not for her or her sons, and Steban had to make do with the little she gave him as she held her arm out and pointed toward the road.

"You see that road? He went that way. To the end, the very end. You can't see him anymore. He's not coming back."

The boy had looked. And then he turned toward the stable and pointed at the criollos, and his mother felt her heart sink. Then immediately reasoned with herself. Nipped it in the bud. With her black eyes crushing Steban, eyes like a certainty, like a threat.

"He went on his own. He didn't take a horse."

The older boys got the same explanation. As far as the mother was concerned, the chapter on the father was closed. She had burned any clothes that could no longer be put to use, and a few forgotten items, she'd buried his dinner bowl and metal tumbler behind the house, as a sign of repudiation. She'd erased him down to the last trace, making him disappear from the world, the unworthy man, the reveler, the coward. An absolute blackout in their life.

Of course the days grew longer, suddenly exhausting when the hay season arrived, then the shearing. But by then the father'd been gone for months, and in the valley everyone knew. A few guys showed up to lend a hand in exchange for a little money—they must have been hard up, for they sure weren't paid much. Mauro and Joaquin learned to shear the ewes with them. At the age of six they were the men of the house and they played their role conscientiously. In the region, the shepherds respected their efforts in silence. No one repeated what was on everyone's lips in San León: that the mother wouldn't last long on her own, and that her land would soon be up for sale.

That's because they had no idea of the spite that gnawed away at the old lady, deep in her belly. With a man or without one life was the same, the usual hardship—it was so normal that it no longer hurt. And besides, the mother never got up in the morning complaining about the ferocity of the world, because she'd never known anything else. She didn't expect anything better. The day the father left she made note of the fact the same way she made note of the cooler temperatures or the sun's shorter passage across the sky when autumn was coming. Nor did she run to town to inform everyone of her imminent poverty; she had no one to talk to. Would that have brought the father back? It'd surely be better if it didn't.

So one day she found herself obliged to take off her apron,

saddle up Rufian, and make the journey to San León to buy bags of seed—spring was coming—and a supply of spirits, and to pay her outstanding debts. After her errands she went into the bar and sat down heavily on a chair, ignoring the astonished gazes shot her way, banging her fist on the table to order a Fernet. That was when the rumor got started, and young Trabor went out to tell his brother to go right away for the banker Gomez, who dealt with everyone here, because something was afoot.

Gomez sat down at the table with her. He snapped his fingers, and Alejo brought him a glass. He drank to her health.

"What brings you here, little sister?"

An hour later, the news spread through the entire village. The abandoned mother had ridden away again, holding her belly with one hand and her sacks of supplies with the other, which they'd insisted on giving her. She also promised to send Mauro when her waters broke. But she never sent for anyone, in the end, and the little brother was born in the month of December at two o'clock in the morning, by the grace of God, said the priest, because they all got off lightly. What he didn't say was that a sad twist of fate would surely have been preferable, because the mother hardly needed a fourth mouth to feed, and more than once she'd worried about the future, with this little brother coming at the worst possible time, smack during birthing season—but in this case, she meant her sheep. However, the damage was done, and the mother had given birth on her own, on her feet. At daybreak the brothers found the newborn baby in his cradle. They asked no questions, went no closer. The mother, somewhat pale, served them dried beef with eggs and a mug of coffee, and assigned the work for the day. She herself rearranged a few things in the house, then after breakfast she went to plant two hundred feet of potatoes, with the little brother bundled on her back.

In the evening Steban noticed that the newcomer cried a lot, but as usual, he said nothing.

"Don't look at him," scolded the mother when she caught him staring into the baby basket. "You'll bring him bad luck."

And he turned away.

With the father gone, the mother closed the house to visitors. It was not like they'd ever had a lot of visits, and now there were even fewer. From time to time an uncle, particularly in the beginning, to show that they looked after their kin. More often, a buyer for cattle or wool, or a breeder who wanted to negotiate access for his beasts to graze on the mother's lands— she earned a few more pennies that way, renting out her meager pastureland. But most of the time the days passed and no one but she or her sons ever crossed the threshold. Even when they ordered her to put the boys in school she didn't budge. They weren't about to come out and get them with a rifle in their hand, now, were they.

So, for the first time in years, she had peace. Even if it was at the cost of backbreaking labor: she accepted it.

When she'd married the father and come to live on the estancia, she knew that her husband's old man lived there, too. What she didn't know was that he'd last so long. In San León everyone had assured her that the old geezer wasn't long for this world, given the quantity of alcohol he consumed. Drunk from morning to night—as soon as she arrived she could see that it was true. But as for his allotted time, that was another matter altogether. The twins were born three years later, and the old man was still tippling to his heart's content. Then Steban, two years after that, on whom the old man spilled a glass of whiskey, stumbling as he went to view the newborn swaddled in his crib. He drank up half of all their income. Sometimes the mother said something to the father, and they had it out. The next day she had a bruise on her cheek, a

swollen eye, and nothing had changed. Worse than that: the
father had begun drinking, too. Sprawled across the table he
filled one glass after the other, telling incoherent stories to the
old man's approval. They lured each other into tales only they
could understand, in their drunkard's dialect, and the brothers
looked at them askance, fascinated and vaguely disapproving,
until eventually the mother took the bottle away, shouting that
that was enough. Some evenings there were fights, because the
men clung to their glasses, and they bellowed insults the boys
did not understand.

"Go to bed!" roared the mother, and they ran straight to
their rooms, and for a long time they listened to the shouts and
insults coming down the corridor, the sounds of bodies clash-
ing, thumping.

So when at last the old man died, the night the twins cele-
brated their fifth birthday, the mother felt the relief spread all
the way through her, to the marrow of her bones. A sort of evil,
radiant joy, which could have set her dancing had the fear of
being seen by the father not prevented her. She'd found the
vile old man lying stiff on the floor next to the woodstove, with
an injury to his temple. A nasty fall, which he wouldn't have
had if he hadn't drunk so much, she told the father, who was
weeping his eyes out. That same night she'd let her husband
back into her bed, to console him.

But the evil was there now and her man, on his own now,
went on drinking for the both of them. He would put a glass
down in front of him and pour as if the old man still had his
ass glued to the other chair. And in fact it seemed to the
mother as if the old man must be laughing all the way from the
hell he'd surely landed in, that swine of a man who'd almost
ruined them and was still hard at his devil's work. When she
wiped down the table in the evening, using vinegar to remove
the smell of alcohol encrusted in the wood, she ruminated,
champing at the bit. She'd waited eight years for the old man

to croak; but if she had to put up with a drunk of a husband for the rest of her life, she wouldn't make it. He was working less and less, searching for the bottles she hid with the obstinacy of a hunting dog on the trail of some wounded game. Mauro and Joaquin often found him at the edge of a pasture, vomiting bile and brandy. He'd jabbed a horse, trying to shoe it, leaving it incapacitated for two weeks. He screamed at the mother every day. And things weren't getting better.

And yet that night when the mother had struck the first blow, regardless of all the spite she'd accumulated and the urgency that had gone into it, she did not think the father would die of it.

She'd found him in the barn, collapsed in the hay, an oil lamp at his feet. In his right hand was the bottle of spirits, nearly empty. She'd screamed, because of the alcohol and because of the flame, she'd frightened him gesticulating like that, was how he put it to her afterwards: that was why he had knocked over the fuse. In a few seconds, the fire had caught in the fodder, a terrifying vision, the smoke running all along the bales and its warm breath already upon them. The mother rushed over to pick up an old blanket and tossed it on the burning hay to smother the flames, slapping over and over at the fire that escaped to the left, to the right, burning the skin on her wrists and arms. When she collapsed next to the father, in shock, but with the building safe, he grunted in a thick voice that when she'd burst into the barn he thought she was a she-devil. And he added, "You just never bloody leave me alone."

That was when she began to hit him.

Maybe it had been smoldering for years, this rage that flared up all on its own, without her thinking about it, this fury suddenly taking hold of her, enough to make you wonder if that was all she'd been waiting for, and the father whimpering there beneath her, the man with nothing to say, just silent, and she hit him again and again. And maybe it was the blow she gave him in the end when she kicked him in the throat with the tip of her boot, the rage at seeing her life destroyed, her sheep and cattle sold for bottles of hooch year after year: she only stopped when he was no longer moving.

No longer moving, ever.

In the middle of the night she harnessed Rufian and slung the father's body over the saddle—he was heavy, she had to start over four times before she got him to stay up there where she could lash him on properly. She led him out to the swamp, the only one anywhere around, at the foot of the little chain of mountains, where the will-o'-the-wisps dance, where no one dares to go. The mother knew that was all nonsense, and she knew of no better spot to get rid of the body. Because it didn't take her long to think it through: she didn't want to go to prison or lose the estancia, or even the sons whom she'd now have to raise on her own, including the one who was on the way, who'd stopped her bleeding two months ago now. A free woman, that was what she was—she'd never been more free, and the thought of getting herself locked up at this very moment when the horizon was at last opening to her seemed an unacceptable injustice. She spent the early hours of the night working out her plan. She would say that the father suddenly vanished, on impulse, that he'd abandoned her and her sons, and everyone would acknowledge the fact with a pat on the shoulder to encourage her, because no one would disbelieve her. He'd been up to no good for so long. Some neighbors would try to console her by assuring her he'd be back, he wasn't such a bad fellow; she'd burst into tears, sure she'd never see him again, and in San León people would whisper that the father was a real bastard for leaving a woman who needed him so badly.

Yes, that was how it would all go, without any suspicion, without a hitch. Once she felt calm, the mother led Rufian to the middle of the swampland, trying not to think of what might be clinging to her legs, and for all that she was lifting her knees high as she walked. There was something terrifying about the swamps at night. The quagmire could hide all sorts of creatures, all sorts of traps; the moonlight mingled the territory of sky and water, gray and wan, obscured by the tree branches that were too thin and too dense, and once when the mother looked behind her to make sure the father was properly attached to the horse, the path she had come on had vanished. She would find her way: she was born here. But it made a strange impression, as if the swamp were slowly closing over her, waiting for her to unload her burden in order to snatch her and swallow her in turn. One wrong step and she'd sink in and not be able to get out again. Yet the horse was walking by her side: she had infinite faith in his instinct. She moved closer to him, and with every step the father's legs swung against her hip.

As she slid the body into the muddy sands, she spread wide his arms and legs so he'd be as flat as possible, already half hidden by the rushes. She exerted a slight pressure with the tip of her foot, the better to push him into the welcoming silt. And like a sentry who refuses to be budged, she'd planted herself further back on a patch of solid ground, regularly testing the earth with her foot to make sure it would not give way, pulling the horse forward with her. She wanted to be sure. In a low voice she rehearsed the words she would be saying in the days to come: *He's gone, he just left us, just like that, the kids and me, all alone, yes, he left, I don't know where he went, he didn't say. No, I don't think we'll see him again.*

After an hour had gone by, in the stagnant air of the swamp, the father's body was entirely buried beneath the thick grasses, and the mother knew that no one would ever find him, because the insects and foul beasts that hid in the water would get to him soon enough.

RAFAEL

T he little brother comes tearing around the bend in the road, lying close against his chestnut's mane, urging him to gallop faster. In one hand he's holding the reins. In the other, a hat. Behind him, his three brothers are snapping leather straps on their horses' flanks, yelling, but he knows it's to no avail: none of them can catch Halley. He almost lets slip a cry of wild joy—last year when he laughed too hard with his mouth wide open he swallowed a fly, and there are evenings when he can still feel the nauseating sensation of the insect's legs tickling his tongue at the back of his throat. He half turns in the saddle to look back and senses more than sees Joaquin's face, distorted with rage; he hears Mauro's hollering. Steban is right behind him, following the others in silence, the mute and passive accomplice of the wars waged among the brothers. So Rafael sits up, imperceptibly, slowing his chestnut, the horse balks and shakes his head to protest, spewing drops of foam. Rafael whispers, laying a hand on his shoulder:

"Easy, easy . . . "

Rafael laughs at the tension in the reins, the horse's anger as he refuses to calm down, thrusting his forelegs forward, gathering in his powerful hindquarters. Behind them, the pounding of hooves takes only a few seconds to come closer. Like every time, a wave of fear goes through the little brother, immediately replaced by the excitement of the chase. He waves the hat, arm outstretched, and lets out a cry, and he can hear Joaquin's roar of anger, *You fucking asshole!* and his criollo panting as it reaches Halley's stride, biting his rump. For a hundred yards or more the two horses gallop side by side, ears flattened, lips pulled back from their teeth: only the bit is keeping them from gnashing each other in the cheek. Rafael leans to the right to avoid his chestnut's furious thrusts of the neck, and he can see the reins wet with sweat, and the horse's white nose, almost pink at the corner of his mouth, where there is a gleam of steel. He drives him on, clicking his tongue, *Come on, come on*, is nearly unseated by the horse trying to rear to get away from the hand restraining him, rolling his eyes, intoxicated, exasperated. The little brother gives a sudden tug on the reins and laughs, then some slack, feels giddy with the way Halley propels himself forward now, muscles tense between the boy's thighs as if they were about to explode. Rafael feels the wind in his hair, in his eyes as they narrow against the dazzling sunlight. The wild gallop, and yet he is hardly shaken for all that; both of them are flying, like woodpeckers low to the ground about to soar skyward with a single flap of their wings. Until Mauro shoots them down with his rifle. For no good reason. For a laugh. They don't even eat them.

The horse gallops, pebbles and earth scatter beneath his hooves. How often has the little brother covered this path on foot? Just about every evening, for years, mud and twigs clinging to his trousers, his head ringing from being thrown to the ground by his brothers. He knows the path's every bend, every hole, every flying chip of gravel, from having walked back along it, over and over, after every time Mauro and Joaquin's joyful fury took him there. And even the day his mother gave him the horse, although back then he believed it would stop at last.

His horse. An endless wait, seven years, and during that time he would gaze at the mother's little herd of half-wild horses, which more often than not kept their distance from the farm. Seven years he spent observing the shapes and coats of horses so far away they were the size of ants, seven years being

sure of nothing, counting how many were missing in the
spring, counting the foals still awkward on the steppe with its
host of dangers. How could he determine which one the
mother would choose for him? When, with the twins' reluctant
assistance, she brought the dark chestnut back to the estancia,
not long before he turned seven, the little brother stood there
for a few seconds with his mouth open. From a distance he had
not seen how beautiful the criollo was. A magnificent animal,
with a slightly curving white nose, and four white stockings
that made him look as if he were dancing when he moved.
Rafael knew immediately from the way the mother was looking
at the horse and at him, the little brother, that the animal
would be his; and he'd never seen a prouder, livelier one.
He'd never seen a mane on a horse's neck ripple with such
insolent grace. The brothers were sick with rage. They said that
with such long legs the horse would stumble on the first stone,
and that the plain would get the better of his proud elegance.
His back would sag, his hindquarters would succumb to work.
Worst of all, he had a white hoof. *He won't last,* said Mauro
scornfully. *I'll give him one month before he's walking on three
legs*—and he pointed his index and middle finger at the criollo
as if holding a rifle, pretending to shoot. *Bang.* Rafael shud-
dered. He looked at the horse and thought he was admirable;
he was already getting attached. When he'd finished his chores
in the evening he sat at the edge of the paddock sighing with
impatience, calling softly to his horse. He stole crusts of bread
to give to him. Henceforth this near-black creature was his
responsibility, and he would always come first. When it came
to eating and drinking. And care. Even when the little brother
came home exhausted from the pastures, before he went to
collapse on his bed he would make sure his horse had everything he needed. And sometimes he would sleep next to him
in the stable, to breathe in his smell, and feel that soft nose
against his neck when he came begging for a caress.

On the calendar—which he could not yet read—time passed infinitely slowly. The mother had marked his birthday with a cross, not realizing he was incapable of figuring out when it was, and every morning he asked her to show him what day it was. Fed up, she stopped telling him, but he eventually grasped that you had to move one square at a time. And the cross started getting closer, magically, both near and far away, and he could feel the excitement, his stomach in knots.

Of course all through the spring Mauro, Joaquin, and even Steban went on catching him, lifting him up and passing him from hand to hand to the pounding of their horses' hooves. They threw him in among the thorny bushes with a shrill cry, bent double with laughter in their saddles. The little brother said nothing. He was waiting for his revenge, and not just a little one, the day he would fly away on his incredible criollo.

But things didn't go the way he'd planned. What he had imagined as a morning to celebrate came to a sudden end, an ordinary day like any other, an illusion, a slap in the face. The mother had given him the horse and he'd taken him out, feverish, happy, intimidated; and as he walked and trotted, he looked at the opalescent muzzle against the dark coat, his mouth opening on a deep impulse held in check. He was fascinated by how different this horse was from Jericho and Tierra, the two peaceable, rotund drudges he'd ridden up to now. Perched on the summit of the world, Rafael was jubilant, coming and going, turning round. He didn't go home. He was waiting for the moment when the chestnut would show he'd had enough and rear up; he waited patiently, in vain. He turned his back on the farm, yearning for the horizon as if it were a new departure, casting a gaze full of wonder at the sky reddening with the setting sun, the same sky as every day and at the same time so special. He let out a cry, not too loud to begin with, to be sure he wouldn't be heard, and when he'd ridden further away and was hidden behind a dried thicket, he yelled like a madman, fist raised. Then both hands reaching out to the clouds, taking in the universe all at once, drunk with the sensation of having become untouchable.

As he headed home, the brothers were waiting. On their horses, planted in a row, a good ways up from the farm, blocking the road. The little brother rode up to them, ready to join them and ride back to the house together, the four of them abreast on their spirited criollos, a fine family photograph where the only thing missing was the older boys' smiles.

"So you think this is it?" asked Joaquin.

Rafael raised his eyebrows. The time it took for Mauro's horse to bump into Halley and cause him to swerve to the side.

"We don't want you with us," said the tall twin. "We don't want some brat in the way. Got it?"

Behind him, Joaquin had drawn closer, to knock the little brother's hat from his head, then spit on the ground.

"You didn't even see me coming. You're a real shit."

He had tossed the Stetson far off, into a mud puddle, and Rafael stood in his stirrups hoping in vain that the hat would fall to one side, thinking as fast as he could what his options might be: insult them, or run away. But he didn't have time to do either, because Mauro had reached down to grab Halley's reins, shoving the chestnut and obliging him to step backwards, while Joaquin seized Rafael around the waist and hurled him to the ground. The three brothers let out a whoop of victory, circling around the little brother, almost trampling him, until finally one of the horses bumped into him and made him stumble. Then the older boys galloped off in peals of laughter, Mauro leading Halley behind him. Joaquin hollered something that Rafael didn't hear. A few seconds later there was nothing but dust, and the sound of galloping hooves, hell-bent for leather, fading into the distance.

The dust, settling.

And then silence.

In the end, nothing changed that day.

So Rafael will be like those solitary eagles who never get attached, indifferent to their isolation, hiding in their inaccessible nests. One of those wild beasts that crawl through the swamps avoiding their fellow creatures, reaching their burrow with the prey they've torn from sky or earth for sole companion. Neither the fact of turning seven nor the horse had mended the rift separating him from the other sons. He is not the fourth son of a family: from that day on he knew that nothing could change the fact. He threw in the towel.

So Rafael grows up with that wound inside him, and with every insult he forms his scar tissue, and he licks his wounds for hours on end. Gradually he learns to curb the urge to beg the others to let him be a part of the family. He cuts himself off from his brothers. He keeps them from his territory, however wretched it might be: he works alone. Out of the way, all the time. Even when they are together with the mother for dinner, he moves his chair to one side, leaves a void. Steban is always next to him, impassive and taciturn, a sort of screen, or relay, between him and the twins' violence.

In the morning he whistles to the dogs before going to check the cattle, to look for sickly calves, or ewes about to give birth. Along with the horse, they are his only close companions. From the kitchen the mother hears him calling.

"One! Three!"

Yapping in response, the clatter of claws across the stone in the courtyard. The mastiffs come running, leaping. The little brother grabs them by the scruffs of their necks, almost lifts them off the ground, kisses them. Ends up cuffing them if they try to bite, out of jealousy or excitement. He mounts Halley and calls again, "One, Three! *Vamos!*"

Fastened to a chain, Two whimpers. One of the dogs is

always left behind on the farm, just in case. And anyway, right now he's too young to keep up with the others. He has replaced the old Two, the one they had before, who died gored by a cow. A few days after the accident the mother went to get the puppy from a neighbor whose bitch had had a litter. She named him after his predecessor, the way she'd always done.

Since childhood the mother has always had three dogs, and they've always been called One, Two, and Three. She gets new dogs as old age and death require. She says that this way she doesn't mix up their names. But sometimes she is referring to a dog from the past, and mixes it up with the living. She forgets. She waves her hand. It doesn't matter.

The little brother takes the dogs along.

Three nips at Halley's tail. Cautiously. One day when he wasn't fast enough the horse broke one of his fangs with a kick of his hoof, and the dog now has a lopsided grin as he waits, tongue lolling, for Rafael's orders regarding the ewes.

All day long they inspect the plains, sheltering themselves from the sun or the westerly winds. The animals no longer even look up when they arrive. The horse, the dogs, the little brother: they form a part of their landscape, their smells, the voices they recognize.

When they ride off for two days, they go as far as the first plateaus. From up there, on land so arid that even the stony ground cracks open, Rafael observes worlds overlapping. Dry steppe scattered with twisted thickets, alongside winding streams kept from watering the earth by the rocky terrain. There are few trees. And most of them are stunted, ornery shrubs, even if here and there a *caldén* or sycamore stands out. Virgin land untouched by the hand of man—if you forget the thousands of miles of barbed wire fencing in the estancias. With his hand pointing toward those infinite enclosures, the little brother counts and murmurs, organizes, plans how plots will be changed, herds divided depending on whether they are to be shorn or sold. He dreams of riding further.

The mother won't let him. Only Mauro and Joaquin can go far away. The year Rafael turns eleven, the twins leave for eight whole weeks on a *puesto* to the far reaches of the domain, to inspect and treat a herd of sheep. The little brother is sick with envy. He pictures them living like kings in the wooden shack, laughing their heads off as they drink their maté together, free, finally free. Every day when he jumps down from his horse for lunch, opening his satchel as Three looks at him imploringly, he invents new spaces, transforms the plain into forests and valleys. He sets off down unfamiliar trails and peoples them with lakes, pumas, and immense plants, he is lulled by a delicate music, humming sounds that cause the disconcerted dogs to tilt their heads to the side. He is restless, crushed by the length of time that keeps him at home, disgusted by the smell of the ewes, the wool he has to bag every evening after the older boys have finished shearing. He comes home late, his mother shakes him.

"What's wrong with you, dawdling like this, don't you know we've been waiting for you?"

She shoves him toward the barn.

When he heads back to the farm at nightfall, the effluvia of wool seeping into his sinuses, he doesn't even stop in the kitchen to eat.

Suddenly Halley pulls away with a bound, cutting short the last bend before they reach the house. The little brother is one with him, lying close against his long neck, parting the mane from before his eyes as if it were his own hair. Of the four sons, he is the best horseman. That is why the mother entrusts him more and more frequently with watching the animals, for this, and because she can send him on his own, since he never asks for his brothers to go with him. The other three stay behind and work at the farm. In the beginning Mauro followed him on horseback, stirrup against stirrup as far as the big gate. A terrifying silence, of the kind that comes before a storm. His brutal gaze upon Rafael, on the rifle strapped to the saddle—as if he were about to grab it and take aim. Shoot. *Bang.* The little brother remembers the flights of sparrows, thousands of birds in the sky, thousands of voices chirruping and whistling as if the angels had begun to sing. And suddenly, a first one falling. And a second. Then three, then ten. The cloud of cheeping veers off, abruptly, changing direction to escape the lead shots, fleeing southward.

Bang.

Mauro hates birds.

He also hates the little brother, who showed up when he wasn't wanted, his very presence annoys him.

But he never reached for his rifle. After a few weeks had gone by, he stopped going along with him.

"Giddyup!" shouts Rafael.

In only a few strides Halley is on his own, in the lead. He pulls away, to the cries of his rider, lengthens his stride, curves his back. The little brother closes his eyes. He won't open them again until he feels the horse's slight hesitation when he crosses the channel, the nuance in his gallop.

He stops by the water trough. Has time to turn around and face Joaquin, who is crimson with rage, then he tosses his hat into the water.

"Again!" he cries, a broad smile spreading across his face. "You're really nothing but a shit."

STEBAN

What you gonna d-do, later?"
Sitting tall in his saddle, singling out the grass-fed
calves he'll have to separate from their mothers, out
of the corner of his eye Steban can see that Rafael has blinked
in response to his question and is frowning. The little brother
turns to look at him. It's amazing how whenever the half-wit
says something, which is rare, the others give him a sidelong
glance. You'd think that he's not the one talking, that he has
something written on his face, which is why they're all surprised if he opens his mouth, if he gets half a sentence out
without breaking it off. And yet he says plenty of things, however stingily, if they only knew—but he blurts them out in
silence, articulates them without making a sound, and the
twins burst out laughing when they see his lips fluttering in
vain while deep inside he's murmuring, so that no one can
hear: *Stupid bastards.* It's because he never says anything that
the older boys have gotten into the habit of calling him the
mute or, more frequently, the half-wit; and he can sense it in
Rafael's gaze, too, the condescension, the pity and disgust. And
yet they're going to have to support each other, the two of
them, the half-wit and the little brother, and they both know
why, although they don't speak about it, they erase the images
from inside their eyes by rubbing their eyelids.

Probably, when he was little, before Rafael was born,
Steban had hoped deep down that the twins would accept him,
but back then they already rode ahead of him as if they were a

single being, forgetting him along the way, shaking him off in the steppe. Until that memorable night when everything inside him turned upside down. The next day he had almost stopped talking, and the divide between himself and Mauro and Joaquin had widened, and with it came their mockery, their scorn. Then very soon afterward Rafael arrived. In the beginning Steban had sealed a sort of tacit agreement with his older brothers, all three of them against that little thing that had made their workload heavier, because the mother spent much of her time with it, not that it needed that much attention, but it was always too much, and they wished it'd never been born. But things had changed, and alliances with them; Steban didn't grow closer to the little brother because he liked him, but out of pragmatism. Because everything else had failed. The twins rejected him, insulted him, and in the end they used him. As for the mother, there was no counting on her. He couldn't even talk to her. Because who knew what might happen then.

Rafael has the same suffering deep inside him, and that is why Steban is forcing his way in, obliging him to look at him, answer him. In his question, in the way he has of not taking his eyes off him, he is trying to convince Rafael that if they join forces they'll be stronger. But despite the need, he can understand his reluctance to have to count on someone like him, Steban, with his look of stupor and his mouth always open onto silence, honestly, if he was in Rafael's shoes, he'd be disappointed too, he'd curse the heavens for being so unlucky. To team up with Mauro or Joaquin, yes, that would make sense; they were brutes, but they were solid. But when it came to Steban . . . There are days he can't stand his own presence, he'd like to scream to be left alone, he hunches up his shoulders and lets his arms hang by his side, he is mute, overwhelmed by the fears rising inside him.

Next to him, the little brother is still thinking about his question, and eventually he shrugs.

"Dunno. What about you?"

"I'll l-leave."

"And go where?"

"Dunno. Somewhere . . . they're not."

He juts his chin out, indicating Mauro and Joaquin as they gallop over to the cattle, shouting loudly to annoy the young bulls. And then he turns to look in the direction of the house, no longer visible. And adds: "Somewhere . . . she's not."

He knows that the little brother won't understand his last words, just his inquisitive look, the time it takes to show he's listening, and already his attention has turned to the animals, which have begun mooing, or the dust from the twins' horses, and he's dying to follow them. And at that moment Steban realizes, too, that he is on his own, now and always, because he alone witnessed the mother walking away that night, with the father lying across the saddle, and he alone saw her come back hours later, without him. No one noticed the dark red stain on Rufian's flank, a stain Steban stared at for days, until the dust and the rain got the better of it and every last trace of the father had disappeared. The father ran away. Maybe it seemed like that to others! But Steban never spoke about it, not even to his brothers. He's convinced that if he said anything the mother would take him off in the middle of the night too. He doesn't know where. Doesn't know what would happen. Just that you don't come back. To make sure he won't give himself away, that the words won't escape his lips, he has stopped talking. Nights on end he's been banging his head against the wall of his room, telling himself to keep quiet, not say a thing, never answer. Just to look and to clench his teeth, because he cannot forget the sound of the horse's hooves, like a dark presage in the gloom, that slow plodding of hooves that even now, twelve years later, turns his blood to ice whenever he hears it, what if it were to happen again. Maybe when Rufian dies he will take the fear with him.

Maybe the fear will vanish if he can leave the estancia.

But who will want anything to do with a boy the others have always referred to as *the half-wit*?

"Shall we go?"

The little brother's quivering voice makes him open his eyes. Sometimes he looks at them, the three brothers, and the mother, and the dogs and the cattle, and it's enough to make him burst into tears, because something inside him murmurs that there's nothing to be done, that he is shackled to this life. If he wants to leave he'll have to be like one of those hares caught in a trap that gnaws at its own paw to get free, never knowing if it will stop bleeding, because in that moment it's not a matter of life or death, but just of getting away. But that's another thing Rafael won't understand, and it's useless to try and explain. So Steban falls silent again, pulls the suffering deep inside, and gives the nod of his head the little brother was waiting for; the horses set off, straight ahead.

They ride down the slope to join the twins. Within a few yards the gallop of their horses and the wind rushing over them rouse them and make them laugh. Rafael lets out a joyful cry, he's already forgotten Steban's question, he's breathing in the air as if he could sense the animals' mood upon it. Steban out-flanks him, annoys him, nudges his own mount's shoulder against Halley's, and the little brother shrieks and laughs, he's never afraid when he's up there in the saddle, and he pulls away, rides off, comes back, and even Steban can feel a faint twinge of envy seeing him whirl around the way he does on his criollo, as if they were one, and then he says, after checking in his mind that there's not a single dangerous word, *Let's get, get to work now.*

Ahead of them is a plain, three hundred hectares, and at least a hundred steers they have to round up for a fattener. A godsend for the mother, who gave her orders to her sons this morning with a smile—something so rare that they all took notice. To be sure, the sale means the herd will be reduced by over half. But for all the mother fusses and carries on about not selling her cattle, she said yes right away, because she can tell she's not going to be able to fatten them up. One day she too will have only sheep left, she knows it, even though it's gut-wrenching, a loss of nobility. She'll end up producing only wool. Like everyone else.

Steban and Rafael catch up with the twins, ride close behind them when Mauro whistles and waves them on. They've all got their gazes riveted on the Angus, they ride side by side, exchanging a few words or a joke. A strange truce comes over them when it's time to herd the cattle, their hatred and hidden pacts fade away, they all look intently in the same direction. Even the way they look at Steban seems to lose its arrogance, and Mauro yells orders without anger, without disdain, just get the work done, round them up, take them away, follow some sort of animal instinct. And the dogs circle around the sons, dash over to the herd, their eyes on the stragglers.

"Call the dogs back," Mauro tells the little brother. "It's too soon. They're going to piss them off."

Progressively they move apart, the twins restraining the bulk of the group in the middle of the pastures, keeping the playful animals from getting away. Steban and Rafael go after the loners. For two hours, crossing the immense plain, they approach the solitary steers, scold them, drive them toward the others. And set off again. Start all over. They bring them back in bunches, in small numbers; sometimes it takes the two of them to force a stubborn young bull, and the jumpy horses dodge the horns sweeping the air. Rafael says, "We'll have to keep an eye on this one, he's a nasty piece of work."

Then immediately laughs.

"No we won't, he's going off to be fattened. That makes one less who's got it in for us."

And Steban nods, mindful of the creature's bobbing head,

snaps his whip if the bull gets testy, holds out his arm to send the little brother around to the left side, or to the right, or behind. Last season his criollo was jabbed by a nervous male, and he can feel the horse's reticence when the animal turns toward them, it's almost nothing, a hesitancy he alone can feel, even Rafael next to him doesn't realize. But he strokes the horse's neck, furtively, encourages him in a hushed voice. With his fingertips he caresses the scar you can still see on the chestnut's shoulder, and the horse shudders, loses his concentration, it doesn't take much, an opening to one side and the bull rushes through it. The little brother cries, "What are you doing?"

Steban doesn't answer, he waves his hand to send Rafael after the young bull, and soon he has brought him back, with that crazy Halley of his who's like the devil, all over the bull, this side and that, nudging him with his breast without ever coming within reach of a horn or a hoof, a horse that might have been born from the same womb as the cattle themselves, knowing their every reflex and flaw, and every danger. In the saddle the little brother is so proud of having caught the fugitive, he tries not to show it but his stifled grin distorts his mouth, and he doesn't say anything, not even that it was Steban's mistake, he doesn't need to, Steban knows it only too well. Further along two cows are grazing and don't look up. Steban follows Rafael's gaze.

"No, let's t-take this one . . . first."

They drive the bull ahead of them, it trots reluctantly. Steban places one hand on his criollo's mane. In that voice only he and his horse can hear he murmurs, "Don't worry."

RAFAEL

Gradually, more and more animals join the herd, as the brothers drive them into an ocean of mooing, and the dogs nip at the beasts' hocks to prevent the most stubborn ones from bolting. The animals don't run much, they save their strength. Most of them are young but they already know, thanks to some improbable hereditary awareness, that the day ahead will be a long one. Sometimes they go dozens of miles or more before they reach the corral the mother will close behind them; by then the dogs' tongues are hanging out, the horses are rearing. The little brother enjoys this routine, it has always filled him with a kind of exaltation, to be wedged there in his saddle, merging with Halley's sudden pirouetting stops and half-turns in order to tear after a fleeing heifer or bull-calf. The horse is covered in foam but doesn't tire. He's focused. It's a game for him, too, and the little brother laughs. Out of the corner of his eye he makes sure the dogs aren't getting trampled by the steers, he calls Three when he gets too close, the way he tends to do. The mastiff turns his head the other way. Rafael points his hand toward the ground and shouts, "Three! Come!"

The air is heavy with an animal scent. When they get home their clothes will be full of it, right through to their skin, tonight and every day hereafter, because they won't wash. Once a week the mother heats water for the tubs and they soak, reluctantly. The smell of their own bodies is as much a part of their life as the animals' is, they can't even tell them

apart, smells drowned by the smoke of burned horn when
they've been shoeing the horses, or the pungency of earth if
they've been rolling on the ground to wrestle a calf away from
its mother for branding. Between their sweat and that of ewes
and steers there's so little difference; only a sour whiff betrays
the boys' smell, whereas the animals' is powerful, peaty. After
work, the little brother often inhales the odor of wet fur and
leather, his hands against the horse's damp flank, he raises
them to his nose the better to take it in, to melt into the animal's bulk. Halley turns his head to Rafael and the boy holds
out his sticky palms for the horse to sniff. He listens to the
horse's snuffling as he breathes in the strong perfume, then
looks at him questioningly and licks the familiar effluvia, tickling the boy's skin—in the end, the horse calls quietly in a
quivering of nostrils, and Rafael places his cheek against him
wordlessly.

Steban suddenly gives a long shrill whistle. The entire herd
is there. The four brothers split up again, two behind, two on
either side. The dogs bound from one to the other. The only
horizon left to the animals is straight ahead. And the little
brother shouts to give the signal: *Move on!* It's as if an enormous mass, both unique and ungainly, begins to move there
beside him, causing the earth it is crushing and the sky above
to tremble, and the cows low, the air quivers all at once. Four
hundred hooves, like war drums hammering the ground as
they advance heavily, and the vibrations rise into the horses'
pasterns, and swarm around the brothers' legs and heels like
an immense hive. Rafael places one hand on his belly and
twists his shirt. Every time, the sound resonates so loudly that
it makes him shudder, his guts are in such turmoil he's afraid
they'll spill out, so he presses, hard, the time it takes to get used
to it again, his body shaking from the long stampede, a strange
fever running up his back. All he'd have to do to forget the
herd is close his eyes, keeping only the cadence, this odd piece

of music, monotonous and unending. An impossible rhythm, and he's there, ecstatic and terrified, one hand on his horse's neck to remain here in the world.

When the trembling calms down, he swings his legs forward and Halley begins to trot. The brothers' shouts resonate all at once, along with the cries of the running, worried cattle. The warm safe world into which he had retreated is shattered. He'd like to reach it again, but he knows it's pointless, even if he could, the magic has vanished. He'll have to wait for another time, a new cavalcade. The break is painful.

Red-rimmed eyes.

The cattle's backs undulating like a brown sea.

For four hours they drive the herd ahead of them, across prairies, fording streams. It could go on forever, and they have no more landmarks, they are lost in the plain with its unchanging landscape, they are dulled by the cattle's lowing and the dogs' barking. When the enclosures grow smaller they hardly notice. Mauro and Joaquin have been silent for a long time, they've stifled their shouts, their throats sting from the dust. The cold wind defeats them, dries the corners of their eyes.

The little brother says nothing.

He is thinking about Steban's question, earlier, his voice hoarse from speaking so rarely. *What you gonna do, later?*

He's never thought about it.

For the first time he understands that his life could be different, that he is holding it in his hands. A moment later he spits on the ground. What did he say—and go where?

The mother is his future, the estancia his destiny and his tomb. He doesn't want to think, or to answer. It would spoil too many things. Only the livestock matters, and the work of every moment, the unending repetition, wearying and reassuring, and even the galloping of the horses is the same day after day, and the cattle's breathing, and the light of dawn over the plain. Seen like this, life has no reason to change. It can last the time of humankind, the time of the universe, of certainty. Above all he must not ask himself Steban's question. There is poison behind it.

"Left corridor, left!"

Joaquin rides past him at a furious gallop, driving the cows while Steban prevents them from turning back. The little brother gives a start, urges Halley to follow and waves his whip to thrash the cattle's flanks; he's annoyed the others have gotten ahead. They steer the herd toward the big corral. Like every time, the animals in the lead slow down, hesitate. How much do they sense, the moment the enclosures rise higher around them, that old instinct urging them to turn away from the direction they're headed, bringing that presentiment of capture or death—an instinct the brothers suppress by pushing them from behind, with the dogs gone mad, their fangs nipping at the animals' hocks. The cattle press together, lowing, caught unawares in their forward rush by this sudden stop; they stamp their hooves, begin to turn in circles. They would be ready to go all that way again, back to where they started, if the horses were not forcing them to move ahead by tightening the circle around them and pushing them ever further. So the herd moves forward again, slowly at first and then loping quickly, trying to escape from something invisible, charging straight ahead, into the enclosure, if there were a precipice it would be no different. The earth shudders, seems to sink. The horses, nervous, try to pull away from the reins holding them back. An echo in the sky. The animals' cries, the stamping like a coming storm, thundering, rumbling. The mother closes the gates. Rafael jumps off his horse and helps her to lock them.

In the middle, the cattle are bellowing incessantly and the little brother blocks his ears. He never could stand these cries of distress that echo over the steppe as the animals discover their penned-in state, colliding with the barbed wire, recoiling as they bleed. Every lowing cry causes him to shudder, an ever-increasing clamor that gives him a sort of fever as he runs from one gate to the next, repulsing the most terrified steers, placing his hands back over his eardrums the moment he can. From a distance he hears Mauro insulting him.

"Whip them, whip them, asshole! They'll get through!"

Last year, or maybe it was the year before, a bull managed to jump over the fence, taking with him the barbed wire and the entire herd they'd spent all afternoon rounding up. A whole day for nothing, twice as much work, and the bull had to be slaughtered because it had severed its tendons. So Rafael shakes himself, waves his arms frantically to make them back up, opens his ears to the animal lament, and screams louder so he won't hear them anymore, louder than the steers and the cows combined, and his roar fills the air and his entire head, burning his throat, pounding in his temples. He knows that in the middle of the corral the cows and calves will already be calmer by now; around the edges there are only the rebellious ones, furious and afraid. And after an hour even they see they are the only ones still snorting and bellowing, and they lower their heads to sniff the dust, and seek out the buckets, or some grass or grain. Sometimes when the brothers think the beasts have finally settled they'll raise their muzzles with an enraged thrust of their horns and let out a long moo, which sets a few of them off again.

And then it fades, shrinks, closes over. The sounds vanish. There is less movement among the herd, and the animals are quiet.

Everything returns to silence.

Because at last it's a good day, enhanced by the money the fattener has given the mother, the sons are allowed to kill a steer. The little brother has already seen how Mauro raises the sledgehammer above his head and brings it down with all his might onto the animal's brow to knock him out, but as always the sound of cracking bone and the animal's stifled cry make Rafael open his eyes wide, his mouth is open, too, on a stifled exclamation, as the animal collapses. And Mauro is already on top of the steer, severing its carotids, a blade so sharp that he showed the little brother how he could dissect a fly in full flight, and Rafael knelt on the ground to find the severed insect, and stared at the tall twin who was looking down at him. Mauro nodded.

"You see, for the steer it'll be the same thing."

All four observe the creature and the red puddle spreading underneath his neck, the convulsions shaking him, hardly a whisper. Not one of them says a thing. A moment of suspended time, something in-between where anything could happen and nothing happens, just the normal flow of things, the twittering of anxious birds, the startled breath of the steer, and his fall, in slow motion, as if a thread were still holding him on his feet. The blood oozing into his golden fur, thick and sticky, while his heart surrenders and stops. Whether you're a man or a beast, that is where it all begins and it all ends; that plump, taut flesh pulsating, pumping, beating. All of a sudden, it stops beating. All it takes is for the movement to stop, a stomach and chest to freeze. One sigh, the last, and then nothing. A dead body.

When at last the steer is motionless, its dying spasms have left it, Joaquin gives a final kick to its croup to make sure. He says simply, *That's it.* At first the sight of the blood pouring onto the ground is somewhat daunting, until they get their hands into it and something brutal rises from their guts and makes them laugh, maybe a voracious, inextinguishable hunger, the joy of knowing they'll soon be eating from this red flesh which even now seems to be quivering still, there beneath them, and the smell of grilling meat makes their mouths water even as they are cutting open the skin to pull back the hide. Then they cut up the meat, collect the blood to make blood sausages. Their hands and arms are splattered with the still-warm crimson liquid; with his fingertips, Rafael has drawn lines on his face. War paint. He laughs. Mauro grabs him and smears him from chin to brow, making fun of him. He calls him *the Indian*. He forces his mouth open and makes him swallow some fresh blood.

The little brother vomits onto the ground. A scarlet puddle on the brownish ochre earth.

When he wipes his hand beneath his nose he can see the red streaks on his skin, he smells the dead animal, all the way down into his throat and up into his sinuses. He takes a sip of water, spits it out, then twice more, to rinse out the metallic taste that lingers. Lips pursed, he takes out his knife and begins to cut where Joaquin tells him to. The dogs eye the cheap cuts. Mauro slices the legs at the knees and hocks, tosses a foot to each brother and shouts, *One for each of us!* They fight, laughing, each boy brandishing his piece of leg like a sword, and the little brother finds it hard to lift his up, and yet it's only the foreleg, if it had been a hind leg he'd have given up, forty pounds of carcass that Mauro and Joaquin are swinging around their heads with cries of excitement; Rafael hunches down beneath the blows, wipes his hands that slip on the blood. He swears at his older brothers to attract their attention and get back in the fight. Sometimes one of them gets clobbered on the jaw and has to step aside for a few seconds, the time to recover his wits—bone against bone, and the blows resound in their heads, their tears mix with blood. Their cries echo across the landscape, provocation and laughter. The mother lets them get on with it. Rafael spies on her out of the corner of his eye, sure she'll come and stop them; but she doesn't move.

She is leaning against the guardrail of the house, her hands

on her hips, and watching them, or the plain behind them. Or
even the condors circling in the clouds, drawn to the odor of
death they can smell from the sky, on currents of wind from the
south and parched air. The sons have noticed them, and snarl
that after the fight they'll go and shoot them, those nasty, heavy
birds with their feverish flight, for the boys they're a feast. But
first of all they have to finish the fight, the little brother hopes
to take Mauro by surprise to make him pay for the blood he
made him swallow, so he lines up behind Steban and behind
Joaquin, following them like a gray shadow. Before long the
older boys forget about him. A good blow to the side of the
head, if he can. He circles round and round the twin, waits for
his chance, hopping, talking to the severed leg to urge himself
on. But deep down he knows he'll fail.

The chopped-up body of the steer lies a few feet away.
Sometimes they step over it to escape a blow, or roll over
behind it for protection. The mother is still watching, sees their
arms dripping with blood. She doesn't shudder, doesn't judge.
This is the animals' fate. She waits for the sons to start cutting
up the meat again.

Everything is wild, brutal, even the gaze she casts upon
them.

MAURO

To add to the harshness of life: does he even know why he tries so hard, the tall twin, always some chore to finish, one more than the other brothers, one even the mother would not dare ask him to do. To prove what, exactly: that he's the strongest? They all say as much. That they need him? They would sooner die than tell him that, and yet they're all convinced of it—he is, they are, without Mauro the estancia would not make it, the sheep would be unshorn, the calves would be branded too late. And who would repair the buildings, who would unwind miles of barbed wire without flinching, who would carry sacks of seed and grain, and roof-beams? At the age of eighteen, he's deformed by labor, his arms taut with streaks of blue veins, and already he has to walk swaying from left to right to go easy on his back. His shoulders are so broad that they block the light when he stands in the door, coming in for dinner. Sometimes when he's tired he bumps into the door frame, causing the entire room to shake, yet he doesn't even notice. He instinctively places his hand on the wood as if to steady it; and the little brother could swear it wouldn't take much for him to knock the house over. Every evening his short black hair is full of twigs, and he combs it with his hand, there in the room, and no one protests, because he's done the work of three men. His brothers would never dare raise their voices in his presence, except perhaps Joaquin—but Joaquin couldn't care less whether the floor was swept that morning. Mauro is a giant, a godsend to the mother, despite any careless behavior he might display; to Steban and Rafael he is a monster.

There are evenings when the three other sons, even Joaquin, even the mother, are covered with the gray dust of the steppe, to the point you'd think they'll be buried there, unable to go forward or back, come to a complete halt. Exhaustion grips them like a vise, and getting up, serving the soup, eating it, everything is painful. They don't talk, not that they'd have anything to say: their thoughts escape them. Deep inside them there is only a void, a total absence of thought process, in order to save their energy, rebuild it. And although Mauro always comes home from the plains or the stables with his head held high, eventually his eyes, too, begin to close, sometimes over his cup of maté, and his upper body slips to one side, and Joaquin reaches out to catch him. Then the mother says, "Get to bed now."

And no one moves. The four sons bear the signs of an existence eroded by fatigue—their own, but also that of the animals and the earth. Often there is not enough rain, and the hard soil cracks open beneath their feet, the spindly trees are dry and will never grow into anything more than gray copses. Further north, further east, the pastures are rich: but they've never seen them. All they know is what the mother has told them. Their lands grabbed by the rich, bought for a song, and the herds with them. Mauro cannot understand why the grandfather sold them.

"He didn't sell," barks the mother. "They stole them from him. They made him. All so they could . . . could poison the world with their filthy business."

Beasts in the tens of thousands, so numerous even the pampas was not enough, and they began to ration their grazing, to feed them corn and forage, to fatten them to make them heavy. In San León incredulous men read articles in the paper that heap praise upon the new intensive farming techniques, the future, they write, column after column. They may raise sheep in these parts, but no one's forgotten that above all, the meat has to have room to run. To build up muscle, for the taste, the texture. Nothing to do with the meat that comes from those strange farms they talk about all the time, where the beasts never move and are force-fed, whose flesh stinks of death. The sons spit on the ground whenever the mother talks about those big farms: they're out to get them, she's sure of it now, and she can thank her lucky stars that she had the sixth sense to sell most of her cows in time. Mauro shouts, clenching his fists: "But their meat is worthless!"

And so what? They begin to suspect that meat eaters couldn't give a damn about quality, provided they have enough to stuff their guts. It can be fatty and white, but provided they get it full to overflowing, they'll say it melts in their mouth—that's another thing the mother brings back to their incredulous ears, when she returns from the town. Soft meat. They joke about it among themselves, shocked, furious. They'd rather regurgitate this gelatinous flesh than swallow it; and the day the mother comes home and tells them she tasted it in San León they look at her as if she'd said something blasphemous. The meat was good, she says; they don't believe her. Mauro bursts out laughing, she's playing a trick on them. But deep down they know the mother isn't the joking kind, and it worries them. Since the sale to the fattener she hasn't bought any more cattle. The tall twin pounds on the table.

"So you're going to make do with sheep, you too!"

"And why not?"

"You promised you'd hold out. You said it wouldn't happen in your lifetime."

"I've thought it over. I can't go losing with steer what I gain with wool."

"You gave your word."

"And what does that change?"

Mauro made a face.

"It means we'll be shepherds. Shit-faced shepherds. That's not a life for us."

"Your life is what I decide."

"We could go on like before."

"There's no more before."

The mother was born shortly before the great droughts of the second half of the nineteenth century. Oddly enough, she doesn't remember them, even though her parents lost a third of their livestock. Forty years later everyone still talks about it. The old folks say the climate has changed since back then. The steppe has become too arid for life to take hold. Too much wind, too many animals, and the rain that never comes often enough. The land is dying from its pastures.

One day there'll be nothing left, not even a spiny shrub to feed the sheep that scrape the ground by the millions. Not a drop of water for a whole year, or two. Everything will die, men dried up, animals devoured from within, trees scorched. Only rats and grasshoppers—like in Brazil, in 1877, they'll end up like that, they'll die from that rainless sun and wind; they dream of the flood. Tremble at the thought of losing everything.

The mother goes on with her story. A world is disintegrating. She raises one finger in the air.

"Maybe it's time for me to take you to San León. You have to see. Before everything disappears."

The town. Mauro won't want to remember the first time the mother takes them there, Joaquin and him. They are afraid. Too many people, too much noise. Too many shouts, everywhere at once, greetings or insults, men and horses, and steers, and sheep. Donkeys too, and the cacophony of voices calling loudly to each other, each one alone in the world, drowning out the other voices that are raised in turn to make themselves heard. Hammers pounding on houses, rattling; the squealing of cartwheels passing by. The way people hail them, joke with them, not really them but the mother—she knows everyone, she doesn't introduce her sons because she figures it's obvious, and the men look at them, holding their hands above their eyes to shield them from the sunlight, and they talk about the boys as if they weren't there.

"Is that little Mauro who's grown so tall? Good lord, what a bruiser he's turned into."

The mother nods, gives a quick laugh, with that way she has of half-heartedly sketching a sentence.

"Wanted to see the town. So . . . "

She drags them from shop to store, inflicts on them her interminable haggling, down to the last peso, obliges them to check the invoices, makes them carry her shopping and her bags. In the street they hear the gibes: *So you found yourself some slaves to help ya?* Joaquin murmurs:

"What are slaves?"

The mother ignores him and raises her head, with her proud look, and answers back, for all to hear: *I'll have you know these boys work hard, I'm the one who trained them.* They feel awkward. When he gets home Joaquin will lie to Steban and Rafael about how huge the city is, how busy and full of light, how they caught a bull-calf that had gotten loose and was causing panic in the streets. He'll roll his biceps and talk about San León as if they had conquered it; Mauro will nod in silent agreement. In fact, they are fascinated and impressed by the town, it is as tough as they themselves are, a famished, thirsty place.

Slowly, with subsequent visits, they become more accustomed; the mother has decided to take them along to help from now on, so every month they leave the two younger boys in charge of the estancia while the three of them set off for the day. Mauro reminds his twin to keep his mouth shut so he won't look as idiotic as that numbskull Steban, and forbids him from looking around, and especially from pointing.

"It makes us look stupid, as if we didn't know anything. So the people in town laugh at us when they see us. Shit, Joaquin, behave yourself."

At the bar, they watch their mother gambling, the men slapping her on the shoulder when she makes a smart move. She raises her glass, drinks it down in one. She's the only woman ever to set foot in the bar. Sometimes when she's had a lot to drink she bursts out laughing and says she's become a man like all the others.

With the same rigidity. And the same faults. She drinks as much as the men, we all get our turn, she thinks, her eyes raised to the sky, a mean smile on her face. She's a vengeful poker player. It's her reward when she's finished her errands— questioning every invoice, filling the cart with stocks of food, grain, coal, horseshoes, and barbed wire: invariably, she ends up at the bar and rolls her cigarettes in her callous hands, orders a Fernet or a whisky, then another one, tosses down the cards, kills her demons, bets again—no one finds any cause for complaint, she has even acquired a certain local notoriety.

There are evenings when girls sing and dance on the stage at the back. In the beginning the twins don't dare look at them.

Until now the only woman they've ever known is their mother, with her broad hips, patched skirts, and filthy apron. Her brown hair, long and flat, framing a face with perpetually drawn features. They recall seeing other women at Mass on Sundays, also dressed in dreary colors; some were prettier, and shapely, and wore a smile. But when they turned six they stopped going to church. Too much work on the estancia. The mother put a statuette of Santa Maria in the house, and they had to pretend to pray to her every evening. The mother, and the Virgin. Nothing else. They've never seen lipstick on a girl's lips, or makeup around her eyes. Let alone blond curls, and of course they have no way of knowing they are fake. And that smile. It takes their breath away. They can't even grasp whether this thing standing there singing in front of them really is a woman, or some species they know nothing about. They are so visibly shaken by what they see on stage that people make fun of them again. The mother calls them to order and they run back to her, yet they can't help stealing glances at the girls. Mauro stutters with a nervous laugh:

"But . . . "

She interrupts him with a swipe of her hand.

"*Putas. Jodete!*"

They huddle next to her. Just hearing those vibrant voices at the far end of the room causes something to stir inside them. The girls are amused, they wave to them as they sing. The boys blush. Sit closer together. An abyss opens inside them, a devastating temptation. Stupor, too: so, this exists. There they are by the mother, their mouths hanging open, their eyes almost popping out of their sockets from staring. Shivers all over. They squeeze their abdomens. When, at the end of the show, a tipsy customer goes to slip a bill into the bodice of one of the girls, grasping her breasts in each hand to kiss them, Mauro lets out a cry and takes hold of Joaquin's arm. They are burning inside, they picture themselves on the crest separating paradise from hell. The heat is suffocating.

And they know that the mother will never let them kiss the girls' breasts. She will never give them the money.

RAFAEL

So there are these dark moments on the estancia, the twins' agitation floating in the air like a warm current, wafting by the two younger boys who stand back, hidden behind the barn, fascinated by the strange spectacle. They know instinctively what is happening, their elder brothers standing pressed against a ewe's rear end, twitching furiously, it doesn't last long, the animals don't react once they've been caught.

Mauro pulls his trousers back up, head lowered, he never looks at Joaquin, who is slow to copy him. He closes the gate behind him, not saying a word.

It's always in the evening. The mother is snoring in her armchair, stunned with fatigue and alcohol. They know she got up that morning before they did.

Since Rafael continues to shadow the twins, of course one day he gets caught—was it Steban's loud giggle or the ewes turning their heads, the older boys give a start, grab hold of them. *Filthy little spies, how long have you been watching us?*

After they're done what's left are two battered bodies making their way back to their room, and the pain, and the stifled tears. Steban moans, holding his jaw. The little brother, in his corner, make his lips bleed, so hard has he bitten them to keep from crying. The twins hit hard. The humiliation and rage at having been caught in the act. With their kicks in the belly they buy silence.

Now the twins are more violent than ever before. For weeks

Rafael and Steban have stopped watching them in the ewes'
paddock; in vain. The sting of shame doesn't go away. It only
feels better during the time it takes to fight, to tense one's muscles and make others suffer.

The older boys hit them where it won't show, sparing their
faces. They don't want the mother to find out, above all. She
might notice how, some mornings, the younger boys walk bent
over, how they avert their eyes when they walk past the twins.
Not even. She gives her orders for the day without looking at
them, she never interrupts a chore she's in the middle of.
Mauro and Joaquin snicker.

Rafael darts away, scurries, goes to his horse, the dogs.
Curls up in one corner of the barn, with Three half lying on his
legs, and he waits for the older boys to forget him. He buries
his nose in the mastiff's fur, and he wishes the caress would
never end, that his arms never had to let go. No matter how
much he ruminates, then murmurs his plans into the dog's
ear—plant the pickets, unroll the barbed wire, clean out the
stable and the barn—nothing works. His body is becoming
wiry, but refuses to fill out, and Rafael despairs of ever bursting with muscles with which to confront the twins. Next to him
Mauro looks like an ogre on the prowl, terrifying with his
instinct for knowing where the boy is working, where he is hiding while he's cleaning the leather. Joaquin is never far behind,
catching up the moment his twin gives a faint whistle. *Here he
is, I got him.* Steban runs away and curls up—every time, the
little brother finds him lying under the bed as if he were dead.
He doesn't blame him. The half-wit, whimpering as he rolls in
a ball on the ground, is of no interest to the twins. No fighting.
It's no fun. Whereas Rafael . . .

So he gets used to their blows, now and again he strikes
back, and for a moment he forgets the pain. He always ends up
on the ground, his back and belly stomped on by the older
boys' boots. He sobs while Mauro and Joaquin laugh as they

give him his hiding, he waits for the pain to come, the real pain, when his horizon will be reduced to the rhythm of his heart trying to beat, and his paltry dreams of revenge.

What if he killed them. What if he kept his rifle with him all day, even for the most menial chores, with two cartridges, one each, he wouldn't need more, he won't miss. He can see himself with the rifle on his shoulder, carefully taking aim in the direction of their footsteps, their stifled chuckling. He can feel the trembling of his forefinger on the trigger, the clinging thoughts, the mother, the estancia, prison. Does he want to throw his life out the window for two bastards, he's not sure, even if he is panicky with spite, or he has to do it better, then, somewhere else, far away, next to a ditch he'll have been digging for days, lure them there, tip them in, one bullet each in the head. For months the idea obsesses him.

On nights when the moon is full, he goes out and roams the steppe, perched on Halley's back. Their ghostly form drifts through the dry black grass. Rafael ties old cloths around his horse's hooves to stifle the sound; he takes a shovel with him, rides into the distance. The first weeks he tries to dig in fifty different spots, or is it a hundred. But every attempt ends with a hole so small he despairs of ever finding a patch of soft earth, where the rock will not get the better of his anger and his deadened arms; even when he takes a pickaxe, the stoniness of the earth resonates through his body, leaving him exhausted by dawn of the next day. At the very best spots he manages to dig a foot or two. On the days that preceded he often measured Mauro, walking by his side, a few steps, casual as could be, the time it took to reckon his height and width. Anything less than twenty inches deep is a waste of time: the carrion eaters would soon unearth a body so close to the surface. Sometimes with the first shove of the spade he senses the hostility of the rock. He climbs back on his horse and searches elsewhere.

Of course there are the swamps. But it takes almost two hours to get there, and a bit longer to come back, when he and Halley are overcome by tiredness, to go there and back every night is impossible. He does try once, however. The atmosphere, the stinking breath of the earth, the strange glow deep below, it all repels him. The shiver up and down his spine tells him that this territory is cursed, already, as deadly a trap as quicksand, a place that will open the way only the better to close over him, a place infested with insects and stagnant water. Something holds him back, something like a presentiment, or fear. The horse, too, hesitates at the edge of the swamp: Rafael sees this as a sign. He turns back. Forget it. In any case it was too far away.

Night after night, increasingly disheartened, he traces long, useless serpentines, to be sure not to miss the patch of land he so hopes to find. For a moment he is tempted by the orchards or the kitchen garden, then decides against it. Now that would be too close; the mother is always working there, and she'd see right away that someone had been tampering with the soil. So he criss-crosses the plain without really believing in it anymore, it's become a sort of rite, not to give in. To drive back the nightmares. He sometimes drifts off to sleep on horseback. One night he is so tired he falls off. The fall wakens him: he no longer knows what he's doing there or what he's looking for. He instinctively remounts and Halley heads for the stables; Rafael lies down in the stall with him. Another time he sees three young foxes sitting next to a rock pile, and they don't move as he comes nearer. From a distance he talks to them, wants to tame them. He slows his horse, not to frighten them, continues his monologue in a low voice, almost humming. The little foxes wait, unbelievably still. He thinks they are under a spell; they're nothing but stones. When he rides up to the pile he shuts his eyes with disappointment.

Halley walks for hours every night, tirelessly. The little brother and the horse are used to this yellow and blue and silvery steppe, with its baroque shadows, its silence scarcely troubled by the falling wind or the muffled hooves. They ride aimlessly, indefinable entities forming one body, they are stubborn, weary of their pointless quest; Rafael no longer even takes the shovel. They ride like legendary creatures punished by the gods, doomed by some unknown sin to wander forever. They do not rebel. The little brother leans to one side to turn the horse, follows a long imaginary line, shifts to the other side to come back along a parallel line, not ten yards further. The plain lies under the grid of their steps. They know it by heart. But it grants them nothing, offers only the harshness of its rocky surface, where Halley's hooves leave no trace. It too is unyielding.

Where you been? The twins corner him, some mornings, in the stable, when they see the sweat on Halley's flanks. *Where you been, idiot? You want us to tell the mother?* He doesn't answer, his fatigue has broken him, he cannot even keep his eyes focused on them. Tell the mother, tell her what?

The moon burns the plain, patiently, and his body, his eyes reddened by that consuming white light that has left a strange scar on his neck where the buckle of his satchel has been pressing. Henceforth Rafael hides from the nocturnal rays and their hunger for skin and metal; he is fascinated by the sting of the evil star, and he rolls his sleeves down his arms, lowers his head beneath his hat, treats the wound on his neck with some neatsfoot oil. Imperceptibly, the iris of his pale eyes, the mane of his horse turn even paler, as if the moon were whitening them to expel them from the world; or perhaps, muses the little brother, the moon also is seeking to destroy them. But for the time being, they are alone.

They might be the last inhabitants of this deserted land, and yet the steppe is swarming with infinitesimal, insignificant life, flying, crawling, hissing life. Their ears and feet buzz with them. They can hear the owls hooting in the distance, the foxes barking. But nothing seems alive but them and their long silent march, and their shadow cast ahead of them by the stars. Nothing stops them. They could walk to the end of time, were it not for the events about to befall them, and which no one has seen coming.

JOAQUIN

Of course Mauro was right when he said that the mother would never give them a peso, would never allow them to dream a bit in town. And of course Joaquin knew that his twin was right, but he could not help but have faith, a little scrap of hope no bigger than a fly squashed in his palm, no higher than a barb you pinch between your fingers, not much at all, a little scrap of nothing, or just about. But what came instead was even less than that. The void. Zero.

The mother drove them jolting along to San León, did her errands, then installed Mauro and Joaquin next to her at the bar while she made ready to gamble, rubbing her hands with pleasure, any more and she'd be purring, and she sits down with some guys who already have their cards out, and it goes on, and on, and then some. If they weren't there it would be no different.

They are allowed three beers each. That's what they've earned.

So after a while they start to complain. And make demands. They do the math, mainly Joaquin who's better with numbers, and who explains it all to Mauro—and sure enough, it sends him into a rage to work out how much the mother is earning at their expense, exploiting them fifteen hours a day just so they can wet their whistle with six beers one evening once a month, it would be stupid not to say something. He wants to live, too, the world is there at his fingertips, right there within his grasp, and it drives him crazy not to be able to reach out and really touch it, it gives him pins and needles under his fingernails, he can feel the blood pulsing. Just the thought that they'll go home again as always, vanquished, and try to drown their frustration by wedging a ewe's legs between their boots to keep her from moving, it makes Joaquin want to vomit, he's had his fill of sheep's asses, they deserve something more, the mother has got to understand this. Therefore, because she placed a cautious hand on her wallet when he asked her for some money, he leans closer to her again now, in the middle of the game, she hates it when he does this, he doesn't care. Mauro reached out to stop him but Joaquin shoved him away. Mauro is always trying to give orders, as if he knew better than his brother what to do and what not to do, why doesn't he say something, the loudmouth, because he doesn't think it's the right moment, and so what?—since that's the way things are, he, Joaquin, is beside himself now, and he'll say something, will demand his due from the mother, so he mutters angrily:

"And if you didn't have us, if you had to hire some guys like us, it would cost you a lot more than a few beers, huh?"

But that just goes to show how poorly he knows the old lady: tipsy with her first glasses of Fernet, she turns red, and stands up and holds out a threatening finger, and shouts loudly for all to hear:

"And what if I asked you to pay for your room and board from the time you were born, my boy, how much do you think would be left over? How many years would you have to slave away for me, if you had to pay it all back?"

Around the table the other players start to joke, and tongues begin to wag. Joaquin gives a hollow, mock gallant laugh.

"But I'm your son . . . "

"My son? So what? I don't owe you a thing. Whereas you."

"Without us you couldn't keep the estancia going."

"Without me, you and your brothers would be nothing but vagabonds, scarcely fit to do anything but ride a horse."

"But—"

"You can pack your bags and leave tomorrow if you like. And you, too, Mauro! If you think I need you so bad. I give you ten days to come back whining and begging me to take you back."

"Damn true!" shouts an old man next to them.

The others nod, exchanging glances and making acquiescent noises in their throats. Suddenly the entire room is humming with murmurs like an insect's buzzing, faces set in agreement, looking at Joaquin full of reproach, but what do they know about the life the mother leads, and that they pretend to envy, let them come have a look, and then we'll talk again, and at that moment Joaquin wishes he could run away, so he wouldn't see them or hear them, but voices are raised, words spin in the smoky air of the bar, heavy, clinging words, pounding against his temples.

"When you think of all your mother had to put up with to raise you all on her own."

"And don't those kids make their demands, blackmail even."

"All youngsters are like that. Look at Federico's."

"It didn't take him long, did it."

"He'd give anything to come back, now."

And the same old man, shouting and laughing and pointing at them. *You too would give anything to come back!* In the midst of their stories and exclamations someone grabs Joaquin by the shoulder and leads him away, shakes him, opens the door to let him out, goes out with him and lights a cigarette, hands it to him. Joaquin inhales the smoke in silence. Their breathing in the night. The noise grows fainter when the door has closed and peace and quiet fold around them at last. Next to him, Mauro is leaning against the fence, rolling a cigarette for himself. He closes his eyes and says:

"You shouldn't do that. It's pointless."

"I know."

"So?"

"I dunno . . . I couldn't help myself."

"That's the mother, huh. That's the way she is."

"Yup."

"Someday we'll manage to convince her, if we have to protest we will."

Joaquin shrugs. The cool night air feels good on his burning cheeks, but does nothing for his resentment, and yet something has died inside him, there's a hateful resignation, nothing but compromises, sentences starting with *It doesn't matter . . .* For a long time he stays there with Mauro, who lights one cigarette after the other, he sits on the steps leading to the bar, his head spinning a little after three beers, and he laughs joylessly.

"Three glasses and I'm already pissed, I don't need any more than this, to be honest, what else can I possibly want?"

Mauro's voice, hardly audible in the night, distant, muffled.

"Well, otherwise, we leave."

"What?"

"Go work somewhere else. We can always find something."

"You mean it?"

"Hell, yes. Don't you?"

Joaquin opens his mouth, doesn't answer right away. He knows his twin only too well, he can flare up without thinking, irreversibly; he's an animal, a hothead who'll never set foot on the estancia again if he decides he's done with it. That's where the old guys in the bar are mistaken, when they say the two brothers will beg the mother to take them back: Mauro never looks back. And as for Joaquin, he doesn't know if deep down this is what he really wants, if he really asks himself, without lying, swallowing his pride. So he plays for time. To chuck it all in—sure, he's tempted, but he'd also like a promise that he'll have a better future. Yet nothing could be less certain, however much he tries to convince himself, or maybe it will be better, but that's still a maybe, and the uncertainty forms a knot in his stomach.

Mauro crushes his cigarette under his heel.

"Don't worry, hey, I understand."

Joaquin protests. *I didn't say anything.*

"Yeah, you didn't say anything. And I understood."

"No, you didn't."

The older twin gives a sudden laugh.

"Hey, don't take me for a fool. You're scared stiff. Drop it."

And Joaquin says no more. He has no choice. If it's to confess in the end that he's got no guts, he'd rather just leave it there. He lowers his head. Doesn't want to meet Mauro's gaze. He mimes smoking and says, *Got another one?* They wait together, a wordless reconciliation, brothers above and beyond all else, beyond even the mother, who divides them. Joaquin can feel the tension between them vanishing; Mauro gives him a friendly tap on the back, which he reciprocates with a smile.

"I can be a real moron, right?"

"Hell, no."

When the mother finally comes out in the middle of the night, they get to their feet without speaking and support her over to the cart. Half-amused, half-disgusted, they set her sprawling on the seat. Joaquin tosses a blanket over her, frowning.

"Just look at that."

"Yup. That's the mother for you."

"We should leave her in the ditch. She wouldn't even wake up."

Mauro guffaws as he picks up the reins.

"Yeah, old witch stinking of alcohol. She must've lost the equivalent of three hundred beers playing poker."

"Why don't we throw her overboard, she'd have to crawl all the way home in the state she's in."

"If she doesn't get shot by some fella thinks she's a peccary."

"Chrissake, she'd be moaning her head off the next day. We'd be in for it, man."

"Well we'd still have a good time while we're at it."

And it comforts them to mutter and heap insults on her, insults that burn their tongues while she snores there behind them, even though they do glance now and again at the shape beneath the blanket, because with the mother you never know, it may seem like nothing and then she'll hear what she's not supposed to hear, and her hand is quicker than anything. When she slaps them, or hits them, they curl up like children, and yet any of the brothers could fend her off, even the youngest, skinny as a rake that he is. Any one of them could knock her over. Trample her. Beat her, in the end, so she'd understand that it can happen to her, too, and not just to them, the mother too can receive a good hiding.

Truth is, they will never touch her.

Whether they hate her or adore her, depending on the day and on her mood, the mother is the sacred woman. They come from her, they have drunk her milk, they've been tiny, puling, crying infants and she's made them into men. They are revolted by her authority and yet they submit; they know that without her the estancia would be a vast, uncultivated desert, and they would be wild children no better than those aimless foxes in search of little rodents. Who would have fed them? Who would have taught them to tend the livestock, when the father ran off and left them to their fate? The mother is everything to them. They may insult her but respect paralyzes them, holds them back. Time and work and worries have spoiled her looks; they don't care. They don't look at her. The mother is both the woman and not a woman. She brought them into the world, she protects them, she barks her orders, shows them no consideration; she incarnates male and female at the same time. In that alone her perfection amazes them. She ends up being a universal, asexual creature, and if someone asked they could hardly describe her. The mother is the mother. Grounded and solid, terrifyingly constant; they can replay her intonations and threats, and the words that will come. But if they try to describe her features, she vanishes as if in a dream, as blurry as a ghost, a shapeless form, without boundaries. The mother is everywhere, above and beyond the world.

Deep down even Joaquin is proud of the way she mocks the *putas* singing in the bar.

And yet. Incredulous, he will be the first one sacrificed, along with his stupid faith in the bonds of blood—because the only blood the mother believes in is the blood of violence and of animals. Joaquin is no more than a pawn in her life, one of four, one she will do without if she has to, and she will erase him from the estancia, and spit on his absence the way she would spit on his grave if she could—and for sure she would have preferred to see him six feet under, eaten by worms, and have everyone forget him, forget how it happened, how, ultimately, she was the one who caused the storm.

THE MOTHER

The sons are wrong if they think the mother goes into a trance at the very thought of the bar, that it is the only real excuse for their trip to town every month. Because the bar, at the outset, is merely a reaction to the vexation she feels after her visit, just before, to another establishment: the bank.

In the course of a long day in San León, the bills, errands, alcohol, and gambling are nothing compared to that austere building, with its talent for sending her back into the street in a rage. She wanted things to go better: but there's nothing for it, that pig of a banker robs her every time. And ever since she told him there were as many holes in his vaults as there are vermin in his worm-eaten floorboards, he's had it in for her. But even if he happened to be amenable one day, the mother would not even notice; her eyes narrow the moment she charges through the door, a mean look on her face. It never fails. He looks at her papers, opens the iron gate to show her, gives a sigh. Shortly after that the mother slams the door behind her, crosses the street with her cheeks on fire, and goes to join the twins, vociferating as if it were them she was mad at, shouting her lungs out: *Gomez, Gomez, one day I'll dry the skin from your ass on the same line as the hide from my steers!*

She sees her sons looking down to avoid the sight of her mouth twisted with anger, her eyes darting flames. And the gazes of passersby, staring at the mother as if she were some old lunatic, with her trembling cheeks and her hands in the air and the words that spill out higgledy-piggledy, and there are days when she feels that searing shiver down her back and the bad smell in her armpits, and the hatred inside her, and Mauro and Joaquin stubbornly contemplate the ground, rejecting her in silence. But this is life, you refuse to let others stomp on your feet, the boys have to learn this if they don't want the estancia to end up in the hands of those bastards in the neat and tidy clothes. *I'm going to check my accounts,* chimes the mother every time, as she pushes the door and goes in. Sometimes she stays for a long time, and outside they must be thinking they've had her for dinner in there and she'll never come out; to hope that maybe this time things have worked out and they're keeping her in there for a drink or to celebrate the sale of the herd, now that would make her laugh, and on this particular day she's taking so long she can imagine Mauro getting impatient and saying, "Did she come out and we missed her?"

But how could she go past them, with her sons outside the bank like two guard dogs that don't miss a thing, their senses on the alert, their gazes riveted on the door until everything blurs, their eyes sting, and Joaquin shakes his head.

"She's still in there."

"What's she doing?"

The mother, in fact, doesn't have the leisure to waste time imagining her boys, sitting there with that crafty swine and his bad news, telling her what she doesn't want to hear, and she springs to her feet with a shout, what right do they have to take—and that bastard answering: *The right that gives them the right,* and what else while we're at it, pretty soon they'll be stealing what she doesn't even have, she'd do better to keep her money at home, at least it wouldn't disappear. No one will give her any credit now? Tell me another! It's up to her? Yes, just you wait and see.

Out she comes, practically tearing the door from its hinges, appearing in a halo of rage—although nothing is really apparent, the twins can sense her fury all the way from where they are sitting, it's like a draft, a hot wind the mother contains inside her and which boils in her bloodshot eyes, in her cavernous voice when she is next to them and says, with a ferocious look:

"Nothin' left."

They hesitate for a moment before they dare speak.

"Nothing?"

"They've taken everything."

Mauro stamps his foot on the ground.

"But how could they? With the herd we just sold."

"There were debts. They helped themselves. They all did."

The mother gives a scornful sniff, turns to look toward the town. A mean smile on her lips. Like a kettle about to explode, and she murmurs, so that it doesn't burst as it passes her lips, so that the words will calm down, otherwise she'd go back into the bank and slit Gomez's throat right there where he's sitting in his armchair:

"The father was right to leave. There's no hope in this damn place, they take everything you've got, down to your last peso. We should have left, too."

She lets out a stifled cry, the anger overflowing, even more than resignation. To the twins she has suddenly become incandescent, a live torch. It wouldn't take much for her to split in two, taking the town, its inhabitants, and its banker with her, a burning tidal wave, a flow of lava. They don't even dare to touch her. She tosses her satchel down next to her. Rubs her face, hard. Her cheeks are red.

Joaquin whispers, "What are we gonna do?"

"What?"

He repeats his words in the same tone. The mother gets annoyed, *Talk louder*.

"So tell me, there's no shame! What are we gonna do. *What are we gonna do.*"

"Yeah," he mutters.

"Yeah, what?"

"This."

"I can't hear you. Are you afraid these people"—she turns, waves her arm to include the street, the passersby—"will make fun of us?"

And Joaquin looks imploringly at the bystanders who are beginning to stop and listen.

"No, no."

"So?"

"So."

"What have you got to tell me, loud and clear?"

Looking lost, he observes the mother.

"I dunno, I dunno!"

"Well, I know. We're going to start over. Come on."

She had untied Rufian, then thinks better of it. Hitches him back to the post and heads toward the bar in a few determined strides. Inside her the rage has formed a ball of fire that only gambling and alcohol will quell. In the meantime, it is devouring her. At the end of the street there are children squabbling, and she gazes at them for a few moments and thinks about other things: the exhausting work, the days making her old before her time. Her wretched life. But never mind, tonight she'll give fate a kick in the ass, she can tell. Behind her, Mauro is calling out.

"Ma . . . "

She hesitates. He calls again, he's the only one she might listen to, she's drifting, one leg poised in midair. *Ma, please . . .* So she stops and looks at them, Joaquin and him, clinging to the cart as if someone were about to steal it. In the end they're still just kids. For a split second she almost goes back to them, to ruffle their hair and sit next to them, to urge the horse homeward. But there is her anger. She forgets everything and shouts, "Come on."

She doesn't wait for them. She knows they'll obey her. At the bar, she's invited to sit down to a game, far away from the window. She joins in, picks up her cards, trembling.

"Watch me now," she says.

Across from her, old Emiliano smiles and stretches. And says, *Some movement at last. I'm in.* The others nod and murmur. She hands the cards to Leo.

"Go on, shuffle."

Her surly expression has not left her. The mother is on the warpath. To take on the banks, injustice. To take on the world. And with a beer in her hand. With her untidy hair and her face still red with fury, she looks like a gorgon straight out of hell. And indeed no one really dares look at her or ask her what's wrong. They're not interested; and her answer would be stinging, because everyone ought to sweep their own doorstep before they come ferreting around hers. The only thing that everyone can see is that she is in a very foul temper. She is the first to know that at times like this you ought to withdraw, because you play badly. But there's honor. And rage. She is above it all. She picks up her cards.

She loses.

Shuffles, deals, loses again. And again. In the beginning the guys laugh at her, tease her. The stakes aren't high. Then they go higher with each new game. The mother persists. In the room there's heavy drinking and smoking. A white cloud floats above the gamblers, there's a mingled smell of sweat. As time passes the table is littered with chips and cards, gazes grow either keener or unfocused by alcohol. There's less talk. The men follow the game, lay down their cards, pick them up. Make a joke before the next round. The mother's pile of chips is dwindling relentlessly; sometimes she can add to it, but not much. The next round and she loses everything. Sitting across from her they feel awkward, as if, all things considered, she was trying her best to lose. Determined to play the worst hand possible. Her eyes are bloodshot. She's drunk eight or ten beers.

"Playin' real well now, aren't you," grunts Emiliano.

The mother pounds her fist on the table. *How dare you talk to me like that!*

"What you up to, trying to go bust tonight?"

"Play. Play!"

They continue, with a sigh. The excitement is gone: even the old rascals who usually fleece the mother, with moderation, don't like this predictable succession of games, and their victories are bitter. They protest, exhaling noisily. The mother couldn't care less, leaning low on her elbows, her gaze unfocused. She hovers over her cards without seeing them, talks to herself in a mumbled voice. The twins sense her morbid jubilation as she throws her chips in with a flourish of outrage, demands a new game, slaps down her cards. The smoke from the cigarillos makes her cough.

"Open the window," orders Alejo.

The lukewarm draft of air gives them a shiver of pleasure. Mauro and Joaquin get to their feet and go and sit at a table at the far end of the bar. They had taken the mother by the arm and told her to stop, to no avail. What the hell do those two know? She shoved them away, calling them idiots.

"Never. I got too much money at stake. I have to get it back."

"Ma, and what if you lose everything?"

"Luck can turn. It's my turn soon. Leave me alone."

She shouts at Alejo to give them some empanadas, to keep them busy. The aroma of grilled beef and baked pastry fills the air, makes their mouths water. They sit down, and the mother can return to her cards, forget those sons of hers who bother her with their worried looks, who have finally left her alone, muttering that they have nothing to lose, so they think, and she's not about to prove them wrong when all she wants is some peace and quiet so she can get on with the cards. From one distracted ear, confused by the beer and the late hour, she hears customers commenting on the game, doesn't understand that they are shaking with laughter; doubt makes her hesitate. She plays a straight, six-seven-eight-six, confusing the last card, upside down, with a nine, her eyes blurred with alcohol. Night fell hours ago. From where she sits she can make out figures hurrying along the street, opening the door to the bar to come in or go out, and it all evens out, those who arrive and those who leave, like births and deaths, and there are still just as many people inside, just as many people watching her, shaking their heads and making remarks, she'd rather not hear, she studies her hand.

There are entire spells when she is unaware of her surroundings. Her chest is tight as if her heart were struggling, and it keeps her from concentrating, as surely as if Mauro and Joaquin were there, and not across the room, and yet she can sense their watchfulness, why the hell don't they stop spying on her and judging her like that—she spills her beer, wipes it up with the back of her sleeve. She turns around all of a sudden, furious, sees them three tables further along. She shouts at them because it's clearly their fault if she's losing so much tonight.

"Are you gonna stop or what?"

They give a start. Because they didn't think she could see them. She has eyes in the back of her head. For the poker game it's the same, and with her gaze still riveted on her sons, she hears the bid and says, as usual, *I'm in*.

But this time Emiliano taps on the table next to her, gives her a nudge in the shoulder.

"You got nothing left," he says.

The mother turns around and no matter where she looks, however much she searches, her side of the table is empty, all her chips have vanished. She begins to sob.

"It can't be, I was going to make up my losses."

Emiliano shakes his head and says again, *You're all out.*

And that is when the mother falls.

MAURO

I n the sweltering heat of the bar at night he waits, watching
the mother out of the corner of his eye, sharing cigarettes
with Joaquin, sucking at the last drops of the beer he finished hours ago. The tall twin has been used to this, ever since
the father's departure thirteen years ago. The brothers, the
mother, the animals, the family, so to speak: he's the one who
watches over them all. It's not that it's exactly pleasant every
day, but in a way it's part of his work. And while the mother
gives the orders, the brothers turn to him when it comes to
learning how to reach inside a cow's womb to bring out a calf,
or how to manage with a ram that doesn't want to go from one
herd to another. Even Joaquin lets him take over, he knows
what's what: there are evenings when he is tormented by the
decisions he has to make, particularly during the birthing season, a season he hates, for it forces him to hand down verdicts
written in blood, do we save the ewe or the lamb, slaughter the
bull whose castration went wrong or let him live on, maybe we
can sell him before he dies. He never lets emotion get the better of him: but the question constantly hounds him, maybe he
could have done better. Sometimes he tries. Often he ends up
with his arms and hands dripping in blood, and the animal
dying at his feet; sometimes, against all expectation, it gets
back on its feet, a miraculous, tremulous survivor, and something powerful vibrates in his own belly, he looks at the brothers there next to him and says, simply, "There you go."

And they nod. He towers over them—not just his size, his

faith, too. He is the estancia. Together with Joaquin. It's not that he really needs his twin for the work, but it's something you can't control, maybe it's from being together in the mother's entrails before they even came into the world, so they can't ever be separated, anyway that's the way it is, Mauro and Joaquin always two by two, it's not right otherwise. Joaquin is there to look at his brother with pride, to assume some part of his strength, his labor, but above all to walk by his side, whatever happens, even when the older brother is wrong and Joaquin says nothing.

"Well?"

Mauro blinks, returns to the night in the smoky bar, to Joaquin sitting next to him, the empty plates from which they've scraped the tiniest crumbs.

"What?"

"I said, we have to shoe Salvaje. He's thrown his right front shoe, did you see?"

"Yes."

"We'll take care of it tomorrow."

"Okay."

"Remember the first time we shod him? We had to get him to lie down to do it."

"He's a good horse."

"I know, he's mine, I know him. But he's stubborn as a mule, too."

"Always takes a bit of mule to make a good horse."

"Like the mother."

Mauro laughs joylessly. *Just what I was gonna say.* He pushes back his plate, looking in vain for another crumb, a tiny morsel of forgotten meat.

"Lambing season soon," continues Joaquin, twiddling his fingertips on the table—and Mauro realizes how much their thoughts wander into the same spaces, the same subjects.

"Yeah, I saw."

The ewes' swollen udders, their bellies expanding with the lambs' kicks. In one week, two at the most, the brothers will ride across their land from dawn to sunset, counting the newborns, checking to make sure the sheep are healthy. It will take three months or so until the births are over, because after the sheep the cows will start; three months endlessly riding, caring, slaughtering if necessary, if they're unlucky. When that's done they'll round up the herds to brand the lambs and the calves; but first of all there's this period of delivery, with the smell of mucus and blood. Sometimes they don't make it home for two or three days, and their hands are stained with sickly sweet effluvia and black clots which they try to clean by rubbing them in the dust on the trail. When they heat up their mess tins at night, their fingers stink and every spoonful they swallow reminds them of the awkward creatures they pulled from their mothers' entrails, and they end up leaving half the meal, vaguely nauseated, inhaling the animal smell on their trousers and shirts. And yet they are proud of having, in their way, given birth, all through those scorching days. Joaquin puts his head down on his forearm and looks at his brother.

"How many, you reckon?"

"I don't know. Maybe two thousand, if we're lucky."

Tired, they doze in spurts. They would like to keep their eyes open but their eyelids close despite them, and the room begins to spin as if they'd had too much to drink, or were whirling in place, round and round, the way they used to when they were kids to make themselves dizzy, arms spread, laughing out loud, Joaquin keeling over first. Mauro went on, staggering, clinging to the passing air. Afterward, lying side by side, they would gaze at the sky and wait for the nausea to pass. The clouds retreated, returned, tilted; Joaquin would often sit up with a shout, because suddenly it felt as if he were falling into the void, but it was only the rolling inside him, and Mauro would grab him by the sleeve to calm him down. Then they would tell each other stories about the horses and the steppe. Until they eventually drifted into a hesitant half-sleep, and then the mother would be shouting for them at the top of her lungs, to make sure they could hear her wherever they were.

Mauro gives a start.

The mother.

He shakes Joaquin and turns toward her at the same time. He's never heard her scream like this, he's never seen her in such a state. Her howls pierce the noise, shocking the men, who pull away from her as if to avoid something dangerous. She is on her feet, roaring, tearing out her long straight hair, waving her arms, her eyes red with fatigue and anger. Emiliano tries in vain to calm her down. Alejo puts a glass of alcohol in front of her; she swallows it down in one. And then she collapses on her chair. The bar goes dead silent.

Mauro shoves a few men aside without apology.

"What's going on?"

She doesn't reply. Her gaze has drifted into the distance, foggy, despondent. The twins kneel down next to her.

"Ma?"

Slowly she turns her head, looks at them. She says, *Joaquin.* But it's Mauro who replies.

"I'm here, Ma."

"Joaquin?"

"He's here."

Tears stream down her face, old too soon. It's the first time he's ever seen her cry. Something snaps inside him, and he stands up straight, immense, and turns to face the gathering.

"What happened, for Chrissake?"

Emiliano gathers up his cards and hands them to Alejo to put away.

"Well, she lost."

The boy frowns, fumbles for words.

"Everything?"

The old man nods. *Yup. And then some.*

"I don't understand."

"Are you Joaquin?"

"No, it's him."

Emiliano's strange blue eyes shift to the other twin. Gauge him. He clicks his tongue.

"Son, you'd better pack your bags. Your mother lost you in the game. I'll come and get you tomorrow at daybreak."

The mother has collapsed on the seat of the cart, inert, snoring. Rufian is trotting at a good clip, glad to be on the way home; his breathing gives rhythm to the night. Clouds hide the moon but he knows the way by heart, as if he can smell the familiar house, the stable, his feed. His hooves seem to fly over the ground and the pebbles at a steady pace, *clop clop clop*. He knows nothing about the abyss that has opened in the belly of the boys sitting next to their sleeping mother.

Mauro is holding the reins. He doesn't see the road. Cannot see it. All he can see is his brother.

"Don't worry," murmurs Joaquin.

But his voice is trembling.

They have never been apart. They were born twins, just as they were born with dark hair and black eyes: inseparably. Mauro cannot imagine a life without Joaquin. It would be the same if he had lost a hand or a foot. He grunts: "She won't let you leave."

Joaquin casts a scornful look at the mother.

"Her? So it's not enough for you, what she did tonight?"

"She'll work it out with Emiliano tomorrow."

"There's nothing to work out, Mauro. She gambled me. *Gambled.* Like money or cattle. You hear me?"

They fall silent. Joaquin shoves the mother with his foot, and she half slips onto the floor of the cart, twisted in a ridiculous position. He spits on her.

"*Me*. You can be sure she knew what she was doing, the old lady, didn't she. It wasn't you she gambled, Mauro. She needs you, you're the strongest, you do the work of two men, she could never manage without you. But I'm nothing to her. Any old seasonal hand can replace me when she needs extra labor, she'll check her budget and see it'll cost her less than to feed me year in year out, and she'll think that luck was on her side after all."

"Don't say that."

"Wait and see."

"You'll be back."

"She'll never have the money to get me back."

Mauro opens his mouth to speak, then swallows his words. He tries to put himself in his brother's position. Of course the mother won't do anything tomorrow: he stops trying to reassure Joaquin. His brother will leave, like Emiliano said. At the thought of it, he feels the burning in his guts again. He imagines the old man showing up with a new horse for his twin, who will then saddle it with his own tack, and strap on his kit—he has so little, a few items of clothing, a knife, his lasso. He whispers:

"And Salvaje?"

In the dark, Joaquin's hands are twisted so tight that Mauro takes his arm and shakes it.

"Ma will never let you take him with you, will she."

"I know. He's worth more than I am, that horse, even if she does nothing with him."

"If you want, I'll take him back out to the plains. He'll be better off out there than ending up a workhorse."

Joaquin does not answer right away. His dun criollo. Mauro knows that this upsets Joaquin as much as leaving him, his brother, he can sense the temptation in Joaquin's eyes, to beg the mother to give him the horse, if he has to he'll set aside his dignity, his pride, for a horse, for a friend. Who else could remind him of the estancia, who could stay with him other than Salvaje—a warm, vibrant memory of his life up until that evening, the thick mane for consolation, the damp coat to dry his tears, in the early days. And for sure the mother doesn't give a damn about that horse, and after what she agreed to this evening it would be the least she could do. But she won't give Joaquin the horse, Mauro is sure of that. She has never given any of them anything. It's all for her bloody self, for Chrissake, it drives him insane, the fact she could lose his brother at a poker game, you'd think she doesn't know how to do anything but destroy, she is headed for a place in hell, dragging them with her, to fix things and slave away in silence. And yet he can sense Joaquin next to him, slowly breathing, gathering his momentum, and how can he hold it against him, he would have done the same. Uttering the words in a quiet voice to get used to them, to give himself courage, and the older brother hears them and it hurts: *Ma, by the way, about Salvaje . . .*

But when the grunting under the blanket she has wrapped herself in reaches their ears, Joaquin suddenly hunches over and decides against it. *Look, Mauro*, and the tall twin nods his head with a sorrowful smile.

"I wouldn't have said anything, but since you got it on your own: you're right to drop it. No point in humiliating yourself."

"She won't let me, huh."

"No."

"What's she going to do with him?"

"Nothing."

"Yup. That's what I think, too. She just wants him to belong to her."

"That's right."

"Because I'm a stranger now."

"That's bullshit."

"Didn't you see the way she looked at me, back there, when

we left the bar? I'm not part of the family anymore. I could see it in her eyes. Shit, as if I was the one betraying her!"

"The day she can buy you back, she'll do it right away, I'm sure. That's all she'll be thinking about."

"Well, let her think."

Mauro hesitates; what's the point of more lies—he too is aware that the mother has sold them, that in all likelihood she would do so again if she had to. Wipe them off the face of the earth for a game of poker. For a fit of anger that's of no concern to them. She looked at Joaquin as they headed back to the cart, he saw her turn away from him, and it was the same as when she turns for home again after she's witnessed the death of an animal—without sadness, just something she saw on her way home. She'll order the sons to go bury the creature. And that's it, forgotten. How many days will it take the mother to wipe Joaquin from her memory? Something inside Mauro melts with relief at the thought that, of the two of them, he is the one who will be staying behind. He feels slightly guilty. And murmurs:

"I'll see you in San León, don't you think?"

Joaquin doesn't answer. He is already gone.

RAFAEL

T he first night after Joaquin left, the little brother rides out on Halley. Until the very last moment he didn't think Emiliano would show up. The story was too appalling, and the mother said nothing, as expressionless as a corpse. And yet, on seeing the twins' despondent faces, Rafael clenched his fists and waited, suppressing his emotions, so that nothing would show. He went to hide in a corner of the barn. Fell to his knees in a sort of prayer. The estancia was trapped in a heavy silence that seemed doomed to last forever. He gave himself a time beyond which he would lose all hope; and just when he no longer believed it could, it happened.

Mid-morning, the old man was there at the end of the road. Mauro whistled between his teeth the moment he saw him: *Here he is, the vulture.* And Rafael watched him come toward them, bathed in light, his handsome, wrinkled face full of promises, he heard something singing in the sky, and he joined his hands. *Make it be true.*

Up until that final moment, too, he was afraid that Mauro, livid with anger, would take his rifle and kill Emiliano. That the mother would take out a wad of bills. That Joaquin would run away and swear he'd be back later. But none of that happened, and the old man slapped his hand on the shoulder of the smaller twin.

"Don't make such a face! I'm not taking you to the slaughterhouse."

Then they were gone. Silence and emptiness left behind like

a veil over the estancia, and even Rafael is not as pleased as he'd hoped he'd be. He'd have to wait for his nighttime refuge on the steppe and the quiet hoof fall of his horse: only then would he feel his throat relax and his hands open, and the acrid sweat evaporate, how many hours had it been sticking to his temples. The moon is slender but he doesn't care, he can see well enough. The universe sparkles. He rides across the plain, laughing, locates the spots where he had tried to dig graves in weeks gone by. He leans forward and into his horse's ear he says:

"One down."

The estancia without Joaquin slowly closes upon itself again. The remaining brothers keep busy. In the beginning they sleep badly at night, disturbed by this strange change to their immutable world. Something is destabilizing them, causing them to cry out. At daybreak, when it's time to go and sad-dle the horses, they instinctively wait for Joaquin. And when they circle around the cattle, or see to the calves or the newborn lambs, they look for the absent pair of arms. The dogs are disoriented, and don't know whether to follow Mauro or the other two; if no one calls them, they keep to themselves, off to one side.

Sometimes the sons stare out at the arid plains stretching all the way to the horizon, to the mountains: that's where Joaquin is living now, where he's doing the same gaucho work they're doing, but elsewhere, and without them. Out there, the westerly winds blow harder, cold and damp, and the cordillera of the Andes doesn't protect those who live in the foothills. Emiliano is a sheep farmer. They picture Joaquin on horseback, herding the animals, or on foot, cutting their thick wool and putting it in sacks. They feel privileged, the fact that with the mother they still have bovines, and they know only too well how nauseating the acrid smell of sheep can be, how it makes you sick, even after years of it, and how the tiny filaments of wool can irritate your throat and eyes, making you spit and cough when it's shearing season.

"Rotten luck," laughs the little brother, but he instantly falls silent when Mauro shoots him a dark look.

Once again he learns how to pretend: that he misses Joaquin, and his eyes fill with tears when they talk about him. He asks the mother how long she thinks it will take to make enough money to go and get him, this same mother who, from the day she gambled her son, has stopped going to sit at the poker tables. Mauro keeps an eye on her, goes with her to town every time, hoping to see his twin. And when they come back at night he obliges the old lady to put the money she hasn't lost at cards into a jar. Rafael counts along with them. It doesn't add up to much. The older brother says the mother is drinking half again as much as before, eating away at the savings he'd hoped they'd accumulate. She says it's so she won't succumb to the temptation to gamble. A fine excuse. Now she drinks glass after glass, her eyes glued to the games going on around her, without her, she whines her approval or dissent, waving her fingers which long to caress the cards. But she stands firm. It tears her heart out, and her guts, that's how, to restore her dignity, she describes it the next morning to the two younger boys, her voice furry with the residue of alcohol. Rafael gives her a sidelong glance, while Mauro glares at her and grumbles, *You should stop drinking, too.* The little brother nods vigorously, he agrees. And what else do you want, shouts the mother, for there to be nothing left she's allowed to do, not the least little entertainment in this dull existence, do they want her to croak already, joylessly, and not even forty years old, just to put three extra pesos in the jar, and what else while you're at it.

They give up. Make do with her promise she won't gamble them, too—for Rafael, that's enough. If he had to, he'd go and steal from the money saved, to delay Joaquin's return, but there's so little, they'd notice. He suspects the mother herself dips into the jar now and again, in anticipation of her drinking expenses; Joaquin isn't about to come back to the estancia any time soon.

And yet the old lady goes on working, cooking, selling, without flinching. She's started saying "my three sons"—and that's about the only thing that's changed. She has never given an explanation or an apology for that disastrous evening at poker; she's walled up in a stubborn silence. The little brother would have liked to hear her tell the story, but all he gets is gestures of irritation. He often asks Mauro to tell him about that terrible night. Tormented, the tall twin repeats the story relentlessly, convinced as he is that his brothers are mourning the way he is. In his heart of hearts, Rafael is purring. He says, *Tell it again*. And once again Mauro sets the stage, the noisy bar, the alcohol, and the cards on the tables.

"Goddamn," murmurs the little brother in conclusion, every time.

The tall twin nods. *Yup. It's rotten.*

Rotten. When he thinks about it in his bed at night, Rafael has to keep from laughing. Before, they went two by two; before, the older brothers dealt out punches, orders, humiliation. So for that reason alone, Joaquin's departure is beyond Steban and Rafael's wildest expectations. Even if at times the sudden void he left behind him derails them, that void has put an end to the terrible beatings. Mauro hasn't once tried to corner them and thrash them; in his twin's absence he's lost, paralyzed. In the beginning the little brother can scarcely believe it, and when he's rubbing down his horse at the end of the day he is still startled if there's a creaking sound in the barn or he thinks he sees the tall twin's terrifying silhouette in the doorway. As for Steban, he's counting the days. Their older brother's desertion is more alarming than the way he used to beat them: they're afraid that once Mauro recovers from his twin's loss he will come down upon them more cruelly than ever. And even though before long he does start shaking them when they're too slow at what they're doing, never again does he indulge in the violent episodes he found so entertaining. Little by little, Steban and Rafael are amazed to see they can sleep through the night, their bodies going limp, and they don't wake up with their hearts pounding at the chilling thought that it's all going to start up again. It takes weeks, but for the first time in years the little brother is able to luxuriate in sleep, to discover the ecstasy of feeling his body harrowed by nothing more than work. No longer do his eyes shine with the anxious gleam of trapped prey; every evening he is amazed to be able to spread his arms and legs out on the lumpy mattress and wrap himself in a blanket, and a sensation not unlike happiness comes over him while he trembles with joy. In silence he applauds the mother who drinks too much and saves nothing. He works himself into the ground all day long, harder than ever, so she won't be sorry she's lost Joaquin. He prays it won't all turn out to be a dream—and since Joaquin left not a day has gone by without him thanking the Santa María standing on the dresser.

The way he looks at the world has changed. He celebrates his fourteenth birthday without fear. He realizes that for as long as he can remember he has always been flanked by anxiety. The apprehension of the next blow, the insults. And everything else. Maybe if he had not grown up in this savage environment he would not savor so deeply the strange freedom Joaquin's departure has given him. But he measures his luck, their luck, and standing in his stirrups as he looks out at the landscape, he spreads his arms out in front of Steban and bellows:

"Didn't I tell you he'd leave?"

His brother smiles crookedly, revealing his ruined teeth,

and grunts, *Yup,* hoarsely, motioning to him to keep his voice down.

"You mean Mauro might hear us from here?"

The little brother bursts out laughing.

"Mauro is at Las Pointas. Two hours south of here. No danger. You're still scared, aren't you."

"Nah."

"Yes, you are, you idiot."

"Nah, I said."

"Watch out, that was three words in a row."

"Asshole."

A flock of birds rises up before them, frightened by Rafael's shout. He watches them soaring into the sky in a noisy cloud, finding their places and gradually aligning themselves in a V formation, a few birds in the lead then the rest of the flock following, hundreds of vibrant black dots, and they're peeping their hearts out, a noise, a song—the little brother closes his eyes. No sound of a rifle being fired to startle him. Mauro stopped that, too: when the passerines land in the thickets, he observes them while finishing his cigarette, and no spark lights up his tired face, he doesn't reach for his rifle or hurl insults at these creatures he's always hated. He simply turns away so he doesn't see them. He is sick of the world; the wound of Joaquin's departure is not healing. In the evening when he comes home from work he sits down on the front stoop and waits for supper, not saying a word. He eats quickly, leaves the table, and shuts himself in his room. In the beginning the mother pestered him. And then she stopped. Steban and Rafael watch him leave, dragging his feet, and to see how stooped he's become in the space of a few weeks they wonder if he hasn't shrunk. To each other they call him Sad-Mauro.

Sad-Mauro doesn't speak. He learns to gaze at the sky, expecting nothing. How can the little brothers possibly understand the twin's deep, burning wound? What do they know of the extreme feelings of brotherhood—the affection they show that is like a young puppy's: unconscious, volatile, they are no more attached to each other than they are to their livestock, and even less than to their horses. The older boy observes them, full of scorn, and Rafael often notes a gleam in his eye that makes him tremble for fear of seeing the anger and violence return. But now he realizes the gleam vanishes too quickly for Mauro to come at them every time, he'd have to be consumed by anger, bolt upright in a flourish of rage, but fortunately for Steban and him something has snapped, because the only thing that makes the older brother feel good is to set off at gallop and round up the heifers or ewes, in a physical struggle he knows he will win. Or to plunge his head in the river to ease the torment. Or strike out at them, his little brothers, naturally, never imagining for an instant how they will laugh to themselves afterward at how insignificant it feels compared to before—and this despite the fact that he hits hard, deliberately.

The mother and Mauro go at each other too, not often, but from time to time, when he reproaches her for forgetting about Joaquin—and even Rafael is surprised to find he forgets how there used to be four of them, as if he'd erased the second twin from his life, the way he forgets the rain the morning after, as soon as his clothes are dry. Mauro is no fool when he lets fly at them too, and not just the mother, although with her he reminds her that she gave birth to twins, and raised both of them, not just Mauro the firstborn, as he shouts:

"Do you remember him? Do you remember there were two of us, right from the start, and that you went and ruined it?"

But the mother doesn't even answer, and Rafael can see in her gaze that she is waiting for Mauro to be quiet, his distress leaves her indifferent. Joaquin belongs to the past. The tall twin is not mistaken when he argues with her, when she refuses to say how much money she has put aside since she lost her son at poker, since she decided to keep the jar in her room, away from prying eyes. The little brother has been placing bets to himself. A few dozen pesos. Fifty. Nothing. How much is Joaquin worth? Rafael's only benchmark is the price of a ewe or a cow. Somewhere in between? Does it go by weight? Fifteen pesos the pound. But with Joaquin's know-how, surely a lot more. He decides on fifty thousand pesos, because he hopes the mother will never have that much. And yet he reckons all she'd have to do would be to sell five head of cattle. The thought of it, so easy, fills him with dread. Try not to think about it any more, so as not to let it drift through the air, within reach, but the mother is bound to know, and he tries to reassure himself, there has to be something else, some trouble, some lapse of time, an old resentment, so that in the end Joaquin won't come back.

Gradually life goes back to the old routine, spread among them the work gets done. From the outside, nothing has changed on the mother's estancia. And just as the surface of a pond becomes smooth again, and concentric circles vanish once the pebble has fallen to the bottom, the four of them who are left, mother and sons, breathe and grow calm at last. Little ripples. Fewer and fewer. And then nothing. Joaquin is gone for good.

JOAQUIN

No more smiles, ever. That will be his revenge, his way of being faithful, of showing Emiliano that you don't gamble for a boy when there's nothing else to take. He won't be a source of shame to his mother: he knows how to work. He knows he'll have to make do with sheep now and he already misses the smell of cows, but when it comes to herding, rounding up, shearing, and butchering, he already knows all that. He is afraid of no one. The only person who could humiliate him with his robust build and endurance has stayed behind at the estancia.

But smile, that he won't. And when the old man leaves him at the end of the day to his three gauchos and there he is alone with them he makes no effort—he almost felt like clinging to Emiliano to get away from them, he doesn't want to see the others or speak to them. And they don't either, they just touched the brims of their hats in greeting when he arrived, and then they picked up their conversation where they'd left off, if he'd been a passing dog they'd have done no differently. So, seething with bitterness, Joaquin sits on his own on the steps to the house and looks at the sky, counting the hours until it's time to go to bed, not even sure he'll have any dinner. The mother did give him a hunk of dried meat but he doesn't dare take it out. He doesn't understand why the guys already stopped working when there are still two hours of daylight, and he has heard they'll get up early the next morning—but anyway, the mother would say, is that any reason. After an hour has gone by, he's as bored as a dead rat; if he weren't so tense, for sure he would have fallen asleep, never mind his empty stomach. So when one of the gauchos calls out to him, he gives a start.

"So old Emiliano has brought us a baby."

Joaquin makes a face and doesn't reply. He stares at the young man who has stopped speaking, he'd be surprised if he's even five years older than him, and a heavy silence falls over them all, the way it used to with Mauro sometimes, and his long face with its drawn features looks from one man to the next, with a blank expression.

"Heard tell he won you at poker."

It was the oldest man who spoke, a dark, wrinkled little man whose eyes shine beneath eyelids grown heavy with work and sun, and the twin thinks that this is the first time he has heard that word, won, not lost, for the first time his ears can put up with it, so he nods and murmurs, "Yup."

The old gaucho nods.

"That's a blow. I suppose you're not too happy about it."

"It shows," says the one who called him a baby.

"Let me ask him, Fabricio, you always go too fast, what does it cost just to ask him?"

"We don't care, Eduardo, that's all."

"Don't listen to him, baby."

The old gaucho looks at Joaquin, laughing to himself at his joke and adds: "You don't mind if I call you that? Fabricio's right, you look like a kid."

And Joaquin bites his lips not to call them assholes, claws at his knees with his hands not to get up and punch them, all of them, he's sure he could beat all three of them, every last one, old or not old. He hunches over in silence. Keeps his teeth clenched, even when they go in to heat up a bowl of beans for dinner, he picks at his food. The others try to tease him once or twice, but soon give up—they have other fish to fry.

After the meal, they go out again to smoke. Unsure, Joaquin stays there in the corridor, his satchel at his feet with all his meager belongings. Eduardo sees him from outside and comes back into the house.

"I'll show you where you sleep."

He opens the door at the end of the corridor. *Here you are, this is it. And we're good guys here, you'll see. Things will be better tomorrow.*

"Who else sleeps in here?"

"Well, we each have our own room, what did you think. This room is your home. No one comes in here besides you."

On his own, Joaquin sits on the bed. He misses Mauro, and the mother, and even the little brother and that half-wit Steban; he wishes he could cry to get rid of the stinging in his throat, so he could breathe better. But nothing comes, just a dryness that causes his heart to flutter, his cheeks to flush, something dead in his chest, because all of them back there at the estancia have closed the door on him. He was hoping, he really believed, if he's honest, that if the mother herself didn't, Mauro would do something when Emiliano came. But he had waited in vain. In a hushed voice he'd begged, but his tall twin didn't budge, not even a sign of anxiety on his face, no regret. Just a few words: *I'll come back and get you.* And he'd have to take his word for it.

He can sense that the guys outside in the darkness are sitting down now. One of them is playing a guitar. Soundlessly Joaquin opens the window and listens; at the estancia there was never any music. It's nothing like the bawdy or raucous songs at the bar in San León; what he hears calms him, lulls him on the evening of this difficult day. With his elbows on the wooden sill he puts his cheek on his arms. He wishes he could fall asleep and that it would go on, the plucking of chords resonating deep inside him, the voice humming, almost murmuring. He feels as if he's been listening for hours, he's with them in the dark, whispering the refrains, trying to memorize bits of lyrics so he can say them again, too.

"Hey, kid."

He opens his eyes without even raising his head. Eduardo is waving to him through the window.

"Come on out."

Joaquin slowly shakes his head. He doesn't feel like it. No strength. But the old man insists, eventually comes in the house and knocks on the door. Doesn't open it; speaks through the wooden panel.

"Don't stay there worrying about things, son. Come on out, why don't you."

Joaquin looks at the closed door, hears the voice coming through it. At the estancia no one ever knocks; doors are made to be opened as you burst in practically tearing them from their hinges. And shouts go with it. Never before could he sit in a room like this and hear someone asking from beyond a closed door:

"Can I come in?"

So for the first time in his life Joaquin says, *Yes.*

He wakes up outside in the middle of the night. For a fraction of a second he thinks he can still hear the music and the men laughing around him, then realizes he's alone. He rubs his eyes to come to his senses. A moment later he knows the others have had a good laugh at his expense, leaving him to sleep on the ground while they have gone back to their beds, once Arcangel put the guitar down—he can't remember dropping off, he has no idea how he could have been sleeping so soundly that he didn't hear them leave, wasn't wary of these strangers.

He sits bolt upright and feels the blanket sliding off him, and realizes they put it there so he wouldn't be cold. And then Eduardo's voice behind him:

"You awake, kid? You should go inside."

Joaquin gives a start and jerks around on his butt to face him.

"Hey, old man, aren't you going to sleep?"

"I haven't had a real night's sleep in ages."

"Did you put this blanket on me?"

"It's cold, don't you think?"

Joaquin stands up and wraps the cloth around him to preserve the warmth. His feet are frozen.

"Yup, I think it's even colder than where I'm from."

"The Andes. That's where the damp comes from."

"I'm going to bed."

Eduardo nods, reaches for his pouch of tobacco, and Joaquin looks at him.

"Are you staying here?"

"I've got a few more to smoke, I think."

"Okay."

On the threshold he pauses.

"Thanks. For the blanket."

He doesn't say it, but he thinks: *No one has ever done that for me.*

Thousands of sheep, even more of them and whiter than the mother's. You can't see the ground for the herds, with a few brown rams dotted here and there. They smell different to Joaquin, there's an intoxicating smell of dried turd, maybe the air sweeps away the stench of urine and sweat-clumped wool here, and Fabricio laughs.

"Look at them all with their asses to the wind. No need to ask which way the wind's blowing."

Whether they're eating, sleeping, or playing, the sheep all stand facing the same way, their rumps to the west, their heads low or tucked in their shoulders to keep out of the gusts. From where they are, slightly above them, the gauchos can look down on them as if they were dominos stacked side by side in a huge box, and Joaquin imagines that if a gust of wind knocked over the first one, they're so tightly packed that they'd all fall, one after the other, carried off by a pointless wave, prevented by their physical closeness from getting away—a sea of legs waving from upturned bellies: he bursts out laughing. The others look at him, he breaks off and says, "Shall we go?"

"Let's go," says Eduardo.

They join the herd, their criollos at a walk; Joaquin's mount is the cream color of an unwashed ewe, weary and stoical, worn by years of working the steppe. But no doubt the horse hasn't worked for a while now, because the muscles in his back have slackened, and when the twin runs a hand over his flank he can feel the ribs undulating beneath his palm, like unwelcome little waves. Fabricio notices his gesture and nods.

"Have to get that one back in shape. For two years now he's been out there just wandering around the plain."

"I can tell."

"He's a good nag, otherwise, I saw him at work when I first got here. Mosquito."

He rides in front of him, snapping his fingers, and the horse snorts, shakes his head, and the gaucho laughs.

"A hundred more pounds and he'll be a real devil."

"Plain devil's fine with me," says Joaquin.

"I suspect it is."

"You suspect?"

"Yup."

"How's that?"

"Well, we all know where you come from, kid."

"I still don't get it."

"The men say your estancia is hell on earth."

Joaquin turns toward the herds, not answering, puzzled. Hell. Shit, where'd they get that from, as if they knew the mother and the farm, to talk about where he came from as if it were an abyss—or maybe some of them had worked there as seasonal hands, he can't place them, it would have been a long time ago because the mother decided years ago that her sons were enough to get the work done, but all the same, Joaquin has a good memory, especially for faces: did they ever come for the shearing? Hell.

The image of the old lady hounds him, with her outbursts and tantrums. Sometimes he and Mauro used to look at the statuette of the Virgin on the dresser and neither one of them could believe she was made from the same stuff as the mother, there wasn't the slightest resemblance, so either they'd been lied to, or they'd been mistaken, but no one should try to make them swallow some story about some putative kinship: on the one hand that mass of flesh almost as wide as it was tall, with her thinning hair and her mastiff's jowls, who only knows how to be silent or how to yell, and on the other hand that slender, smiling silhouette, just touching her made you feel better, no, honestly, no. For Joaquin and Mauro there are women, there are men, and there is the mother.

The Virgin in heaven and the mother in hell.

This morning he got up and got ready in a house without shouting, no one nagging in his ear to hurry up, you lazybones, no one grabbing his bowl of maté from him before he's finished because there's no more time, or bellowing for no reason before the day has even started, to spur them on, they're always in a rush, and it's never good and never enough. There's something so different about this place that it leaves him stunned, just wait, it's bound to change.

But all day long they split up the herds, drive them into their pastures to let a bit of wild grass grow elsewhere, you never know when you might need some sheaves of hay for injured or sick animals you've had to take back to the fold. All day long he is patient, relentlessly riding his ill-tempered cremello, sharing the contents of the pail Emiliano's wife prepared for them, taking part in the bets about the evening's menu. *Don't be stupid,* says Eduardo, *you're going to eat up all your pay.* —*I won't be getting any pay.* —*And what do you think, that we work just for the boss lady's soup?*

So for the first time he'll have some money, pesos of his own, Emiliano confirmed it that evening, he said, *To buy back your freedom, in a year you can leave, or stay on.* And Joaquin can hardly believe it, not the fact of leaving, but that he'll be paid, because in that instant the mother's estancia shifts further away in his mind and represents nothing more that a minute preoccupation, giving way at last to a dream, if they don't take it away from him, as always—but this time he hopes with all his might, because this world is different, he can tell, he can yearn for it, and as he runs behind the ewes, his mouth closed over an insane hopefulness, in his mind he cries, "Hell . . . hell!"

MAURO

Hay-making season is over. In the barn, there is a fragrance of dried grass. How such arid soil and poor pastureland are able to join forces to yield a fodder with this dizzying perfume: it never fails, every year, to astound the tall twin. He can also see how much room is left in the barn, and he knows the harvest was meager, the mother will have to buy four or five tons to make up the shortfall; maybe they won't even need it, but if they wait it will be sold out and they won't find any. It hasn't rained in almost three months, the prairies are gray and yellow; the scant grass has not grown properly, yielding a thin, coarse hay that scratches the animals' mouths. Sometimes in winter they have to remove a stem that has stayed planted like an arrow in an animal's gum, causing it to chew the air and shake its head for days. When the season isn't too cold, the herd has no appetite for such dreary food and they prefer to wander for hours, snuffling through the thickets of *neneos*—and Mauro knows he'll have to bring back the herds scheduled for slaughter a few weeks earlier, to leave them in the healthy pastures so that the meat won't have the acrid smell of those spiny plants.

With the end of his pitchfork he gathers the bits of hay that have fallen here and there, and piles them loosely in a corner: the important thing is not to let it go to waste. He tries to work out just how short they'll be exactly, but there are too many things he doesn't know—how many sick animals they'll have to bring back next season, or whether there will be rain or not, because without the rain the food crop won't grow. Despite the heady smell of the hay, the dust makes him cough, dust from the earth they cannot help but harvest along with the grasses, because here, whatever you do, there is always dust—beneath the horses' hooves, behind the carts, on the cows' rumps. Mauro can feel the warmth of the forage he has just stored. In daytime, in the sun, it makes him and the others itch so badly they could scratch their flesh to shreds and clamber into the watering trough to calm the irritation, although none of them do, because they know that the moment their skin dries it will itch all the worse. So they learn to live with it, their skin shivers as if they had a fever, they endure the sweat and, for once, are glad of a bit of breeze to ease their burning arms and neck. In the evening red blotches still sting all the way to their cheeks.

On the other side of the barn the horses whinny suddenly and Mauro looks up, retreats soundlessly into the shadow. This is why he has been lingering here for an hour; he knew the little brother would be stupid enough to come. And surely he doesn't even think about it anymore, otherwise he would not have bothered to open the stable doors to give some grain to the criollos, and yet he ought to remember that his older brother is horribly spiteful. But maybe he didn't notice that Mauro overheard him that morning, when he and Steban were making fun of him, maybe the half-wit—who did see him behind the door and went pale—had actually obeyed the twin's warning gesture, a finger to his lips: *Shhh*—and was too petrified to say anything to Rafael, too cowardly to warn him. And the little brother, so cheerful since Joaquin left: does he think his solitary, grieving older brother doesn't realize that the kid has been imitating him? He thinks he's well hidden when he cries out, and gives a thrust of his hips: *Well! In the ass, Mauro, and in the ass, Joaquin!* Yes, since this morning the tall twin has been waiting to grab him and give him a reason to think twice before he makes fun, he's seething with rage, and if he followed his instincts he'd have rushed at his brother already, but the mother was behind him, she would have heard, he missed his chance. For hours he's been ruminating, working all on his own, because Steban and the little brother would have noticed something just by looking at him, his clenched jaws working incessantly in his ravaged face, but he knows he's right.

Now the mother is in the kitchen, and daylight is fading.

And the little brother has just come into the barn.

Mauro goes toward him, stealing silently across the ground; even the horses don't hear him, munching their grain with a peaceable sound, the sighs of animals that have eaten their fill, and their nostrils in the bucket between two mouthfuls, water splashing, then they shake themselves.

Even the horses have no inkling.

From his hiding place, Mauro observes Rafael in Halley's stable, caressing the criollo, rubbing his hands over his back, under his belly, along his legs, to make sure there are no open wounds. He checks the nails on the horseshoes—they've come slightly loose from the hoof, he keeps an eye, planning no doubt to change them in the next two or three days, never imagining he won't be able to, because right now there's nothing stopping him, nothing to make him suppose anything might change dramatically, change his paltry little everyday plans, he can always go ahead and plan his endless chores. As he leans against his horse he is half-dreaming, tired by his days spent in the scythed prairies, moving his hands to loosen the boils that burst on his palms. Happy as they all are that the harvest is over, his cheek against Halley's flank; the animal perfume drifts over to Mauro.

So the older brother takes a few steps back, just for the pleasure of walking forward again, dragging his feet and seeing the abject little worm jump with fright, immediately guessing it's him, Mauro, with his slow, heavy tread, the boy looks all around in search of a way out that doesn't exist, he's like a mouse in a trap, and the twin can hardly keep from laughing. He continues his act a little longer and sees him stirring in vain, trying to reach the little overhead light then thinking better of it—too late to blow it out, it's pointless, everything's pointless—and finally he slides down the wall, hidden by the horse who has started chewing again; if only he could be invisible.

Mauro plays the game, calls out.

"Rafael?"

He imagines the boy's heart beating wildly and he says it again, speaking in that drawl, like on those evenings when he steals the mother's alcohol:

"Rafael . . ."

The anger grips him, makes him boil inside, the same as when an animal resists him and he's about to flatten it to the ground to give it a lesson, to show who's in charge, a rope, a slipknot around the forelegs and a sudden jerk, hard, bringing the animal down as it falls with a cry. They're all the same, steers and little brothers, they still try, and Mauro has to use force to remind them who gives the orders, now and always, if that's what they want.

Bending almost double not to be seen, he trots soundlessly toward the stable, stands up straight in the precise spot where Rafael, on the other side, has huddled up to wait for his older brother to go away; he's so frightened he could wait for hours, but Mauro is there on the other side of the partition, only a few inches behind him, and looking down on him now from his full height he bellows:

"What do you think you're doing here?"

The little brother gives a cry of surprise. Halley starts, swerves. Mauro leans over the stable door and snickers.

"You thought I wouldn't see you, didn't you, little shit?"

"No, that's not it."

"Then what are you doing down there?"

The little brother stands up.

"I . . . I had a stomachache."

"And what else?"

"Nothing, I was just waiting for it to go away."

"Yeah, right."

The tall twin laughs, and drags him by force from the stable. *Let's wait together, why don't we, as it happens I have to talk to you, you don't see a problem with that, do you?*

"I was going to go home."

"Without an explanation? That's not good."

"An explanation for what?"

"Are you trying to make fun of me?"

In the little brother's gaze there is that fear that keeps him from thinking and would make him say anything just to find an excuse, the fear that stings his eyes and never fails to delight Mauro. The twin knows that Rafael will try to confuse him, either by trying to defend himself or by figuring the older boy will feel sorry for him, so to destroy any hope he puts a stop to it at once.

"What were you saying to Steban this morning when you were making fun of Joaquin and me?"

The little brother looks at him, amazed.

"Nothing! I didn't say anything!"

"Try and remember."

"I swear I didn't."

"Wait a minute, let me help you." And he shifts his hips forward and backward in an obscene movement. "'In the ass, Mauro,' does that remind you of anything?"

Now Rafael goes to pieces. He doesn't try to deny it; his eyes go red and his vision blurs, and he immediately puts his hands around his head to protect himself—too late, because Mauro throws him against the stable door and his cheek slams into the door frame, nearly knocking him out. He collapses without a sound, not even a whimper. Gets to his knees. His hands reach for the wall so he can support himself and wait for the dizziness to fade. Breathing hard, Mauro kicks him. He falls over again. Crawls backwards to a shower of insults.

"You think you're going to rule the roost here, is that it, asshole?"

"No, I promise—"

"Shut up!"

The kick in his ribs takes his breath away, and Mauro himself, despite his anger, hesitates for a split second, as if he's kicked him too hard, as if he wants to make sure the little brother isn't dead, lying on the dirt floor, his hands curled back upon themselves. In his gesture there is something of the submission of a fighting dog, the moment the weaker dog lies on his back in a gesture of abdication, and Rafael, dazed with pain, rolls over on his side, hiccupping, giving Mauro the sign he wanted: he is still alive. So the twin, enjoying himself too much to be satisfied with such an easy victory, pummels the little brother on the ground, drags him from one thrashing to the next until he flattens him against the cart at the back of the stable, where he tramples him, flinging his heels, grunting and grimacing.

"Are you going to do it again, worm?"

"No! No!"

"I know you'll do it again."

"No, never! Never! I swear!"

"And why should I believe you?"

"I promise!"

Mauro grabs Rafael by his shirt, so violently it tears, then slaps him hard, precisely, and drops him on the ground where he curls up.

"If I catch you at it again I'll kill you? Understand?"

"Yes."

"I will do it and you know it."

"Yes."

"Stop looking at me like a trapped rabbit, you annoy me."

"Okay."

Mauro kneels down and tilts his head to stare right at the little brother, far too close: for a moment, he's tempted to give him one last blow, but finally it is enough to delight in his terrified expression. With disgust he says, "Your nose is bleeding, you little shit. You'll have to wash."

A murmur. *Yes, Mauro.*

He trembles on hearing the older brother's grunting, a hoarseness like that of a wild animal unsure whether to attack or to flee, circling around him, frothing at the mouth. The older brother blows his heavy breath in his face, surrounds him with his huge shadow. The horses don't move, huddle at the back of their stalls with an anxious look, and Mauro knows he frightens them, but let this be a lesson: no one, neither man nor beast, can make fun of him, this applies to the animals too. At his feet the little brother is breathing jerkily, his nostrils pinched, one hand under his nose to stop the bleeding. He moves as little as possible, eyes down. He no longer exists, he's transparent, vanished into the manure, the earth, and the older brother nods and straightens up.

"You're gonna stay here for a while."

The little brother nods, exhales.

"Because this is where you belong, in the shit. I want to hear you say yes."

"Yes."

"No making fun of me, ever, got it?"

"Yes."

"Okay. If you tell the mother, you're dead."

Rafael

The older brother walks away and Rafael hears his footsteps fading. For a long while he lies on the ground. The coolness of the earth on his cheek, which is turning blue; his fingers clasping a pebble, to think about something besides the pain. When he opens his eyes the stable is whirling about him. He crawls outside, his mouth open to swallow some air, he leans against the wooden planks they repaired last spring. A sound of something running reaches him but he doesn't look, he retreats into the dark as if he could disappear.

Something breathing. Just there.

The dog's moist nose, suddenly by his face.

Tears are flowing down the little brother's face. Delicately, Three licks them, in an effort to console him. The tears are salty on his cheeks and the dog draws back when he recognizes the smell of blood, looks at the boy, head tilting to one side. A plaintive whine. The little brother would like to reassure him but the words won't come. All he can do is try to stand, holding his side, and the dog's presence encourages him, without him he'd have lain slumped there for hours under the stars he cannot see.

Three escorts him to the house. A moment of hesitation before entering—but the lights are out. His head still buzzing, Rafael gropes his way, finds the latch. The smell of food and tobacco in the room make him nauseous. He pours some water from the pitcher above the sink and carefully cleans himself, sponging his face, patting himself with his fingertips. Banishes the thought telling him that it hurts: he has grown accustomed to pain, not the pain that radiates in a hail of blows, but the throbbing pain of the hours and days to follow—migraines, swollen wounds. When the mother asks him what happened, invariably he says,

"I bumped into something."

And that's enough for her. Basically, she doesn't give a damn.

When the door to the bedroom is flung open, it takes Rafael a few seconds to emerge from exhausted sleep and find his way out of the limbo of his dreamless night; no doubt he thinks it's a mistake, or a nightmare, because what else could it be, this door smashing against the wall and the angry cry—and right away, the mother's voice upon him.

"Get up!"

And as he opens his eyes and the darkness does not leave one side of his face, the time it takes him to realize that his cheek is so swollen it is blocking his view, she grabs him by the hair and he jumps up with a moan. Adrenaline instantly revives the pain, bursts into his head and along his veins. He gets up to escape but the mother has him in a brutal vise, drags him out of the room, garbling her words of fury, spluttering imprecations he does not understand, his whimpering answers limited to lost spurts of "Ma?" They go down the narrow corridor, past the kitchen where Mauro and Steban are sitting motionless at the table, on out of the house, nearly falling down the three steps of the stoop, so entangled are they, and twisted with pain and rage.

"See! See!" screams the mother, dragging him into the stable.

And before they even enter the building, he knows.

The mother has stopped across from him, next to the stable, her face purple with rage, her hair disheveled. The little

brother rushes toward Halley's box. The chestnut shudders.
Looks at him. In Rafael's eyes, tears of relief: he stayed. Despite
the open doors.

But the mother grabs him again by the shoulder and spins
him around, and he can feel her acrid breath in his nose when
she yells:

"Here! What's missing, here?"

On the other side, the two stalls are empty. The horses are
gone. The little brother opens his mouth, makes as if to hurry
out: *Outside?*

"I already looked."

"They're not there?"

"No."

"In the field, behind?"

"I already looked, I said! They're gone. Gone!"

"Ma . . . "

He falls silent. To tell her what? That yesterday after Mauro
thrashed him, he forgot? That it was all he could do to stagger
into the house and lie down weeping on his bed? He knows
he's in the wrong. He's the one who's in charge of the horses.
If he can't look after them, he shouldn't have asked to. That's
the only thing that will make sense to the mother. She won't listen to excuses or complaints. Standing immobilized outside
the deserted stables, the little brother looks with his one eye at
the soiled bedding, the turds neatly piled at the far end of the
stall, the unfinished hay to one side. He pictures Jericho and
Nordeste setting off down the lane that leads out of the
estancia, trotting over earth and pebbles, their noses in the air:
free. Heading west, toward the *mesetas*. Into the wind. Entire
days before they will encounter a living soul. For a moment he
envies them. If it was him, he would never come back.

Rafael secures the leather satchels to the saddle, makes sure
he hasn't forgotten anything. It's impossible to know how long

he'll be gone. Logically, he should be home tonight, but he doesn't want to leave it to chance. So he makes his list one more time. Dawdles a little. Eventually climbs into the saddle and doesn't move. In the house there is no sign of life. Steban and Mauro have gone to their work, but the mother is still in there. Hiding? No. Indifferent. Punishing. She won't come out to see him leave, she won't encourage him, this son who has promised to come back with the horses. He bites his lips. A murmur of resignation to Halley. *Hey.*

The chestnut moves forward. Behind him, Three springs up. The little brother cries, "Go home!"

The dog pauses, undecided. Rafael too, hesitates, because if he listened to his heart he'd take the dog with him. But he knows it's not allowed. Like all of them, Three belongs to the estancia. It is up to the mother to decide, and the mother would say no—of course. So he repeats his order, barking, "Home!"

The dog doesn't insist, and reluctantly heads back the way he's come. He often turns to look at them riding away, the little brother and the horse, and he sways on his paws as if he doesn't know where to run. His master's command seems to be disintegrating in his brain.

In the distance the sky has turned gloomy, streaked with black clouds, and Rafael can feel the tension in the air. A magnetic storm? Torrential summer rains, furrowing along the rocks, swallowing the earth without soaking it? All the farmers must be looking up right now, hands joined in prayer. God only knows they need the water. But maybe it will pass them by, borne away by the fickle winds, and they'll look at the bellies of the clouds and dream of shattering them with a rifle—some will even try, certainly, in an insane surge of hope.

The little brother picks up the horses' trail. Westward, as he thought. The lure of the plateaus, of the lakes, maybe, farther away, if they go straight without stopping, intoxicated with the improbable promise of better grazing. He himself has only dreamt of those places, knows only what he's heard about them from the rare gauchos like himself who've ridden in search of lost animals, as far as the Andean lands. At the outermost bounds of the country reigns the cold forest, moist and exuberant. *Nalcas* with huge leaves, the size of a man, plants he sees as something out of a fairy tale whenever the guys recall with a shiver the lianas that, in places, make the undergrowth impenetrable.

In the early hours of his search, the little brother hopes the fugitive horses will lead him into those unknown territories, among those giant conifers he's never seen, to hear the song of hidden birds, the fleeing footfall of invisible creatures. Then his gaze adjusts, measures the horizon. Inaccessible. And his own body is shattered, tossed to and fro, wracked with pain at every jolt in the saddle, while his eye, still swollen, hinders him from seeing the tiny trail the horses have left. If they did go that way, it will take him days of wandering before he can catch up with them, and it enrages him to know they are ten hours ahead of him but he cannot spur Halley on to catch them, because he has to keep his eye out for every infinitesimal trace on the rocky ground, every fork in the way, every hesitation; and maybe the horses themselves are already lost, too, in those places without landmarks. What's more, all through that first day he is wasting time. The plateaus oblige him to backtrack and go around whenever the trails that would have led him straight across have crumbled away, or are too steep for Halley. Sometimes he loses Jericho and Nordeste's trail altogether, and has to walk with his nose to the ground until he picks it up again—and even then, he is not entirely sure it is their trail, and he wagers that there are only those two horses in this deserted place, because otherwise he would have gone back to the estancia ten times over. But that's not something he can conceive of. He will go back with the horses, or not go back at all, because the mother is perfectly capable of beating him to death.

He observes the nature around him, semi-arid, hard pastureland, low plateaus. Wherever he looks, a vast emptiness. Doubt often causes him to rein Halley in. He wonders whether the two nags decided to gallop to the ends of the earth. Instead of going around in circles, nibbling at a bit of grass when a river irrigates the land, he senses the horses have shot straight ahead without stopping. Or else he's completely lost their trail, misled by the hoofmarks of guanacos.

It can't be. He'd never take a llama's hoofprint for a horse's, that he is sure of. He spurs Halley on. The chestnut moves forward, then balks. He doesn't know this place, but he does know, instinctively, how long they've been away, and he realizes they can no longer turn back before nightfall. Sniffing the air, he detects wild smells—foxes, a few rodents, predators, too, of the kind that terrify the herds when they give chase in order to isolate the weakest member. And he smells the water, turns back down the mountain to head toward it, and the little brother lets him go until they can make out the brown glimmer of the swamps. When they reach the edge of the swamps the boy hobbles Halley, breaks up some barberry branches to make a fire, some dead wood he finds under the trees that grow in the sodden soil. Since morning the wind has been blowing at them, draining them, and Rafael wants to be sure to find a place that is sheltered, up against some yellow boulders. In the tiny cook pan he brought with him he stews some dried beans and cuts a slice of smoked meat. Around him, in the dark, he hears his horse gnawing at rushes and probably the leaves on the bushes as well, and when the chestnut snorts, Rafael feels his presence and finds some comfort there. Later, wrapped in a blanket by the fire, his head against the saddle, he almost feels happy; but the uncertainty of finding Jericho and Nordeste twists his gut. He listens to the night birds, their squawks and cries, the rush of wings. The furtive scampering of little mammals, the constant rustling of the wind in the branches of the *mayten* trees. He feels alone and extraordinarily free, in the middle of the world. He reaches his hand up to the stars, he could be touching them. He holds that optical illusion and passes from one to another, as if he were caressing them with his fingertips, as if he were brushing against sparks, trying to herd them together, the only thing he knows how to do, and he does this until his arm begins to ache. Then he puts it under the blanket again and pushes the saddle closer to the fire, and the flames flicker over his face in long, hot orange tongues, he gazes at the embers, the incandescent light. When he closes his eyes, the red sparks dance and crackle behind his lids, and again he looks at the sky, the fire, he shivers in the cooling air, fatigued by this vagabond day. And he thinks again of the runaway horses.

Did they stop, too, or did they go on in the night, walking carefully? Maybe they'll retrace their steps, maybe they're already tired of this freedom that brings them neither grain nor clean water, terrified by the sound of the creatures hiding at the edge of the forest and the smell of pumas carried by the whirling wind. The little brother laid some branches across the trail to block the path but he doesn't really believe it will do any good, that they'll come back, that would be too easy, to wake up and find them there grazing next to Halley as if nothing had happened, ready to go home. Tomorrow he will follow their tracks into the great forest he saw from a distance, and leave the low-lying plateaus. He should have brought an extra blanket. Twice he gets up, shivering, and adds wood to the fire. When the wind veers, he has to move farther from the fire, fearful of being burned in his sleep. He sleeps poorly, stirred by a strange excitement, a clarity that allows him to hear thousands of rustling noises, the dull clamor of nocturnal creatures, insects and prairie mice, raptors and hunters. In the middle of the night it all falls quiet and the sounds fade. He is woken by a silence so heavy that it seeps into his ears, like the shells from the ocean the nomadic gauchos let him listen to but never gave him. He tosses more branches onto the fire, damp wood that whistles and cracks, to cover the world's silence. He is convinced that nothing can happen behind his back as long as the embers are still singing like this, but his eyes are open and his senses on the alert. He could count the hours. It is enough just to keep an eye on the fire, until gradually his eyelids itch and grow heavy, he is not even aware of it, and eventually they close altogether. His breathing is so peaceful that he might seem dead, lying there by the flames then the burning branches of wood. Then the ashes. When dawn startles him awake, he is on his back with his arms spread wide, he is warm, and stiff, and his first gesture is to stir the embers, but there is no warmth left there, not a cinder, nothing.

These strange, solitary days, the only rhythm that of the horse's hooves, while Rafael dozes for hours on end, still groggy from Mauro's blows. Terribly monotonous, time goes by, without him noticing.

On the third day he enters the forest. The change of landscape leaves him stunned; all he has ever known is the treeless steppe. He looks up at the magnificent boughs, the changing hues of entire regions where the rain has ventured. The *arrayáns* display their golden trunks, their silvery foliage mingled with the cypress trees that grow among their roots. With his fingertip he touches the low-lying branches of the araucarias, of a green so dark he thought they were black. He jabs his finger. Is startled. Gazes all around him at the sparse undergrowth woven with sun and wind, their new, unreal colors. Something inside him fills with a wonder so deep it is stifling, saturated with impossible visions, smells of humus and resin.

His eyes open wide, red with staring. He spreads his arms. Breathes. And nothing comes to disturb the magical beauty of the forest, neither the eagerness to find his horses nor the thought that at the estancia the mother is already waiting, muttering about how slow he's always been.

Halley walks soundlessly. The rocky surface gradually yields to a dust of earth and sand, crumbling into broken pebbles at the trail's edge. He easily picks up the horses' prints again. He stops.

Goes and sits down.

If he was at the farm he would never do this, but solitude and freedom propel him; he gathers a few branches, lights a fire, and puts some water on to boil. He feels like having some maté. He doesn't need it: he feels like it. No one is here to forbid him. It's like taking a break. At the estancia he never could have. But here. His eyes glued to the little pot, he lets his mind wander. Time goes by, liquid, lazy. When the horse comes and sniffs him from behind, he can feel his nose tickling him, the warm breath, it makes him close his eyes. He laughs, gently pushes him away. Plays with his fingers on the horse's white nose, on the pink lips that try to catch him, and he says, *No, no.* After a few moments Halley moves away, goes back to grazing; Rafael throws a few leaves into the simmering water.

Again he listens to distant sounds, and knows that after the last forest the landscape will change yet again. The lakes. Perhaps the horses have gone there to drink. He reins in the urge to hurry there; he is feeling drowsy, replete with sensations. The birds' calls arrive in waves, shatter against the trees. The earth is gray like the wind.

Suddenly the lake is there without warning, offering its irregular immensity to the little brother's gaze of stupefaction. It is surrounded by grasses and thickets, and in places it narrows into winding fords, while in others it opens out onto large blue expanses, where tiny beaches provide access. Rafael jumps off his horse and strips, runs toward the shallow water, so transparent he can see the flat pebbles beneath his feet. He runs farther then at last goes into the water, it is bracing against his skin, then he surfaces, shivering. He laughs to himself, waves his arms to splash the water. All around him the lake is white, frothing, the shrubs are a pale green, and there is the blue of the sky. He cries out. The joy is too great to stay in his gut or his throat, indescribable, but it has to be let out, otherwise he will explode, and what he roars is how splendid the world is, an unbelievable discovery, which takes his breath away and makes his temples throb. With his mouth open on incredulous laughter he gradually falls silent, keeping only the dizziness and dazzle of it. He turns round and round in the tranquil water, feels the movement of the water against his hips. He spins again, and again, and staggers. Stands still in a last cry.

A raptor takes flight, disturbed, a black form against the sun. The little brother holds his hands visor-like and watches the bird fly away. Calls to it, in vain. He plays with the water again, swishes it, forces his way through, and comes out on the shore, returns, leaping, until the pressure on his legs makes him lose his balance and he falls. Then with his heart pounding, breathless from so much laughter and shouting, he floats a few feet from the edge, making sure he always has his depth. The light exalts him, reverberating on the lake, the groves of trees, the almost-sand. He closes his eyes and a strange melody comes to lull him, so intangible he is not quite sure he has heard it, but he pretends he has, delights in the crystalline notes, never mind if they are merely the fruit of his imagination. Something grazes his leg beneath the water, tickling, and suddenly he is afraid. What unknown creatures live here and dream of luring him to the bottom—the question courses through him, and all at once he rushes forward, using his arms to propel himself through the lake, stepping high to run, to get out of there, breathless.

On his knees on the shore, wheezing, he rolls himself up in the blanket and laughs at the thought that he has escaped from some imaginary monsters; he is so glad he is safe. Narrowing his eyes he looks at the smooth surface of the water, sees nothing, not the slightest movement, only the wind stirring the tiniest ripples.

But below the surface the lake was readying its wyvern-like creatures, of that much he is sure.

He abandons the idea of sleeping on the shore and moves inland to find the shelter of a boulder. No creatures will find him there, or drag him out and back into the consuming depths. He lights a fire. Behind him, in perspective, the lake sleeps, barely troubled by the faintest lapping. The little brother observes it, still wary. He gradually feels peace descend as night folds around him, and he forgets his fears, lulled by the soothing firelight. Sleep gathers him, he lets go. His dreams are inhabited by miraculous visions, but none of them come close to the enchantment of the landscapes he has discovered these last days.

THE MOTHER

And these days on the estancia are wearing out her
hands and her back, with two sons gone, even if there's
Mauro, with his strength, and her own pride at having
given birth to such a colossus, but alas when he's the only
one—because even if Steban does his work without a fuss, they
can't leave him on his own, can't trust him, they're never sure.
In a way, the only ones left are the mother and the tall twin.
The other son helps the way the dogs do, obeying orders, and
you always have to check on him, you never know. On one
hand the half-wit, on the other the good animals, and basically
they're equal, it doesn't bother her anymore to admit it, that's
how life has ordained it. If only Steban could run as fast as the
dogs.

This is why the mother sighs when she says there are only
two of them left to run the estancia, which needs five pairs of
arms, or better six, and Steban doesn't react, leaning over his
plate, you wonder if he even heard her, if he thinks he's
included in the two the mother is referring to, or simply
whether the numbers have confused him, two, five, or six,
whereas when he himself thinks about it he comes up with
three—like the dogs, but maybe he's wrong, and he continues
to sit there in silence.

Fortunately, it's not shearing season yet, otherwise the runaway horses could have gone to the devil, the mother wouldn't
have let Rafael leave, and that would have earned him a few
sleepless nights, the time it would take for the horses to come

back on their own or get lost for good. Because it's the ewes before anything, they are what they live off of, they are what the mother needs if she's to go drinking in San León as much as the father drank at home, basically fate has simply shifted from one to the other, but the family curse doesn't affect her, no, not her, and there is a hush all around her when she sits at the bar and calls for a drink.

And so to banish this strange ennui that has come over her on the deserted estancia, one morning she hastily harnesses the horse and heads off to town. She has left Mauro behind: someone has to stay. He protests:

"Why not Steban?"

The mother gives him a nasty look. *Don't be ridiculous.*

"I'll drink up your reserve."

"I'll be back before nightfall. Don't let me catch you at it. Don't forget the heifers."

Crack of the whip and she's gone, speeding along the road, only too happy to get away from the gloomy day. It's not so much monotony that bothers her as the void, two fewer sons to yell at, she can't get used to it. Not enough people to give orders to. Not enough orders to bark, and the steers don't run enough, even the dogs go around with their heads drooping. Maybe when she gets home the little brother will be back, that bloody dreamer, he's bound to be lolling along the trail gazing at the sky.

In town she does some hasty business in the shops, to keep her conscience clear, then rushes to the bar as soon as the time seems right. There's a buzz in the air and this surprises her, and yet she's early, and already there is a crowd laughing and talking loudly, she goes up to the table where Emiliano is sitting, he's called out to her, and as she sits down next to him she says, "Must be something going on, for it to be this crowded."

He gives a quiet laugh.

"You know this lot. Least little thing and they're excited."

"I'd like to know why that is, myself."

"Ah ha."

"Ah ha?"

"It's worth a beer, isn't it?"

When Alejo sets the glasses down in front of them, Emiliano thanks him, blows on the foam. Takes a swig then starts laughing again already.

"So here's the thing. First of all, there's this big breeder from the pampa who got robbed last week, maybe you heard about it. Millions of fresh banknotes from his safe, vanished, bound to be one of his men. So word has it that the robber is in the area. A posse came through here yesterday, they've lost his trail. In my opinion they lost him a while ago; when a guy's been on the run for two hundred miles it's a bad sign. For sure they were about to give up and head back. So you know how it is, the minute one of those bastards has a rough time, the likes of us are all glad, aren't we. As for his men, we rode with them right to the gates of the town and made fun of them all the way. You bet! The whole business just tickles me pink."

The mother smiles, too.

"So there's justice after all. Filthy meat men."

"They think they own the place."

"Their pockets are so full they don't give a damn if the country goes to rack and ruin."

"Well, there's one who's not about to fill them up again any time soon."

"*Dios mio*, does me good to hear things like this, Emiliano."

"Yup. But the best yet—"

He breaks off and the mother opens her eyes wide.

"Well?"

"This is a true story, I swear: Juan's wife gave birth to a dark-skinned baby."

"Huh?"

"Yup, a Negro. A black baby. You see all these morons

drinking all around us and falling off their seats laughing? That's why."

The mother cannot believe it.

"You mean . . . Juan from the bank?"

"Exactly."

"Juan Gomez?"

"Yes, I said!"

"Land sakes! Hey, Alejo! We need some drinks over here! On me!"

Afterward, the mother goes and knocks at the door of the bank. But since she's been drinking for a while, the door is already locked. She hammers on the door, singing, *Gomez, show me your little dark-skinned baby, let me see your dark eyes* . . . She stands there like a witch, bent double with laughter, and she walks back and forth outside the locked building, drunken, determined, thinking up the worst jibes and jokes she's heard this evening, and there sure were plenty there in the bar, the worst ones so she can say them again, arms spread in a hesitant, joyful dance, she shouts herself hoarse, *Gomez, Gomez, how does it feel now it's your turn?*

Behind her, a sob in the night.

She looks around.

Juan's wife is there, sitting against the wall, the baby in her arms—or at least the mother thinks it's the baby, because in the dark she can hardly see. The mother opens her mouth, thinks for a moment before speaking; the words are buried deep in her brain. And at first all she manages is an alcoholic grunt, followed by a question mark, no doubt, but who could guess? She tries to focus: *Well, well. What have we here.* Steps backward as the weeping grows louder, mingled with words she does not understand. She reaches out to pull aside the blanket protecting the infant's face. Raises an eyebrow: he's not as dark as she expected, she thought he'd be black as coal, but maybe she can't see because of the obscurity, or the moonlight, and she stands up straight, meets the woman's helpless gaze, and with a shudder hears the trembling voice murmuring, "Help me, please."

And the mother doesn't like those words, she's a person who has never asked, never begged, she gazes silently at the huddled figure before her and it makes her think of a pile of wool after the ewes have been shorn, shapeless, crumbling, that's all it puts her in mind of, she doesn't answer.

"Please."

Now the woman holds the baby out to the mother, and the mother understands. That she could take it. Do what she wants with it, the guilty woman doesn't care, she fucks black men, she just wants someone to take the child, wants it to disappear from her life. Just then the mother would tell her that she'll leave it out for the pumas—God willing one will come along some day soon—or that she'll tell Mauro to bang it against a wall to kill it, then bury it, Mauro would do that, no questions asked. Anything rather than keep it. And the woman herself, couldn't she harness her horse, with her banker husband, and ride off to abandon it outside the church in some other village? Oh, the mother knows she'd have to go a long way to find a place where no one has heard the story, so they wouldn't bring the baby straight back the next day, and she can already imagine the jibes: "Hey, Gomez, you lose something?"

That would mean too far away; of course it's impossible.

"Señora . . . "

The mother studies the woman gazing imploringly at her. Of course she, the mother, is the best solution, she's poor and already old, who else is there to ask when you don't want to get your hands dirty. This fine lady would never have called her señora if she didn't have a knife to her throat, but she's glad to find her there tonight, and she'll add a full purse if she has to, all the mother has to do is nod her head and say yes. This is the way it has always been, the rich get the poor to wash their sins away for them, they discharge their blood and shame on them, because the poor don't care, and the poor in turn transform dirt into money. It doesn't bother them to hold out their hands; they've been doing it for centuries, like washing away shit, and they may hold their noses but in the end they do it and it's always good enough for them.

The mother stands there in the dark swaying from side to side, and anyone who saw her would think she's hesitating, that she's about to topple, and it's true, it would be no sweat off her brow to drown the infant, no worse than a kitten, now that she knows how much better it is to get rid of them. What she's trying to work out is how much the woman will offer her. How much Gomez is prepared to give to wipe away yesterday and the day before, as if it were possible, as if people won't snicker every time he crosses the street ahead of them, with or without a little dark-faced child, and everything that goes with it. She wonders if the Negroes in San León have already fled, for fear of being lynched, or has the guilty man stepped forward.

Ten thousand pesos.

As if they think life will go back to normal, afterward. It will take years for people to stop talking. Years of coming up with more or less improbable theories about the child's fate. Did they kill it? Did they sell it as a slave? Did they abandon it somewhere; if so, where, to whom? To get those wagging tongues to fall silent, the only remedy is time.

Twenty thousand.

And even if this is the way things have always been, the mother feels a surge of rage to see herself as the villain in the story, an inferior woman who isn't offended by anything anyone asks of her, because God knows how those people imagine she lives, and how many other undesirable children she would have already killed for a few coins, children and cats, and fathers—has that fine lady sitting there before her thought about fathers? If she only knew.

The mother recalls that it is not a hard thing, to kill. Sometimes it comes without thinking, without doing it on purpose. And if you have to do it on purpose, what does that change? Mauro will bash it—like bleeding a rabbit. One blow to the back of the neck. A hole in the ground. No risk it'll wake up once it's buried in there. Filthy rich people.

Whereas if the mother says no. She suddenly intuits that this is where her power lies, in her ability to refuse, the strength of her obstruction, her strength, period, not to go down on her knees this time. It would be too easy to take the money and bury the infant; ever so easy to get rid of it for them. All she has to do is say no.

Even for thirty thousand.

Good God, thirty thousand.

She almost chokes imagining the full purse gradually receding from her, and all the while she's pushing it out of her mind she can feel her fingers curling back as if they could get hold of some of it, grab the leather edge, as if it were nothing, slip her finger in it, bring out a coin or two. To make her victory total. As she stares at the starry sky, without seeing it, with her strange thoughts, the woman there beneath her whimpers, her face wretched, the pain in her eyes so powerful you could weep. But the mother is unacquainted with pity; she will never return a thing she has never been given. Who would have come to her aid rather than spit on her if she'd had a bastard child like that? She would have dealt with it, she'd have had to, because no one would have helped her. Of course she would have thought of killing it. But she would have done it all on her own. Not by choice, but because there was no one there to wash away the sins of people like her.

And so, gently, to see hope light up in the woman's eyes, she leans closer to them, the woman and the little Negro. And forms her lips into a round "o" to say the word.

And she says no.

The mother dances all night outside the bank, and her shoes beat the rhythm of her slow farandole on the wood, her arms spread for balance like the wings of a large bird, gray and opaque. There are no sounds other than her heavy leaping on the threshold of the house, not even the woman's sobbing, she left long ago with the little dark-skinned infant in her arms, from way up there behind her window she must be able to hear the mother, going crazy as she counts the steps and leaps, and it doesn't stop, it doesn't stop, the mother hopes that Juan, too, up in his room, is clenching his fists, waiting for the old witch to get it over with.

She's had her revenge, it's a paltry consolation to be honest, but she won't have it spoiled. Tonight she's the winner. At last she can breathe, there's a spark, and the chill of the night does not reach her, she's burning, both inside and out. She dances and gestures to the window upstairs, laughing and stumbling, convinced they're watching her. At times the moon casts a glow on her squat form, and it catches the white light in her eyes, opens her mouth so her teeth shine—teeth like a predator's. When was the last time she felt this light, if ever? When was the last time she reveled in the sight of a creature more unfortunate than she herself?

The mother dances, still, always, like a drunken old bear.

She feels mean. Alive.

RAFAEL

On the fourth morning—or is it already the fifth?—the little brother begins to hunt. Even if he finds the horses today, his food supply has dwindled, he won't make it back to the estancia. Taking his rifle, he leaves Halley by the riverside, his nose buried in the damp grass, and he heads off in silence. He doesn't know the game in this region. On previous days he came across rodents, hares. The guanacos vanished once he entered the forested zone, and he doesn't know what is making the fleeing sounds he hears on his way. Careful. There's no sign the pumas have deserted the area to stay near the llamas, their favorite prey. Solitary creatures wandering outside their territory are often the most dangerous, and he advances with his loaded rifle on his shoulder, ready to fire.

Around him the fauna has gradually fallen silent, alerted by a troubling instinct; never since he reached the trees and the lakes has there been such a silence, even when he talks out loud to Halley or sings his lungs out. Until now the birds have always gone on chattering as if they were alone on the planet, and some of the little mammals he met looked at him for a few seconds before continuing calmly on their way. But here. One by one the woodpeckers, blackbirds, and *chucaos* all leave off their chatter, and nothing is moving, either in the leaves or on the ground. The forest is utterly silent. The little brother looks all around, listens, fails to understand. His breathing is the only sound he can hear, then now and again a bird's chirring, or a cry of alarm—and then, again, silence.

He parts the lianas. When he looks behind him, the path has already closed on him and he makes marks on the tree trunks to be able to find his way back. He is intrigued by the density of growth, and glances in vain at the sky in hopes of more light. Bamboo bars the way: he's never seen it before. After an hour has gone by he becomes despondent. The forest has surrounded him, is tightening its hold, eating up the space—the place is too dense even for animals, a fox could hardly squeeze its way through, it would scrape its flanks on the fallen branches. And yet these woods are full of life, and the huge effort of the silent creatures is palpable, they won't hold out against him for long, he thinks, he can almost sense them wriggling with impatience as they wait for his departure. Sometimes he hears a cry, a lament, immediately stifled. The sound of paws rustling over the ground. Immobility is the worst ordeal for these running, flying creatures, more used to flight than cunning. The boy is impressed by the trap, but he won't be taken in. He stays there. Sits on a gray moss-covered tree trunk that has been there for years, half rotten. He doesn't move. He remembers stories he's heard, days of despair when the game outthinks, outsmarts the poacher, when all the other solutions have been exhausted: he will hunt blind. It's not that he enjoys staying there in the same place for hours without moving, leaning against a tree or hiding in the hollow of a boulder. If he had any choice. Even exasperated by silence, he'll have to melt into the landscape, make himself invisible—until the animals believe the lie and the forest comes to life again. And gradually the little brother feels the foliage closing around him, the hastily woven spiderwebs shrouding him, he can scarcely believe it. His hands stay motionless despite the insect bites, the itching; he breathes without making a sound. Nature envelops him. For a moment, he wonders if he will be able to get away again. If the lianas are not going to grab his ankles and hold him there forever. He resists the temptation to fight his way out of there. In his mind he says, over and over, *I am a tree. I am a tree . . .*

Halley is waiting for him, he knows, grazing by the water. Maybe he could boil some grass and eat it, too. But fresh meat . . . for Chrissake. His mouth is watering, he runs his tongue over his lips, as if he might be able to taste that imaginary smell of grilling, the mother's lamb with spices, the fat making it tender; the sizzling of the oil and laurel leaf in the pan when you put the chops in. Only the mother knows how to sear the meat on the outside and keep it pink within, with its fragrant aroma, and the juice running out onto the potatoes. God how hungry he is all of a sudden.

And then the sound is there, right nearby, on the other side of the bamboo curtain. At first, still engrossed by his vision, he thinks he's hallucinating, and he doesn't look. But the shape is coming closer, he can no longer ignore it. He fires. Instinctively, without even knowing what he has fired at. Not a whimper, not a breath. He rushes over.

The little brother has never seen such a big mara—on the steppe, they are skinnier—but the meat is tasty, and all night he smokes the leftovers to have the next day. He takes his time. The horses' hoofprints are getting sharper on the ground: the end of the chase is drawing near. They're bound to be slowing down, they're indecisive, there's nothing calling them to go farther. They've slackened their pace, lowered their horizon. They must have stopped, they sniff the air and its lack of promise, they turn their heads to try and recognize the landscape. But they are lost, and nothing is the same. If the little brother wasn't riding after them, would they know how to get home? They sneeze, rub their noses. Their neighing pierces the silence. But there is no answer, and they doze to forget their solitude, then set off again, uncertain. Some hours behind them, Rafael thinks of the horses. They've been on a long journey, and they will surely have injuries to tend to—sores from thorns, pasterns hurt from so much walking. He thinks he won't go back right away, give them time to recover. A day or so. Deep down he is reluctant to go back to the estancia, the mother, his two remaining brothers. The punishment he'll get at the same time, for having taken so long; no matter how he tries to memorize the places he sees, to prove he's been to the ends of the earth, his welcome will be a bitter one. He already misses his freedom. If only the horses would find a new burst of energy, and the trail would grow fainter, leading away, up into the mountains ahead of him.

Nordeste and Jericho, their backs to the wind, look down on the slope they have just climbed, scattering pebbles downhill with their hooves. Once again the trees grow scarcer, hampered by altitude, the rock shows through and reclaims its territory, with the echo of every infinitesimal noise. There are still groves, thick and light-colored, their roots running along the surface of the soil, anchored in the most invisible cracks.

On the ground there is blood.

Ears back, the horses look all around, alternating moments of vigilance and rest. No one can say why they stopped there, why they decided not to go any further. No one can know if they heard the little brother's voice ring out in the distance, or the thud of Halley's horseshoes. Perhaps it's some familiar smell that has brought them to a halt. Perhaps they are nervous because of the presence behind them.

Nordeste turns his head, clacks his teeth to stop the third horse from coming any closer.

The little brother has to walk up the steep slope, leading Halley. As they make their way he frowns, disoriented by the tracks he has just seen on the ground.

There are three sets.

Three, that's not right. Something has changed.

He reaches for the rifle. Abandons the effort of silence as they move through this place, surrounded by mountains, an echo betraying him with every step. He feels as if he is about to fall into a huge trap. He does not slow his steps. The proximity of the horses has electrified him.

Standing slightly off to one side from the others, the bay is the first to notice him. Nordeste and Jericho sense the horse's attention and turn. A faint whinnying. At last.

Scanning the space around him, the little brother stands back.

He looks. Counts—of course it's idiotic, they're there before him.

The third horse has no saddle but is still wearing a bridle and bit, his reins dragging on the ground. What the little brother is looking for is his rider.

He stays under cover for a long while, and listens out for sounds, registers every detail on the face of the mountain. If it was up to him, he would wait for hours, but the horses draw nearer, intrigued by his motionless form, they stretch out their noses to sniff at him. They must recognize him because they stand at his side, their gaze telling him they're relieved to let him take charge again at last. They don't move when the little brother slips the halters over them. Never taking his eyes off the third horse.

He hitches the horses, then hobbles the bay once he's removed his bridle; how long has he been on the loose, for the scabs of blood to have dried at the corners of his mouth? The hills all around abound in caves and recesses, their entrances often hidden by thick shrubbery. Dozens of places for a man to hide in, and, his rifle still in his hand, the little brother decides to explore, even if he does not know what he's looking for—

doesn't know beyond the fact that a bridled horse doesn't wander around on its own, and he wants to find whoever was with him. Every time he approaches a cave he looks around fearfully, keeps himself well to one side, in case someone tries to jump him; then he calls out, not too loudly, enough to be heard from where he is but no farther, give no clues, attract no attention. There is clearly something wrong, because no one in this country would let his criollo go free with his bit in his mouth, hurting him, injuring his mouth like this.

If he were keeping track, Rafael would make a note that it is in the seventeenth hiding place that he spots the form on the ground. He springs back.

His heart is pounding like never before, his thoughts evaporate. Like a young animal he huddles against the mountainside, stops everything: voice, breathing, thoughts. It takes him several minutes before he dares to cock his rifle, and a few more before he whispers, pressed up against the orange rock and its protection:

"Hey?"

No sound in response, and yet he is sure he saw something. So he says it again, twice, ten times, relentlessly, the way he does with a frightened animal, until it calms down and looks at him. So he can touch it, or slip the lasso over. *Hey.*

And all at once he hears a grunt. Not an answer, not a word, no, a grumbling, a gurgle, and he cannot tell if it is from a man or an animal, and he has to stop himself from shouting, recoiling, running away. In there, something is moving, the sound of something dragging on, a loathsome breathing. His voice is trembling now when he says again, "Hey? Is anybody there?"

And this time he understands, beneath the rustling.

" . . . help."

THE OLD MAN

In the cave, the old man tries to call out. He's fucked, may as well. At that moment anything seems better than dying there all on his own, and yet that wouldn't be the worst thing, the worst thing would be to die slowly, to feel how he is taking his leave, day after day, with this wretched pain that never goes away and is eating away at him even worse than the wound itself. He doesn't know how long he's been hiding in this place that smells of blood and damp stone; he's lost all awareness. He can tell he's passed out more than once, that he's been awake at night, in the morning, never knowing which was which, because that's the least of his worries, because the hours and days go by, regardless of what he might want to do about it, and the only thing on his mind is suffering.

He didn't believe in pain. He didn't believe Nivaldo, years ago, when a bull gored him and they were waiting for a useless doctor, both of them knew it would be pointless, but the old man would have felt guilty if he'd just stood there without moving while his fellow worker passed away. Now and again Nivaldo murmured how it hurt. Every time he parted his clenched lips to spit out a word, blood trickled onto his cheek. He spoke of the terrifying vise of his body, and the tempest inside, and the sensation that everything was draining out of him. He even wished he could stop breathing, so that the pain and the panicky fear would go away, God knows if he could have, and maybe it was a silent prayer to the old man, but he didn't want to hear it, he didn't want that blood on his hands, and he went on waiting, saying nothing. The old man could see the intestines throbbing in Nivaldo's hands like a strange animal that could barely struggle, and he'd looked away. He wished it would be over with sooner. He hoped the doctor wouldn't come, wouldn't try anything. Let Nivaldo die without opening him even more, without touching the body that was already gone. But he didn't understand the pain. The sweat, the ravaged features, he hardly recognized him, flesh curling in upon itself, he could see it all but didn't believe in it. It was just death, announcing its arrival. The pain Nivaldo was whispering about didn't exist. He wasn't even listening anymore, he blocked his ears and merely put a hand here or there on his shoulder, until the man said, breathlessly, "Don't touch me. It hurts too much."

Nivaldo died the moment the doctor leaned over him. Maybe he felt a great rush of hope when he saw him, because his veiled gaze suddenly lit up, maybe he thought he'd be saved, that anything was possible. He had moved one hand, not really his hand but a few fingers, his fingertips, and at that moment the old man had also thought that life would hold on to Nivaldo. A second later he expired. It was better that way, for sure. The old man lit a cigarette.

That is what he is thinking about, curled up in a ball on his blanket in the cave, and at last he understands what pain feels like, not the pain of a fractured leg or your nose broken by a stubborn animal, no, real pain, the kind that brings tears, the kind that makes you call out to the man outside, whoever he is, good or evil, and his eyes open wide because his cry is stifled by a moan, no one will ever hear him, no one will ever come. To him it is like a howl exploding in his head, lacerating his flesh, and he tries again and again, he'll pass out, he'll die if need be, Help, help, and life is slowly seeping away, he'd like to take hold of it, put it back inside, this life pouring out.

In his youth he was something to see, on his criollo, and when he rode through the town the girls would flash him sidelong glances and laugh among themselves. He didn't have a penny to his name, but that face, *madre*. He could have done whatever he liked with it, even though there were some guys who thought his features were too delicate, too Indian—yes, those high cheekbones and aquiline nose were a problem, along with the hair as black as the steppe on a moonless night; but he hadn't known either mother or father, and you could get lost in conjecture, no one had any idea. All he or anyone else could be sure of was that he was a fine-looking lad and he drove the women crazy.

For a long time the daughter of a big cattle farmer made eyes at him, and he could have gone no further. He would have gotten used to the life, for sure. They would have gone around calling him *señor* and he would have learned not to notice the mocking little smiles aimed at his bad manners. He thought about it all through one long winter, trying to get used to sitting properly on a chair, when all he had ever known was a saddle. He really did consider it. But he liked wide open spaces, and the wind stinging his eyes and the depths of his throat, and he left the following spring for the seasonal migration. He took with him the only creature he would not leave for anything on earth: his horse. Already back then he had a bay. But there have been three of them since, three bay horses worn by time and chasing cattle, herding the goats from the cows so they won't hurt each other, finding every single animal that's wandered off, not to leave any behind when the herds disperse in September in the upland pastures, or return at the first snow to the lowlands.

The bays have come and gone, and time, and years. He

eventually settled down, not for a woman but a job, a boss who paid a little more decently, and thousands of hectares dotted with brown steers. That was twenty years ago. He never lost his love of the rough life, the freedom of having no possessions, just his horse and saddle. He hasn't changed. He hasn't grown old.

Since his youth he's always worn his hair long, now it is white, tied at the back. As if it were yesterday.

Good Lord, the wound is making him twist inside, and the pain has refused to go away, all these days he's been here in this cave, with his smell infesting even the rock. He doesn't understand how he can still be alive, the way his heart is pounding, and the pain eating away at him inside, deeper and deeper, burning his flesh as it makes its way, it must be emptying him out, a scrap of skin over almost nothing at all, just bones and nerves, a little blood, still. If someone told him he was in hell, he'd believe it. He doesn't see what else it could be, because down here on earth he never imagined, never heard tell of so much pain, except Nivaldo of course, but that was a long time ago, and maybe he's forgotten, maybe he's got it wrong.

Thirst. His flask is next to him and he tries to sip whatever drops might remain, but yesterday he did the same, and his lips are cracking as if they were made of old paper. He would like to run his tongue over them to moisten them, but his tongue, too, is rough and swollen, and nothing relieves it, he can't even swallow, his throat tightens in a spasm over his dry, inflamed membranes. Thirst, or pain. In his confused brain they alternate, mingle, gnaw away at him. Normal life seems far away; he knows he has no more right to it, ever again, until the end.

What got into him, the old man, to go see the boss one morning and ram his rifle up against his temple, acting mean enough for the man to realize he would not hesitate to fire, and that his head wasn't worth much? Impossible to say, a moment's madness, it made no sense, one morning that was different from the twenty years that had come before, and yet nothing had happened, just that the old man got up that day and knocked on the door. He doesn't need the money. That wasn't why he was there. It just came over him, all of a sudden. But it's too late for regrets, and the bag is all he's got left, he protects it like a treasure. In the semi-obscurity of the cave, his eyes sticky with dried tears, he cannot see it. He just knows it's there beneath his head, he can feel the leather against his cheek.

Sometimes he thinks of his bay: he slipped off when he got here, removed the girth just before he lost consciousness, the bay wasn't there when he woke up and he must be wandering around the mountain if he's not already dead, both of them dying together in this shithole, all these miles, all these days on the run, for this.

But now there is this sound, outside.

His body on fire, the old man calls again, in a murmur.

At first when the figure moves cautiously toward him, there is a huge wave of disappointment: it's only a kid. And then immediately afterward, relief. If he doesn't frighten him, he can do what he wants with him. The boy looks the clever type, with his hard face, not too fierce. The exhausted old man waits for him to come closer, keeps silent to preserve his strength. Something muddled is racking his brain and he recalls how Nivaldo died when the doctor arrived, so he opens his eyes wide all of a sudden, as wide as he can, he doesn't want to die now, he refuses to kick the bucket and he's seized by terror, the great void, don't let go, no. Madre, he can understand the fear—and he reaches out to grab the kid, a living creature who can keep him here, as long as he clings to this warm flesh he'll be saved. But the boy steps back, eludes him, and his fingers close over air, and the old man sees the boy ready to flee as if he had the devil there before him, for a moment he wonders, am I really in hell this time? He opens his mouth to say something, to prove to himself he's not dead, not yet, and the pain returns, it had left him for such a brief moment, it courses through him, if he's suffering like this it means he's still got a body that can endure, and he murmurs, trembling, "I'm thirsty."

Maybe he fell asleep while the boy went to get water, maybe he was within a hair's breadth of the abyss and didn't know it, on the edge of the precipice, and wouldn't that be unfair, now that he has the wherewithal to live like a king for a hundred years, he gropes beneath him, the bag is still there. He smiles and his chapped lips bleed and sting, he touches them, sees the blood on his hand. Moves his tongue and there's that metallic taste inflaming his throat, and a sense of urgency comes over him again, he feels so avid, breathless, he could lick the earth, he strikes his fist on the ground, almost in tears. When the kid comes back with the flask he wants to tear it from his hands.

"Not too fast," says the kid, not daring to touch him.

But the old man doesn't care, he's seen worse, and he can't stop drinking this water that is pouring through his body like a river swollen with winter rains, if he were a blade of grass he'd sprout at once, rise, climb to the sky, and he blesses this thirst that nothing can quench, and the water flowing into his mouth and spilling out makes him laugh, he chokes. Again the kid says, "Not so fast. Don't drink too much."

And now the old man feels something strange in his stomach, the impression that the same water that was restoring him to life is suddenly going straight through him, as if it were trying to find the way to his injuries, pressing to get out again, and the wounded flesh opens without resisting—bastard, treacherous flesh. It no longer belongs to him, this body shaken by convulsions, writhing, the pain moves into every vein, all his viscera, and the old man can see it coming, the moment when everything will rip open inside him, all mixed together, just life escaping, and he would like to suck the water back up, all the way to his throat, his mouth, spit it back into the flask and start over again there, let him rewrite what comes next, his eyes wide with terror, let him have a second chance. His hands open and press wide on his belly so nothing will happen, he cries out when the spasms come, so this is the end, he didn't think it would be like this, so wretched. God, for a flask of water: what if the kid has poisoned him?

In that instant, the boy grabs his head and rams his fingers into the corner of his mouth, shoving them in, stifling him. The old man knows he is going to die. He stops fighting. A thought for the bag beneath him, that he'll do nothing with; another thought for the goats and sheep whose throats he cut his whole life without ever stopping to wonder what it meant to know you are dying. Maybe he tries one more time to bite the kid who's crushing his jaws.

And then he feels the fingers all the way down his throat, he can feel the convulsion coming, and the boy steps back all of a sudden. The very next moment the old man throws up what he just swallowed, which was drowning him from inside.

RAFAEL

He kneels in the cave and observes the wounded man, who has just lost consciousness again. A scrap of a man, stinking, ragged, so thirsty that Rafael had to ram his fingers down his disgusting throat to make him vomit the water he'd swallowed, otherwise he'd have been done for, his stomach heaving with the rumblings and the bile and blood. Now Rafael stands to one side. He washed his hands with what was left in the flask, clenching his teeth. He looks at the old man. Listens to his wheezing breath. He can't help it, his nostrils contract, he feels nauseous from the fetid stench of the man's flesh, the excrement under his body, the sweat, but something else, too, that he can recognize a mile away: the odor of an infected wound, it's the same with animals that get gangrene when they're left too long with injuries that are impossible to treat. Outside, the horses are waiting, snorting; reassuring. He goes out to speak to them, to run his hands over them, over the scratches they got during their flight. The bay keeps at a certain distance. Rafael makes sure the scrapes are clean. In the end, put off by the thought of going back to the stench in the cave, he leans against a boulder and closes his eyes.

He rubs his face. Hesitates. Obviously, he didn't foresee something like this. Such a deserted place, and now there they are, two of them at the foot of the mountain. Head off and leave the man, that seems to be the best solution. Put a flask full of water by his side with a bit of food, and clear out. Forget what is bound to happen, because it's none of his business. If he'd gone two hundred yards further to the left, or two hundred yards to the right, he wouldn't even have known the old man was there.

But because of the bay, he can't make up his mind. Whether to leave the horse or take him with him, either way you look at it there are pros and cons. If he abandons them both, the bay and his rider, death will come for them both for sure, for the man because he's half dead already, for the horse in his wandering; Rafael can't make up his mind, since he doesn't know which one of the two is causing him to hesitate. What if he takes the horse with him. Initially he thinks the mother will congratulate him for having found an extra horse. But then, on second thought, she'll start asking questions. Where he found it, who he took it from. Why did he leave the man, an old man. And what if some day someone recognizes the horse—someone who knows where the bay came from, what past he is hiding—anyway there are too many things, and maybe the mother will order him to go back and get the wounded man with his carrion stench, he doesn't want to, doesn't know anymore. So he stays. He's got a supply of meat, and there's a river at the foot of the mountain, and berries on the trees, he saw them, he'll go and pick them. He'll decide tomorrow, whether to leave or not, alone or not—but of one thing he's already sure, the man in the cave won't be able to sit in the saddle; he'll figure it out, for the time being there are too many questions and his head is aching.

Squatting down by the injured man again. He has left some food and drink by his side, now he waits for him to open his eyes. But time passes and the old man goes on snoring, trembling and stiff, murmuring incomprehensible words. When he is wracked by pain, he moves an arm or a leg, and gives off a disgusting stink that doesn't even rouse him.

When night falls, Rafael makes a fire, at the edge of the cave so as not to suffocate. Patches of cloud fray a path across the sky. Among them, a few stars. The wind is still blowing, but he's sheltered by the mountain.

In the morning he sees that while he was sleeping the man ate, soundlessly, without waking him. He could kick himself. Just the thought he could have been caught unawares, robbed, had his throat cut. His knife has vanished. He stares into the feverish eyes of the man lying nearby, and he crouches down, ready to spring up again. No. This thing here can't get up, can't hurt him. So he says, "You gotta give me back my knife."

The man shoots him an exhausted look. He follows his gaze. The blade is where he left it for the old man the night before, by the smoked meat that he must have cut into smaller pieces. With his injuries he probably can't swallow easily, and in spite of the gloom Rafael can make out the bits of food he spat out on the ground, and he shudders when he hears the murmuring voice.

"Chrissake I was nearly done for."

Silence, then the old man goes on speaking, breathless.

"I thought you wanted to suffocate me. But without you I'd be dead twice over by now."

Then: "I'm thirsty."

Rafael slides a half-empty flask over to him, and says quickly,

"That's all there is. I'll go get more at the river."

The old man's croaking stops him in his tracks. *Don't go running away.*

"No. I'll come back."

"Can't leave a poor old guy like me."

"No, I told you I'll be back."

"You have a good reason not to leave me, y'know."

"How's that?"

"You see this bag?"

The old man rolls his head on the leather bag he's used as a pillow, and pats it with the palm of his hand.

"Got any idea what's in there?"

"No, sir."

"No, sir."

The injured man smiles, feels how his lips pull taut, so he rounds them so they won't bleed, opens his mouth wide, and Rafael observes his grimace, wrinkling his nose, waiting for what's next.

"Well, let me tell you, huh," continues the old man. "In that bag, there is . . . happiness."

Rafael says nothing, and the man waits, raises his eyebrows.

"Aren't you gonna ask what it is, happiness?"

"What is it?"

"Something you can't even imagine. Only if you see it, then you'll realize. But I'm not gonna show you. You gotta deserve it. First you have to make me better, okay?"

"Okay."

"So go find some water. And come back."

The boy leaps to his feet and runs out of the cave. He could make neither head nor tail out of what the old man was saying, and the ruined leather bag, splattered with the blood of his wounds, inspires little more than disgust. But he saw the gleam of joy in the face below him, and a man with wounds like his, his beard full of clots and so much blood everywhere you don't know where he's been hurt, doesn't go smiling as if he had the Virgin there before him without good reason, and he mulls the question over as he rides Halley down to the river. To be honest, he doesn't even wonder what there might be in the bag: he's not used to inventing or supposing, he lacks imagination. It's the word that has caught his attention, a word he has never heard. Happiness.

Often, to curse her fate, when faced with a dead animal or a harvest spoiled by bad weather or too many bills to pay all at once, the mother would cry out, *Rotten luck.* That's something he does know about. A broken paw, rotten luck. Carrion in the water reservoir, rotten luck. And more rotten luck, the sons finishing work late, or the wind knocking over the fences so the cattle get out. His entire life has been bathed in this mixture of resignation and a fist raised to the sky, a life choking with fear when the elements are unleashed, rage against a world that is neither fair nor beautiful. Not one day begins without recrimination or a sigh; the mother has never gotten up with a smile, with gentle or joyful words. As for the sons on their own, they display a cautious neutrality when they are not at each other's throats, yet they're always ready to fly off the handle over a biting remark, or because they have a bellyache, in other words over a trifle, something of no importance, sometimes not even identifiable, just a desire to contribute to the ambient evil, to the tension and conflict.

Since that is all they know.

So, happiness, then, on what extraordinary occasion might Rafael have heard that word? From the lips of an old man rotten in body and mind—because for sure his mind must be a wreck, too—in the stench of a cave where the worms are congregating, and yet that is where he discovers the word, instantly, because of the expression on the injured man's face, Rafael makes it his business, makes it into something. God, what is happiness, fuck all if he knows. Except that it fits into a leather bag.

If it moves? If it smells? But if happiness is the source of the nauseating smell in the cave, the boy is prepared to give up on it right away. If it speaks, maybe?

Something magical enough to put a gleam in the old man's eyes when he talks about it, precious enough for Rafael to witness the thin hands gripping the leather, for fear someone will take it from him, or that it will get away.

So he quickly fills up the flasks at the river, to go back and observe happiness. He figures that if the old man is still awake, he'll ask him to describe it, a little—in exchange for the water he's brought, and the meat he's given him. But when he gets back up there the man is lying with his eyes closed, and only his uneven breathing echoes against the walls of the cave. The bag is there, under his head, safeguarded. Rafael gazes at it for a long while, trying to work out whether it is something that can run away, or whether the old man's embrace is preventing it. It doesn't move, isn't breathing. Doesn't shine. You'd think there's nothing in there, except that the bag is full, that's for sure, bulging the way it does in spite of the man's head on it. A mystery. Rafael looks on from a distance, his eyes glowing.

During the day he sets up camp: he doesn't know how long his stay will last, but he senses it could be a good while. What will make it long is not something he thinks about, whether it's the time it will take to look after the old man, the time it will take for him to die, or simply the time for Rafael to decide to leave; regardless, he readies the place, weaves long branches together to make an enclosure for the horses, so they can move freely at night without hobbles; during the day he'll leave the hobbles on so they can graze further afield. In the cave he gathers a supply of dead wood, cleans the ground, puts foliage out to dry for softer bedding, and to hold the berries he's gathered. He scurries like an ant, tireless, scrutinizing, fixing a fence, moving the meat to another spot: it was too near the entrance, within reach of the insects. He finds the best place to build a fire, and works out how long they can last with the food he has. North of the cave he's seen traces of crushed grass, and shrubs that have been parted, signs that animals pass through there regularly: from different paths they are all converging at the river, where there are numerous tracks of deer by the water, and of other animals too, but the trampled, overlapping tracks are almost impossible to identify. They reassure him all the same, because this means there will be a steady supply of meat. In preparation, he whittles a few green branches to use as a spit, to cook or smoke his catch when the time comes. In the cave he piles stones with long branches between them to use as shelves—he mustn't leave the food supplies on the ground.

Now and again the wounded man opens an eye and looks at him, drinks some water, moans as he curls up on himself. At the end of the day, before they are trapped by darkness, Rafael goes over to him and says, puffed up with courage:

"Time to have a look at those wounds."

His whole life he's only ever looked after animals, and the old man is just another animal, no more, no less, that's what he keeps telling himself as he puts the water on the fire, because the wounds stink the same, bleed the same, and hurt the same. When he pulled the shirt back from the torn belly he thought of the grazing animals that get caught in barbed wire, of flesh swollen with pus. That's always a bad place for a wound, because that's where the digestive organs are, intestines and other disgusting things, and it gets infected deep inside, the best is to clean it all, cauterize it all. For lack of anything better he mixes and heats some herbs to make a rough poultice. He picked plants that looked like the ones the mother uses, but he isn't sure they're the same; still, the old man won't know, and Rafael will pretend, give him the impression he's healing him, this herb or that one, in the long run, what difference does it make. First he cleans the wounds as best he can, with the old man waving his hands at him to stop, screaming that it hurts.

"I know, *abuelo*, but to put the dressing on it has to be clean, otherwise the herbs will make things worse instead of removing the infection, I'm almost done, almost there."

During the night the old man is delirious, feverish, and Rafael wakes up every time to change the damp rag around his head, pull up the blanket, kindle the fire since the wounded man is cold, for all that he is burning with fever, and several times the poultice slips off his stomach. Between two naps the boy hums to himself. He finally drops off, then is startled because there's howling on the other side of the fire, and sometimes he thinks that if Mauro were here, for sure he would have settled the old man's score, his shouts and laments would get on Mauro's nerves, for sure the older brother couldn't stand it, he'd sooner choke him with his bare hands, the way Rafael saw him do, once, with a ewe whose stomach had been torn open by a puma. For a moment the boy is tempted by the idea, but he knows he hasn't got the strength, in spite of the state the old man is in, and he doesn't really feel like it, it's just he does think about it, with the fatigue, and that moaning lacerating his sleep and making him clench his teeth, anyway he won't do it, not right away, not today.

By morning the man is calmer, as are all injured people who wake at dawn, relieved to have made it through the night and that the Grim Reaper has not come for them. Their defenses are lowered and panic gives way to exhaustion—and that is often when animals die, when they think they're safe, and night takes a backward leap to wrest their last breath from them, and in their dimmed eyes there is a glint of surprise, a mean trick has been played on them and they didn't see it coming. But Rafael pays no attention to any of that. He too curls up in his blanket and enjoys the calm, slips into a dreamless sleep of a starry blue, like the sky he can see through his parted eyelids when he is roused by thunder, a dry, black storm hurtling against the mountainside, he doesn't care, tucked away in his impregnable shelter, his heart adrift in the middle of the world.

JOAQUIN

They've got the rams held tight together between their shouts and their whips. Sometimes Eduardo clicks his tongue and his criollo pushes a bit harder against the recalcitrant animals, jerkily, keeping well away from the coiled horns that are as hard as rock, horns that can break a horse's bones, and the criollos know it as well as the rams do, they give each other sidelong glances all the way along the road to town. Emiliano is in the lead, already proud. Every year his males win a prize, often even two or three, and on seeing them Joaquin realizes that those rams have nothing at all in common with the mother's. They're monsters, three merinos and two corriedales, straight from the bowels of the earth, all muscle and wool, a nasty gleam in their eyes. They've been bred for reproduction and competition, and at the estancia they never come in contact: galvanized by the presence of the ewes, they would attack each other. Herds are carefully divided, territory is split up. With each new season the gauchos have to keep an eye on the quarrelsome young rams, to separate them from the old chiefs; in spite of their vigilance, from time to time they will find two dead sheep in a corner of a pasture, their horns so entangled they could not free themselves, necks broken, breath depleted by battle, smashed, shattered.

For the first time Joaquin goes into the town without the mother. He feels as if he is discovering it all over again—a fresh gaze on the streets, the people, the large square hosting the fair. There's a festive air, and people hurry about.

Hundreds of animals: steers, rams, she-goats, and billy goats are penned in makeshift enclosures, bellowing, interrupting the powerful buzz of conversation, laughter, shouts. It makes Joaquin's head spin, he's never seen such a crowd, never heard so much noise all at once, not that it bothers him, on the contrary, a sort of excitement wells up inside him, his eyes and ears darting everywhere, he breathes in great lungfuls of the town, and his hands are trembling slightly.

They pen their rams in turn, then Emiliano waves them away, go get something to eat, he'll stay there, already the breeders have recognized him and are calling out to him, and Eduardo murmurs with a smile: *They're gonna cut a few deals.* They'll have to come back at the beginning of the afternoon to show the animals, but for now the gauchos are free, and Joaquin follows the others down the street, they seem to know the way, he follows and his mouth waters from the aroma of asados and empanadas. But they are heading away from the heart of the fair, and he says, "Where are we going?"

He receives no answer. Before long Arcangel, who is in the lead, stops, turns around to face them, and nods.

"It's here. They caught two of 'em."

At first Joaquin, going closer with the others, can't see anything, other than the crowd, which has gathered here too and is talking loudly, and then yes, there are two figures on their knees, and the people are staring at them without touching them, they've just come to have a look, they walk around and go away again. Standing on tiptoe Joaquin asks:

"What is it?"

But he already knows it's two corpses slumped there before them, held with their heads low on their knees by the rope that binds them to a wooden pole, and that's not what he's asking, it's why, an explanation, why these two Negroes are dead and on display here, and Eduardo answers, never taking his eyes from the scene:

152 · SANDRINE COLLETTE

"It's because of Gomez."

Fabricio nods and adds, "His wife got knocked up by a black man, so they've been looking for anyone they can punish. The others must've hightailed it out of here long ago."

Joaquin looks at the limp bodies, the children playing at prodding them with sticks, and the frozen faces swing from left to right as if the wind were swaying them, their torn shirts flap open and closed. He frowns.

"Are they the ones who did it? I mean, did those guys have the woman?"

"Not necessarily."

"I don't get it."

"Not much to get. Just that they're Negroes. Maybe the guilty man is one of 'em, but if he's not, they're paying for him."

"Christ, when the wind blows this way they stink, don't they."

"They've probably been there for a while."

Eduardo, who had gone closer to the corpses, steps back.

"They hanged them on the ground. Like dogs."

"Bah, are they anything more," says Arcangel.

Joaquin looks at their broken necks, imagines the time it took. The mother told them how one day a breeder caught a cattle rustler out on the steppe. Not a tree in sight: no matter. With his men he hanged the man like that. First, two or three gauchos pick him up and hold him horizontal; then the others slip a noose around his neck and pull the opposite direction. It makes everyone laugh, the ones holding the man because they have to struggle to keep their balance when the others pull on the rope, have to stand firm to stay upright, and the ones who have the rope because they can see the man's face distorting, his tongue sticking out, and it takes a while until his neck snaps or he stops breathing, anyway everyone's pleased, and red in the face, and it's time for a drink.

That's why the eyes and tongues are swollen, Joaquin notices, he's often seen dead animals on the estancia, but men, never, he doesn't dare say so, the others are looking without flinching. It seems so normal. So obvious. Then finally Fabricio calls to them, "I'm starving, aren't you?"

"You're right," mutters Eduardo, "we won't have enough time if we spend all day here."

They walk away, weaving their way through the people who've come to see, and suddenly Joaquin feels vaguely nauseous, must be the smell, and the thousands of flies on the corpses, and the huge black wounds they uncover whenever a kid runs by and they fly away for a few seconds in a lugubrious swarm.

When they sit down and order empanadas, he hesitates. But how would that make him look. So he nibbles reluctantly with the men, who are still discussing the affair, and gradually, like for them, his appetite returns, and he washes everything down with a few beers. He ends up not thinking about it any more because already their conversations are focusing on the contests, and the bets to make, they want to be in the right place in time to gamble their pay, the money Emiliano gave them this morning when they set out, and which Joaquin is fingering in his pocket, unsure whether to take it out. Eduardo taps him on the shoulder.

"Since you're new, I'll tell you which one to bet on, okay? Only ten pesos."

And ten pesos, fair enough, he'll have enough left over to buy as much drink as he wants, and maybe with the old man's advice he'll win a bit more; he laughs.

"You're on."

For a moment he feels rich, exultant, as if he'd already played and won the jackpot; he observes Emiliano's rams and points a finger.

"That one?"

Eduardo laughs and stands right next to him.

"You see what I'm looking at, now?"

Joaquin turns his head slightly, opens his eyes. Says no more than, "Oh."

"That one. The merino."

"For Christ's sake, that's not a sheep, it's a steer."

"That's the one that'll win in the wool category. Maybe even meat."

"You sure?"

"Sure."

"And Emiliano's?"

Eduardo shrugs.

"Manolo, among the rams that are younger than three. But for this year that'll be it."

"I can trust you, right?"

"You can."

That evening after the contests they head into the little town, with its lights, its packed streets. Joaquin has a bit more money in his pocket than earlier; Eduardo did not disappoint him. He has drunk some of it and he's humming, trotting along behind the others, his head is spinning. Like that morning, he asks, "Where are we going?"

And once again, no one answers, and he continues to follow them. He stops with the men beneath a sign and looks up, steps back. But Fabricio grabs hold of him.

"Hey, baby, you're not going to run away, are you?"

"I'm not interested."

Eduardo bursts out laughing behind him and shoves him toward the door.

"My mistake, or you never done it?"

He tries to get loose: nothing doing. And then with all the booze. And there is the temptation, even when he's terrified. Eventually he walks forward, acting gallant, his gaze defiant, hands in his pockets.

"Let's go, then."

His voice trembled; he clears his throat. *Goddamn dust.* He goes in, trapped between Eduardo, Arcangel, and Fabricio. The girls look at them. Wave at them.

"They know you," murmurs Joaquin.

Arcangel guffaws. *Yeah, sure, that's it.*

When they come toward them, Joaquin has to force himself not to run away. Sweat down his back, shivers. Panic. Nothing to do with the ewes behind the barn, this time, and the image of woolly asses muddles his thoughts, makes it all seem impossible.

"Gotta look after this one," says Eduardo, loudly. "He's not used to it, the boy. He's still an angel."

Afterward, Joaquin lies naked on the sheets, staring at a long crack in the ceiling. The night is cloudless, there might be a full moon, he doesn't remember. Or else the lights outside, casting shadows inside. The curtain by the open window flutters. The girl has put her clothes back on. He looks at her. A pretty brunette, slightly plump—anything seems pretty compared to what he knows, of course. She must be his age and he hesitates to ask her, remains silent, out of laziness, goes on watching her. She is hastily powdering herself, between two tricks, no point making an effort for the bunch of beggars waiting for her; and yet she doesn't rush Joaquin, and he doesn't dare look at her anymore. Did she realize it was his first time? No doubt. It went too fast, he's mad at himself. He would have liked to make it last. But there was nothing for it. He felt it coming, uncontrollably, and he had time to tell himself he'd screwed up. Then it came. He could never have believed the sensation could be so strong, so whole. So different—but he wipes his brothers from his mind, because that life is over, he's a man now, a man for women. He runs his hand over his eyes.

The girl sits down next to him on the bed, hands him a

cigarette without speaking. Because he was so quick, perhaps, and she doesn't want to go back at it again right away, she's stalling, she knows how long it takes as a rule, how many minutes she has gained with him. He smiles. Basically he feels so good he doesn't care.

From outside there's a smell of grilled meat and lamps burning. Now and again the bellowing of a bull, or a ram braying. He pictures the plains, gray and blue in the night, he doesn't know if the others are already waiting for him.

His arms along his side, Joaquin looks at the crack in the ceiling. His heart is beating full and slow, powerfully. Something new is beginning. He's ready.

THE MOTHER

On the fifth morning, the mother sends Mauro and Steban to look for the little brother. She's given them two days, not a moment more, to find his trail. They come back without him, they'd been able to make out his tracks, but with the southwest winds raising drifts of dust along the paths, they soon disappeared. The little brother was headed toward the *mesetas*, they're sure of that. They didn't see or hear anything else. They didn't find anything either: no body, no horse, Halleys or the others. They don't know.

"Fine," mutters the mother, but it doesn't match the expression on her face, which they find hard to qualify—anger, yes, that's it, anger.

On the days that follow she keeps looking out at the road, not saying a word. In the morning, and in the evening before nightfall, she stands by the kitchen window and waits with her arms crossed, and truly on her face there are no signs of tenderness or sorrow, because when she stands there she is speaking to fate, mischievous fate which never stops giving her a hard time, well then, let it come. Morning and evening the mother steams up the window with her breath, she has no intention of leaving her post until something happens, she doesn't know what—the little brother comes back, or a single horse, or bad news. Hardly matters which. Just so the world stops making fun of her, stops ignoring her; she wants an answer. Her mean gaze embraces the plain as far as the eye can see, and if she could set the thickets ablaze with her fury she certainly would, to show them all who she is, and what she has in store for them—show them, the spirits, the clumsy little gods, she defies them to come and stand there before her so she can talk to them about the misfortune they have wrought, since that's all they know how to do. That is why she raises her eyes to the sky, not in prayer, no, it's a threat, her teeth grinding fit to bust the eardrums of the almighty, and fulmination steaming from her nose and mouth, she has to keep from blaspheming—you never know—by biting her lips.

Now and then when they see her, glued to her chair with her faraway gaze, Mauro and Steban think about the father who went away and never came back, along that very road, and Mauro grunts, *That bastard.* Steban says nothing. He still can never say for certain what happens at night when the mother leads you away on a horse. But she dismisses the two remaining brothers with a wave of her hand.

"Get going."

Get going means, *get to work.* And there's no doubt, it's piling up in every corner of the estancia, and yet even she is forced to admit that they are hard at it, her sons, from dawn to dusk, even Mauro is looking tired. But he doesn't give up, he goes on repairing a pickaxe or a calving harness in the lamplight in the stable at night, and when he comes in, all he says is, "It's done."

Once or twice he added, *It's not so bad, huh.* And the mother knows perfectly well what he's referring to, the second son to leave after Joaquin, the huge void on the estancia, and Mauro doesn't want her to weep or regret. He doesn't give a damn about the little brother, doesn't give a damn that he's gone off, too. Maybe he's lying dead somewhere but that won't change *his* life, or the mother's, that's what he commands with his silence and his hard face, they don't need the little brother. And while for her the sorrow is nearly gone, already, because she is so used to these blows of fate, she bows to them already and works out what she has left to keep on going; worry, on the other hand, gnaws away at her, worry about not having enough hands for the job, because Mauro is wrong, of that she is sure, the three of them won't be enough. She'll have to take on extra hands for the shearing season, she really didn't need this, no, she really didn't. All their efforts going up in smoke.

Because when she adds it all up, two out of four means half, and for nothing. It's enough to make you choke with rage. Years of feeding and bringing those kids up by the sweat of her brow, arching her back in order to cope. Because it all takes a huge effort; because they eat vast amounts. Just when they were all four of them getting strong and assuming their share of the labor, giving her a bit of relief from her burden. Yes, just then, when at last they were beginning to earn more than they cost. Rotten luck. One of the twins, already, hasn't been there for weeks; and now the youngest. Two of them, in a flash. Of course, compared to wild animals it's nothing, everyone knows that eight young rabbits out of ten die before they reach maturity. But it's no consolation to the mother. She forgets that she's the one who lost Joaquin at poker, and that where the little brother is concerned, nothing's sure yet. In her muddled brain she confuses it all: if you're absent, you're dead—that's her way of seeing things, dead doesn't necessarily mean death, it just means gone, that's all. And they sure had something to do with it, too, those two who are gone, thumbing their noses at her, when she's been slaving away relentlessly to turn them into men, not to see them vanish without a trace or run off to work for someone else. Their desertion enrages her, blindly. She is unjust, she can sense it in the way Mauro looks at her when she talks about them, and he clams up because she's swearing. But he's not the one whose efforts are being wiped out one after the other, he's not the one forfeiting years of patience, living from hand to mouth while waiting for the day she'd get her revenge, four solid sons, tough as they come, and at last she'd be able to find some rest for this body of hers, aching and exhausted by this life that's no life for any woman, that's for sure. That's why she cried out, her first words, when Mauro and Steban came back without Rafael:

"Where is that little piece of scum?"

As if the kid were making her angry on purpose, off hiding somewhere and laughing at his joke. But the mother knew perfectly well when he didn't come back that it was no joke: something happened, she knows it did, and what good could happen out in that land, nothing, don't even ask, it's a place full of sorrow. Even the horses never made it. Can three horses just vanish like that when they know their home, when they've always lived there? You'd be bound to find them again, errant, exhausted: but not those ones. It's as if they'd never existed. As if they've been snatched up by the sky or the earth, or by spirits. At night she can hear the sound of hooves, she leaps to her feet. But it's just her imagination playing tricks on her, even when she thinks she can see the little brother down the road, his thin little shape jogging along to come home at last. She waits until her eyes sting and she has to face facts, there's no one there, just twisted trees outside and tears inside, she waits and goes back to bed, and doesn't sleep, he was her youngest, after all.

After one more week has gone by she stops counting, stops mourning, accepts the fact that he will not come back. The best thing for her to do is to banish him from her mind so he won't be in the way, so she won't whine. Still, it doesn't stop her from catching herself at the window morning and evening, her gaze scorching the landscape around her and murmuring new imprecations like some old woman whose mind is reeling. But she's stopped thinking about Rafael. If he fell, if he's been killed and the raptors are already devouring him, there's no point in hoping. There's enough evil every day not to go pointlessly creating more. And they have to go on looking after the sheep. Arch your back, woman. Life doesn't wait until you feel like getting your hands dirty.

After haymaking, it is harvest season on the estancia. The house and barn smell of earth and apple. Everything is tidy. The trays are full and every day Mauro inspects them and removes the spoiled fruit so they won't contaminate the rest with mold. The mother peels them, gives the bad bits to the chickens; they pounce on them. With the good bits she makes pies and preserves, stewed fruit she mixes with potatoes so it fills you up, so the grilled meat will enhance the sweetness. When Mauro and Steban dismount at the end of the day, they breathe in the sugary smell, and their mouths water.

On the sandy plot behind the barn they turned over the potatoes, too, letting them dry all day in the sun and wind. The crop is good and Mauro smiled, even though the mother did no more than grunt, "At least something good."

The storeroom is full, a promise for winter. Usually the mother also looks forward to this season of haymaking and gathering, she measures, calculates, tidies, inspects the sons' work to make sure nothing is going moldy, leans over the reserves, gingerly handles the fruit and the root vegetables, she's like a rodent laying in supplies, almost humming. But this year she hasn't left off her dark mood, and she looks without touching, her hands behind her back, she walks around, blasé, frowning. When Mauro is full of enthusiasm she stays silent, and everything could have been better, she seems to whisper, there could have been more, to make up for the worries that fate has given her, yes, at the very least. She gauges, figures that she hasn't come out ahead, maybe if she'd had two hundred pounds more or so of potatoes, and even then. So she takes a spade and goes to turn the earth to make sure there's nothing left behind, she wanders around the apple trees with her head in the air, shows Mauro a shriveled little fruit hidden among the leaves, and Mauro nods to the half-wit who runs to fetch the ladder. Then she shuts herself in the kitchen, slices and cooks, grumpy, and the sons keep busy on their own, mindless of her bitterness, with that wretched temperament she's always had they hardly notice how it's gotten worse.

The mother almost never goes into San León anymore. There, too, something has died inside her, fortunately for her income, because when she goes into town to pay her debts now she is careful to to avoid the bar. She brings back alcohol and drinks it the way she always has, in the evening after dinner, alone in the kitchen. A little glass so she'll sleep better; she often pours a second one, a glass to lull her, make her sway. Outside, lying up against the door, the dogs hear her inarticulate mumblings. They can sense the acrimony in her voice, it needs no words. They are still waiting for the two absent sons. They wonder. Like the mother, their attention often shifts to the horizon, for a sound or a puff of air, a hope—there they are. After a few moments where nothing moves, they curl and stretch, stifle a whimper. Sometimes they meet the mother's gaze, and all together they peer out at the road, in vain, as if she could do something. Annoyed, she shakes her head and frowns, and picks up a broom if she has to.

"Go on, scram!"

Sprawled in the old armchair before it's time for bed, she takes stock, makes a list, plans how they'll get on without the two missing sons; but fatigue overwhelms her too soon, and she drops off, chin on her blouse. She just has time to curse the banker once again, who has the misfortune he deserves, time to tense her fingers on her dishrag as she thinks of the poker games she almost won, back then, and which would be such a boon to her nowadays. So many pesos she wouldn't have known what to do with them. It made her tremble; they were there within reach. She could have told everything to go hang. Even the estancia, she wouldn't have needed it anymore, neither the cows nor the ewes. Nor her sons, not four, or two, no. Not a one. She could have spent her life with her elbows on the table, a drink at hand and a game in progress, because she misses it, terribly. She would have wasted a fortune, lost, started over, and still she would have had enough. Every day Gomez would have bowed down to her, and she would have hired herself a maid so she'd never have to clean the house or fix a meal again. That old dream, so close, within a hair's breadth she was. Just one card.

Always just one fucking card.

Basically, she's spent her life losing. And lately in the evening it's been driving her crazy, because she can feel the money within reach, if only someone would give her a hand, she'd have luck on her side this time, she's sure she would, and she turns up her palms that are gleaming with such a particular shine, come on, help me, she thinks, but she does not really see those hands. The world is hers. She doesn't know how to explain it, it's something that happens inside, a bright light, a great heat, something telling her that her time has come, for Christ's sake, her fingers fidgeting as she walks round and round the kitchen table, feverishly. She can almost see those goddamn chips, those bills, that treasure.

But that's the problem, in the evening she's at the estancia. She worked all day, yes, she fed the sons, the tall one and the half-wit, she cleaned up after them, tidied, put mugs out for the morning's coffee. Because of them she stayed there hoeing, weeding, cooking, cleaning. If only she'd listened to herself. Right now she'd be winning heaps and heaps. But instead she's there ruminating about all the money she's been losing since she stopped gambling, spreading her hands, the sensation is that strong, making gestures as if she were tossing the cards down, in vain, she's still sitting at the table in the estancia, alone and poor and oh, the anger.

All because of the sons.

Rafael

How many days have they been alone in that place, the old man, the boy, and the horses, no one has thought to keep track, and Rafael, trying to work it out, muddles up the mornings and loses count. If it were just up to him, he'd say seven or eight days, but the old *abuelo*, as he calls him now, shakes his head. More than twenty. The boy laughs.

"You've been raving so much you can't keep track of anything anymore," he protests. "Even in the middle of the night you thought it was daytime, and you counted two days for one, for sure."

"Because of the light from the fire. But I corrected it."

"I know how many times I changed your dressing, and how many times you yelled at me 'cause it hurts."

"Bullshit."

"I can repeat the words you said."

"Shut up, then. Is there any meat left?"

The boy cuts a smoked slice and hands it to him.

"I have to go hunting. In two or three days there'll be nothing left."

"I'll be able to sit in a saddle, soon. We'll go back to your place."

"Yes, *abuelo*. My place."

He doesn't tell him what it's like, at his place: a life of poverty crushed by work and arid land, and the mother who'll have his head if he comes back with this old man who can't walk, one more mouth to feed and nothing in exchange, she'll never agree to it. And so the old man can consider himself lucky that Rafael puts up with his silences and grunts, whenever he asks how he came by his wounds, because that would never be enough for the mother, no way, he'd have to provide an explanation, a wound like that is not something you get sharpening your knife. The boy has his own theory about it—a fight that went wrong, or a settling of scores, maybe even the result of some crime, otherwise the old man wouldn't be so reticent to speak, there's bound to be something fishy about what happened. But from there on it's all conjecture, and no matter how often he brings the matter up, he never gets an answer, just two mean eyes staring at him, sometimes suspicion.

"You're trying to get me into trouble, aren't you."

"No, *abuelo*, I'm just curious, I'd like to know."

Inevitably, at that point the old man has a fit of coughing and clutches his belly, and it goes on, impossible to stop, neither water nor maté nor the boy fanning him, you'd think the old man is about to suffocate there and then, his face turning all purple and gray like that. Eventually he calms down and says, breathlessly, *That time I was nearly done for, God's sake.* He catches his breath, his eyes full of tears. *You see, huh, you see.*

The boy doesn't know what he's talking about. But one thing's for sure, the old man forgot his question. And time passes.

Time passes and the old man is not regaining his strength. In the beginning there was visibly some progress, but then again in the state he was in, getting any worse would have meant bowing out altogether. Regaining consciousness, eating a little, conversing now and again, he was able to do all that normally. But then he stopped improving, despite the food and the treatment, and Rafael was puzzled. When he saw that the old man was beginning to recuperate, he thought, *Great, he's*

166 · SANDRINE COLLETTE

out of the woods, the way he would for the cows or the sheep, either they die, or they get better and that's it. He felt pretty proud of himself at the time, because he was the one who'd made the poultice, even if he did hesitate about the plants, so in the end they must have been the right ones, to make his patient perk up to that degree. And then the wound opened again, the old man began complaining again, and everything went wrong. He doesn't want to get up. He doesn't want to eat. Except to holler when things aren't going his way, to ask for some beer or give the kid a hard time because the wounds are hurting so bad and never stop. He curls up in his corner of the cave, clings to the ground if Rafael tries to sit him in the sun over by the entrance, just for a little while. *It will do you good,* abuelo.

"Shut up. Give me something to drink."

The way he treats him. On that score, the old man's no better than the mother, as soon as he got a bit of life back in him he started barking orders. Worse than that: he never talked about happiness again. And yet twenty times a day he checks to see if the bag is still there under his head—and how could it be otherwise—and he gives a nervous laugh when he touches it, rubs it, moves it to better support his head. It's not for Rafael's lack of trying that he doesn't talk about it: but the minute Rafael says something, the old man puts his arms around the leather and casts a suspicious look at the boy.

"You're not trying to steal it from me, are you?"

"Of course not. I just want to know what it is."

"Not good to be too curious."

"You promised to tell me."

"If I show you, you'll take it from me."

"If I were going to take it I would have already."

So now in addition to sleeping on the bag, the old man has tied the bag's strap to his wrist. The slightest movement and he'll wake up. Impossible to think of a way to open the bag during the night, and yet it nags away at the boy, this desire to see the thing the old man's so afraid of losing. So as not to alarm him, he stops talking about it. He does what he knows how to do so well: wait. Like every great predator he carries within him the conviction that haste yields nothing positive. During the hunt, this can mean stepping on a twig, its cracking sound resonating in the silence; a warning smell, because you've forgotten to stay upwind, and the steppe, with its infinite horizon, is unforgiving, a few leaps and the guanacos get away, retreat, disappear. There are blunders, out of inadvertence, fatigue, or stupidity. The only rule is patience. Hours, days. Weeks, if need be.

But the thought won't leave him alone. At night, or during the day when the wounded man is dozing, he goes closer. He always has a ready excuse: a branch to put on the fire, a nightmare, the blanket to adjust. He is deliberately noisy so the old man will pay him no mind, to get him used to things falling over, to his footsteps right behind his head. When he's sure he's asleep, he kneels down next to him. Now he could pull the bag out from under the old man's head, an inch or two, without waking him up; but two inches is too little to open the bag, not enough to see inside. And he doesn't dare slip his hand in. So he explores from the outside, tries to make out the shape, sniffs the air. The leather's too thick, and the moment there's a warning grunt he gives up. He turns hastily, crouching by the fire as if he'd always been there. Sometimes the old man opens an eye and looks at him. Rafael does not turn his head. *Not me,* abuelo. *Must be a draft.*

It becomes a game. Because in the end all he would have to do is take the rifle and blast the old man's head to bits. More than once Rafael pictures himself taking aim and firing, observing the carcass lying there before him, pushing it over with his toe to free the bag. His heart beats faster. Something stops him, however. Not affection, no, because they are made of the same stuff, the two of them, they are hard, devoid of emotion, each one with his weaknesses so deeply buried that no one will ever find them, unless they dig through flesh all the way to the bone. The boy feels affection for his horse and his dogs; not for man.

But anyway. In spite of the meat, and in spite of the herbs on his wounds, the old man has stopped getting better. For several days already he has been stagnating, and once again the boy thinks of how an animal will vegetate before it dies, as if it is still hesitating over which side will determine its future, as it stands with its head low, appetite gone. Two or three times as he treated the old man's wound he removed worms that were nestled in the flesh, white worms, the same kind you see on carrion, and it seemed really strange to him to be removing those wriggling maggots from a living creature, or maybe in the end the old man is transitioning, maybe it's a sign, the boy keeps an eye out, the worms haven't come back. But he thinks about it every time he lifts up the poultice, and gets used to the idea that one morning it might be swarming with them, and he mustn't cry out, mustn't recoil. Around the wound the skin has turned white, or gray here and there, frayed as if it were about to come to pieces. In the middle the skin isn't closing or scarring; the ragged flesh overlaps but there is still this hole sucking it inwards, and expelling flows of yellowish pus and those horrid smells that made you want to throw up. The old man's face has turned black and yellow, too, and his breath when he speaks . . . He sleeps more and more. Frequently the boy has to shake him to change the dressing, it's a major undertaking, because he has to struggle every time, the poultice has stuck to the flesh, the skin tears, and those hands constantly trying to stop him, as if the wound could heal all on its own, as if all the old man has to do is curl up around it and stop moving.

Rafael no longer knows exactly why he is still taking care of the old man; he does it from routine, from fatigue. He keeps on because the mother taught him never to abandon an injured animal, and that's how he's been trained. His intuition orders him to stay there, to help. The only thing that would make him leave the old man is death; but he's standing there facing it like a rabid dog, driven by an instinct that is beyond reasonable, ready to fight and ward it off because survival is written in his blood. Even if he has to stay there for years.

There are evenings when he thinks about the estancia. He misses Three. He is sorry he didn't let him come along. With his fingertips he pretends to stroke the dog's rough coat. He murmurs, *Good dog.* Opposite him the old man sleeps. Dozes, grumbles, dozes again, you'd think he's hibernating in the middle of summer, the way he's decided to sleep so much, only awake to eat and drink a little, nothing else. The boy wishes he'd move more: an animal that lets itself go and won't get to its feet is done for, otherwise it would struggle to stay upright because deep down it knows that lying down is the posture of death, that is how all dead bodies end up, on your feet you still have a chance. But the old man pushes him away when he tries to take his arm, moans about his wound and begs to be left alone. So he does as he is told, and goes back to sit at the entrance to the cave, where he can see the horses, and the landscape full of light.

But what sort of wound is this that doesn't get better, that oozes for all it's worth, as if it had been absorbing evil instead of rejecting it: the boy is beside himself, here he thinks it's been drying and then he finds that, under the dressing, the wound has opened again. He is mad at the old man for not healing the way he should; he reproaches him for his apathy and his vacant gaze. Without a will, there is no way: and Rafael's will alone will not suffice, the granddad has to pull his weight, he mustn't get the impression he has to be forced to produce scar tissue or let himself be disinfected. The problem is that he wastes all his remaining strength wrapping his scrawny arms around his satchel, stroking it, murmuring incomprehensible words to it. When they're not compressing his belly his feverish fingers flutter over the leather, leaving moist, sticky traces. The boy watches, sitting not far away.

He has no perception of time. One day follows another and he seems to see time passing from inside the cave, in bands of light and color, somewhat later in the morning, somewhat earlier in the evening, particularly on days that are overcast. Inaction weighs heavily upon him, on his shoulders and in his back, which hurts him even though he hasn't been harvesting or reaping, nothing. A feeling of urgency is burning his heart. To move. Maybe the old man's growing immobility is the source of this animal reaction in him—to move on, to leave this place of death. For the first time he is aware that he could have gone for help rather than wait here trying to treat a wound that was way beyond him, with methods that were slapdash at best. He tries to come up with excuses: the old man would have died while he was gone. After all, he was the one who didn't want the boy to leave.

The truth is that Rafael was only too grateful for the diversion, relieved he didn't have to go back with the horses so soon; really, the idea of going home didn't even occur to him. Intoxicated with solitude and freedom, and a sense of being all-powerful—hunting to feed himself, lighting fires, finding water—how can he explain the exaltation he feels every time he has found another way to survive? Some primitive reflex buried deep inside him, brought to light by these weeks where his life is in his own hands and nowhere else; he is the sole agent, the only one responsible. In this respect the old man is no more and no less than the crowning glory of the escapade, the accomplishment of his power over another man. Two lives depend on him now, in addition to the horses'. Never has he been so strong.

But the magic is fading, and he is getting weary of ruling, deciding, waiting. When the old man's health begins to decline on top of it, something snaps inside him, bringing with it anger and discouragement. Try as he might! Sometimes he has to restrain himself from giving the old man a heartfelt kick to wake him and shout in his ear: "On your feet, *abuelo*, walk, walk! Let's get going now."

He pictures himself hoisting the wounded man onto his horse and leading him to the estancia, where he'll leave him to the mother. He dreams of giving up on the old man, and all the failures and constraints along with him, the questioning and doubt. Deep down he knows he'll never find the sort of lightness he experienced before, but he would like to cast off this lead weight which is driving him every day a bit deeper into the earth of the cave. He is sure the mother would know how to treat his wound. When he thinks about it, he rubs his eyes and his face, practically stamping his feet. He wishes he could go back to where he was two weeks earlier, to get up after the thrashing Mauro gave him and go and close the doors to the stable. Then he would wake up from this nightmare. But he understood long ago that life doesn't work like that, you can't go back. Like when he would jab his fingers on the barbed wire in the fields, and his older brothers said, mocking him: "You shoulda thought about that beforehand."

Yet again he's let himself get trapped, the burden is too heavy. He was overambitious. Tears run down his cheeks and he wipes them away with surprise, he didn't feel them coming. So he surrenders, rushes out of the cave, sobbing. In the beginning it takes his breath away, there seems to be so much pain trying to force its way out, and he kneels at the edge of the cave, sure he's about to pass out. And what if the old man hears him; but there's no more time for shame, he doesn't care about the old man. It takes endless minutes, perhaps an hour, for his weeping to subside, then it comes back, then recedes, not a lot at first, then a bit more. Sniffling. Immense sadness, fragile and weary, just waiting to start up again. Through his moaning can be heard the voice of a little child.

He walks on the mountain for a long time, listens to his breathing, which won't grow calmer, the birds around him fly away when he passes by. He didn't bring his rifle, it's as if he were naked in nature, at the mercy of any wandering predator. He feels like a lost animal, too, not knowing what to do or where to go; he pictures the little statue in the corner of the mother's kitchen, and he murmurs a prayer. Let life come to his aid and choose for him. He's afraid of freedom, now, he doesn't want it anymore, he's eager to get back to the estancia, to chores, to the smell of cows and sheep. Maybe the old man could make it through the journey, wrapped up on a stretcher pulled by one of the horses. He needs branches and rope. The idea takes off in his mind all of a sudden. He's already working out a diagram, adjusting straps, strengthening the wooden poles to make it all hold. The granddad might get bumped around a bit, but rather than go on festering here . . . He turns around. Breaks into a run.

When he reaches the cave he curbs his urge to wake the old man, and he begins putting twigs on the dying fire. But he can't help himself. He inches slowly closer, then calls to him. *Abuelo.* It's unbelievable, how much the bastard sleeps. The boy can do all the hunting, and fetching water, and keeping the fire going, but it's the other fellow who lies there snoring. Not even. Because there's not a sound in the cave. Rafael ends up shaking the old man by the shoulder.

"*Abuelo.*"

In vain.

In a rage, the boy kicks over the branches where he had put the supply of berries, scatters the fire. Outside, the horses hear him roaring and turn their heads anxiously toward the cave. There's a tumult in there as if the devil had arrived, and things are getting broken, for sure, to hear the echoing of something banging against the walls of the cave, sounds of wood and metal, flying everywhere, crashing, loudly. And then a duller sound, that of a body being thrown, a soft sound, the same you'd get punching a sack full of sand, or flesh, or guts, the violence in there is ferocious; the boy's voice piercing the air:

"Fucking piece of shit!"

On his knees in the cave. Not next to the old man, who's good and dead now, he knew that right away. There's nothing left to do with him but roll him up tight in a blanket and leave him there, since it's impossible to dig a hole either in the rock or even further away in this soil of pebbles, with no shovel, no ax, don't even think about it. The stench won't bother anyone in this wilderness. But for sure predators will come, intrigued by the smell of dead animal, he'll have to stop them and the blanket won't be enough. For now it's next to the leather satchel that the boy is fulminating and cursing; he doesn't give a damn about the old man.

It took him a few minutes before he dared to open the bag. First he dragged it away from the granddad, for fear that the dead man would leap up from beyond death and grab him in a furious reflex—you know what happens when a stiff gets hold of your leg, it burns and turns purple then black, and you can see through the flesh to the bone, and then the entire body is attacked, devoured by a terrifying force, sucked down by the Grim Reaper, by the endless darkness. So he prodded the bag with a stick, just in case there were any evil spirits lingering in the leather or something inside ready to burst out to grab him. When he felt safe, almost sure, because he wouldn't stake his life on it, but he had to try all the same, he unfastened the buckles, trembling. And recoiled. And kicked the flap closed again, quickly, hard, so he wouldn't get caught.

Jesus Christ, when he saw what was in there; he knows what that is. And it's not happiness.

That's why he's yelling his head off.

Hours later, just as he's about to leave the cave for good, he falters from weariness. It's true that these last few days have not been easy. Looking after the old man, putting up with the stench, touching his wound. And seeing to the water, the fire, the food, the horses outside, making sure nothing happens. Being patient, looking at the bag. Sometimes he had such pins and needles in his legs that he had to go for a walk around the mountain. His head was pounding, a constant refrain of wondering whether he should leave, yes he should leave, but he stayed, knowing he was wrong, incapable of finding the solution that would take care of everything, leave for a while, stay for a while—he couldn't split in two, after all. In a way, he's glad it's over. But who's to say that what lies ahead will be any better?

To protect the granddad as best he could he spent the afternoon burying him under dozens, hundreds, of stones. Big ones, little ones; the ones that were willing, either inside the cave or out, and slowly they pile up, initially it seems the old man is as big as the universe, impossible to bury. But gradually his hands disappear, then his arms, and his feet. When the boy can see nothing but rock, and the granddad's face and chest have collapsed beneath the weight, become invisible, impossible to reach for any creature that does not have hands and fingers, he sits on him. Not in the middle, of course. At the edge, where there is nothing but stones. To catch his breath. To listen. There is not a sound, he's sure of that, but checks again, it comes from deep inside him, and yet he knows the old man has stopped breathing, there's not a sigh trying to seep out through the rocks. It's like a last wariness—a last fear. What if he'd got it all wrong, all along. Preparing the plants, the treatment, and even death. What if the granddad is asleep.

How many stories has he heard about corpses waking up after a day or even two. How many of them were buried alive by people who, like him, believed that . . . So he listens for a long time. And when his ears begin to buzz with concentration, and he's sure nothing is ever going to move again, he stands up. Because the old man could never remove the stones, there are too many, they're too heavy. *Dios mio*, he is dead and dead once and for all. Yes, provided he is. The boy picks up the leather bag and leaves, says nothing, neither goodbye nor sorry, since there is no one to hear him. If the old man waved to him as he was on his way out, he would turn back, but he's buried him and he knows perfectly well that he wasn't moving, and there's already a smell of death, even if he can't be sure since with the wound the place has been stinking for days, anyway it's done, all that's left in the cave is dead, there's no need to go back. He leaves.

The Old Man

He can't say he saw it coming and yet something had been warning him for days, and he figured it would end this way, even if for a time he believed the boy could get him out of there, in the early days, when things were improving, with the kid's stinging plants. But since then his body has given up, and he can't take it anymore, can't stand this pile of stinking flesh, and he wishes he could thump it to get it going again, but has to make do with squeezing it in his arms to contain it, so that the little life remaining, hidden inside, won't sneak out some hole and escape.

He didn't believe, either, that he'd cling to his rag of skin with so much spite and determination: he has thumbed his nose at death any number of times, and so what if it came for him, back then he didn't give a damn, he didn't know it could hurt so much. Or because he'd seen Nivaldo, he suspected it might, up to a point; but it would still hurt less than Lorenza being gone, Lorenza who had given him her life, then taken it back again, and maybe that's what made him decide to go on keeping cattle for others, since his own dream was finished, a farm with Lorenza, that was the past, he had to blot it out of his mind.

And yet she was the first one who understood how he loved the animals and the steppe more than his own life, and she went along with it, she said she would wait for him from one season to the next, between the calving and the migration, it's just they would have to work it out, she didn't want the child to be born in winter, the country was tough enough as it was. And he had laughed, a child, for a man like him who'd only ever held a calf or a lamb in his arms, he couldn't get over the fact that Lorenza expected this of him, but she had stood firm. *He'll keep me company when you're gone.* It was the following fall, just as he was getting ready for the seasonal migration, that Lorenza came to tell him: when he returned there would be three of them. She was sure she was expecting a son, he was already kicking her ribs; and the old man, who wasn't old in those days, was overcome with confusion, because he hadn't suspected a thing, but she kissed him and wished him a good journey.

He had led the herds away, singing. The men made fun of him: all the women say that, in the beginning, they say they won't expect anything of them, won't change anything. And the men, stupid idiots that they are, believe they'll be able to have a family and stay in the plains, all at the same time, never imagining they'll have to choose, and that the pampas wins, every time. You'll see, they asserted—and laughed some more. He remained convinced.

They had spent the season in the *invernadas*, the winter pastures, he'd almost forgotten he had a wife and would soon have a son; the thought came to him when it was time to go back down to the plain, and something strange welled inside him, a sort of impatience, and pride, and anxiety, too. There were days when his urgency made him fidget on his horse, and he rounded up the stray steers relentlessly, and this delayed his return, as if deliberately. Other times he was not even sure he wanted to go back, he was already thinking about the moment he would climb back in the saddle to herd the cattle to the far reaches of the plain. To curb his ruminating, in the evening he drank beer after beer until late at night, then got back on his horse the next morning, his head creaking with a sharp pain.

Fate decided for him.

Lorenza had left two days before his return, taking with her his dream and his son, since it was a son—she had given birth one month earlier. She had gone off with a peddler, he learned; he didn't even ask what he sold. The man could sell chickens or dishrags for all he cared. Lorenza hadn't left word for him. No message with anyone. The little room where she had lived while waiting for him—waiting for him!—was perfectly tidy, no dust, nothing left behind. He had closed the door on leaving and the words spun round his brain. *Well then, it's over, they warned you, didn't they, that it wouldn't work out.*

That must have been thirty years ago and nothing had ever hurt him that much again, and yet he had gone looking for it, fate, playing hide-and-seek with it, taunting it from high up on the plateaus, on crazed horses, within reach of a bull's horns. Every time he got a jab in the hand or leg he hoped the pain would distract him from that other pain moored in his chest. As the years went by, the anguish abated, of course. But in all his living memory, not once did he ever feel such a fire consuming his heart and his guts again, not until these days lying in the cave, with his belly and his life consumed from within, and at first it made him laugh, almost joyfully, to see there was such a thing as a greater suffering. But now . . .

Now he doesn't know how to get rid of it anymore, and surely the pain of Lorenza seems like nothing, and the sorrow he felt back then. Today there is no more room for sadness, no strength, and the wound uses everything up, his thoughts and his energy, even the urge to throw up. When the kid showed up, he could still tell himself that he didn't have much to regret in life, that clearly the cattle had been his best company. But now he can't even tell himself that much. Images scroll past his inner eye and he wishes he could stop them, they're like a bad omen, these forgotten memories reappearing when he didn't even ask them to, these muddled, overlapping thoughts, and even when he closes his eyes they're still there inside and nothing will make them leave, but really they'd better stop, he can't stand them anymore.

The terrible visions of the *saladeros* fill his mind, places he'd worked when he was young, that was before Lorenza, the animals bellowing as they approached the abattoir, entire rooms full of meat plunged in brine then packed in barrels of salt to preserve it. His father had told him how the meat used to spoil, in the old days, the steers were killed only for their leather and fat; and of course they cut off the best pieces, but almost nothing, sometimes just the tongue, to grill it—but the old man, remembering this, does not even feel his mouth water, and yet how he used to love it, grilled tongue.

The rest of the animal was just thrown out, left, abandoned, covering the floor with carcasses still three quarters full, such a waste. Salting the meat was the prime way of preserving it, and he remembers the *desolladores* at the slaughterhouse who separated the hide from the flesh, up to their elbows in death all day long, then in the evening they still stank of it and people would move away from them at the bar. At first they sent the cured meat to Brazil, it was good enough for the slaves, not much else, it made them laugh, the people here, they felt like they were playing a trick on them. But then before long the population took to it. And even later—but this was not something the old man's father had witnessed, because he was dead by then—they invented the means of keeping the victuals cold, and the *saladeros* closed down, one after the other. The old man had witnessed those years that changed the world, and he was stunned to see the bovines come back to replace the sheep, after they too had once been banished from the pampas by the craze for merinos, just whichever would earn the most, the gold of meat or the gold of wool, when it wasn't both at the same time; and you didn't know which way to turn.

Nowadays the cattle farmers exported most of their meat by refrigerated transport. A few small firms still salted, but only for themselves and the locals, cured, aromatic hams that the old man knew by heart for having taken them along for years on end during the migration season. Sometimes he regrets his youth, when the gauchos on the steppe killed a cow or a sheep whenever they needed to, that's the way things were, you got hungry all of a sudden, you slaughtered an animal. And it was true that they left half of it behind when they'd finished their feast, they too were unapologetically wasteful, they weren't even aware of it, everyone was the same, that's the way you did things back then. They ate the *matambre*, the meat between the hide and the ribs, thick and tender. Nobody wanted the rest: all you had to do was kill another animal. Wild dogs and all sorts of predators had a feast once they were gone, there was a sort of tacit agreement, they'd sit there waiting a hundred yards off or so, drawn by the smell, they'd start to howl if the men's feast was taking too long. But the meat had to cook, had to be well grilled on the outside and red inside, and the fire had to have good glowing embers. That all took time.

The old man curls a little closer on himself. The memory of the smell of meat causes his stomach to contract and the pain shoots right through him. He calls out to the kid; no answer. When he manages to lift his head, the cave is empty and he feels terribly alone. It's stupid, this impression he has, that if he's all alone he'll succumb, won't have the strength, and he doesn't dare tell himself why, because it's drifting through his brain, resist, don't let it come for you. He wants to tell the kid to find some way to drag him to his house, never mind if it hurts, the stage where he's at . . . Some makeshift stretcher, a saddle with branches roped around him to keep him in it, anything would do, provided he can get out of this place, he can suddenly sense how evil it is, and the wind is making its way in, has come to chill his hands. He calls out again:

"Niño . . . "

Silence. What if the boy has left. Maybe he's fed up with

caring for him and listening to him yell, because he, the old man, hasn't made much of an effort, except to whine and complain when it hurts; if he were the boy he'd have skedaddled ages ago.

Slowly he stretches his legs, pulling at his guts, but his tetanized muscles can't take any more. An immense fatigue comes over him, and for a moment he recalls the stag he hunted ten years or so ago, a clever old stag that made him travel for miles, going round in circles by the swamps, back-tracking to make him lose the scent, it had taken him three days to find it again. And when he came onto a plateau and saw it, he got the feeling it was not by chance, and the animal was neither surprised nor frightened. It didn't move, as if it were invisible, protected by its absolute immobility, not even an eyelash or a tremor. The old man had observed it, the immense antlers, horns lowered; it must have been fourteen, sixteen years old. Not many made it to that age, given the hunters, and injury, and predators; not many grew that big, five feet at a rough guess, one of the finest specimens he'd ever seen.

He fired. In the same instant he told himself he shouldn't have: the sport on the previous days had been enough of a feast, the hunting, tracking, the way he'd been taken for a ride, his determination to catch up with the animal. How many wrong tracks had he followed? How many hours spent dreaming of capture, sniffing the air, rubbing the ground with his fingertips to figure out which way the stag had gone?

But the thought came too late, the shot had already been fired. Maybe he'd altered the trajectory with his moment of hesitation, because when he went closer the animal was still breathing, shot in the belly. Lying there outstretched, it watched the old man come nearer, and what he saw in the animal's eye was immense fatigue, nothing left for anything else, neither fear nor malice, just that exhaustion that turned his eyes gray and made them shine, and the choppy breathing. He'd finished him off with a bullet to the head. He didn't feel up to cutting its arteries with a knife, not that he was afraid of a bad kick, because he would have held on behind the animal's neck, no, but because his heart just wasn't in it. All the way home he felt sad, saw again the way the creature was startled when he shot it between the eyes, and the gaping wound in its belly, and for the first time he thought that death was not a pretty sight.

Same for him, then, ten years later, and the old man is well aware of the irony of fate, lying there disemboweled in his cave, and this fatigue all the way to his fingertips, to his eyelids which won't open anymore, and his mouth that can't call out, his stiff legs. Between his fingers the dressing leaks a green and yellow liquid, he doesn't know if it's from the plants or if it's all that's left inside him, emptied of blood and flesh, just this discharge he doesn't recognize, he looks at it and doesn't understand. He shifts his rigid palm and is surprised, because suddenly the pain has left him, and he moves again, nothing. Surprised, he begins to laugh; even his shaking does not feel like shards of glass under his skin and he makes a prodigious effort to open his eyes, feels a brutal happiness, as if he were anesthetized. So maybe the kid's simples are working at last. All at once it pours inside him, like a draft of air, a luminous fluidity, and he feels light, almost airborne, whereas his body was dragging him gradually toward the earth, embedding him in every crack in the rock, sucking him in from underneath. Now he is floating, free, his innards are open and calm. He would like to sleep, he is sure he will wake again, cured, to sleep the way you do when you are resting, getting better, when you have nothing to eat and you have to pass the time, when you're injured and your flesh is praying for mercy. So he wraps himself in his blanket like a little animal in its burrow, trying to find the most comfortable position, wedging the bag under his head. He turns his back on everything so the daylight won't disturb him. He would have liked a nibble of the dried meat but the kid isn't there to cut it for him, and he can't shake off this torpor, he doesn't want to lose it, doesn't want to run the risk it might elude him. He can hear the melody in the background. He hasn't felt this good for weeks, and he lets himself go, opens his hands, sighs. He can sense the light footsteps entering the cave, the sound of the fire crackling with dried branches, or maybe it's something else, too late, he drifts off, he still has time to think that everything is coming to an end, and then, nothing more, all is well.

RAFAEL

Rafael heads off home without looking back, taking the horses with him, and before long all he has left in his wake is a long cloud of dust. He can feel the space between himself and the cave expanding, getting wider, and at last it begins to let go of him—the tightness in his belly, in his back, yielding with every step the criollos take. An almost joyful lightness courses through his body, tingling his arms and legs. He is tempted to spur Halley on, to break into a mad gallop as they head down the mountain—but he remembers in time that he won't be able to hold the other three horses, so he keeps himself in check, looks up to determine his route from the position of the sun. His excitement abates, makes him wise. Truth is, he's in no hurry to get back to the estancia; a strange malaise grips his throat as the hours pass. Whether on purpose or not, he keeps Halley on a short rein, at a walk, for hours. The criollos stamp their feet, they are used to galloping, even the old man's horse, which must be a hybrid, so tall with such skinny legs, yes, even that one stumbles and snorts, all three pull on their ropes, and Halley strains against the bit, the boy is getting annoyed.

The first day, he checked every hour to make sure the bag was still securely fastened behind him, and looked around at it constantly to keep an eye on it, running one hand over the buckles, making sure it's closed, tightly lashed. He has no choice but to take it home, the mother will have to believe his story, and for sure she will start arguing before he's even opened his mouth, but when he shows her the bag, she'll shut up there and then, of that he can be sure. And Mauro and Steban will look at him differently, because of the bag, for a start, and also because the little brother has changed over the course of these weeks, he's grown up in spite of himself, living like that in the effluvia of blood and the death of a man, not an animal, a man. Confronted with that evil that devours flesh and clings to the walls of the cave, that oozes and seeks to worm its way into every living thing: how many times did Rafael awake with a start, with the terrifying feeling that a blast of air was peeling his skin to get inside? Thinking about these things consoles him for the fact that he's on the way home, he was bound to have lowered his guard at some point, and one day the worms would have gotten into the folds of his stomach to start eating away at him, too. So he leaves it all behind, the wound, the maggots, and death, and the old man beneath the stones, refusing to wake up. He forgets about the cave. At last he can breathe again—he'd been virtually holding his nose not to throw up from the smell of putrefied flesh, back there; now suddenly his sinuses are open, flooding his body with pure air, he fills his lungs with sky, mouth open, he coughs, sneezes. The tears in his eyes make him laugh. Leaning down onto Halley's neck he lets himself be lulled, he thrusts his hands into the horse's mane to rub off the parasites, if there are any left, it won't matter to the horse, and he rids himself of everything, bad memories too, and they walk on.

He even left the meat behind, for fear of bringing the infection and the fetid stench with him. So he hunts again, fresh meat, he kills a hare and roasts it on the spit at night above the fire, he rediscovers the magic of a time he thought was long gone, before he found the horses, before he tried to heal the granddad. At night the flames rise toward the sky, play with the shrubs in the shadow, revealing the green branches, the silvery thickets; behind him, the river murmurs and he struggles not to fall asleep. The aroma of grilled meat tingles his gums, and he swallows air, wait, it'll be all the better for waiting. Since leaving the cave he does like the old man: he sleeps on the leather bag. Scattering the stones to make a soft patch of ground he sets down the bag and his blanket and goes to sit closer to the fire, his face lit by the embers. With the tip of his knife he cuts a piece from the hare, it's still pink, never mind, the temptation is too strong, his mouth is watering, he feels his teeth ready to tear and grind, he laughs at the prospect. And the meat tastes of carrion.

He spits it out, swearing. Tries another piece and spits that out too, runs his fingers around his mouth to remove the filaments caught in his teeth, suddenly he's nauseous, he drinks for a long time, eats a berry. Puzzled, humiliated, he watches as the meat slowly turns black on the fire, he lies on the bag and shivers under the blanket. From where he is lying, gazing at it from underneath, the hare's carcass seems huge; it blocks the sky like a giant incongruous statue, a mass of hanging flesh without a back, the moon darts in and out through the holes left by the eyes, and the prey becomes a monster, an incoherent shape, a black, ragged dragon. Rafael sits halfway up. He kicks over the spit. The flames leap, throw up a shower of sparks, lick at the meat. A few moments later the fire is crackling around the remnants of something you would never know had been a hare.

When they reach the steppe, Rafael stops to study the landscape. He is much further south than he thought, he'll have to follow the rivers for another day or two. The density of the forest led him astray, as if constantly trying to bring him back, to lose him among its conifers, its arrayáns, or the giant araucarias, from summit to hill, valley to plateau. Now the plain reclaims him, with its rocky ground half covered by the jarilla shrubs, the devil's plant, the mother sometimes says, it'll tear your mouth out or make it indestructible. Now and again the rock yields to a little lagoon, a watering hole for the animals—the horses stop to drink there. But it's the wind which the little brother had almost forgotten, the wind hurtling down the ancient glacial valleys, veering up the jagged mountainsides, whipping faces and manes. He puts his hand on his hat to keep it from blowing away, he looks at the clouds, it's as if the summer had gone by while he was looking after the old man in the cave, he's missed it, and yet he didn't stay there that long. In a few weeks the leaves on the bushes will turn brown and shrivel up, will blow all along the pastureland, and he won't be able to do a thing about it, neither catch the leaves nor bring back time, and the mother will shout at him that he is behind with his work, of course he is, almost three weeks behind, what does she expect. The first thing he'll do when he gets back is lay in the wood for next season, every year that's his job, and if this year Mauro and Steban have already done it, thinking he wouldn't be coming back, he'll sort the late calves and lambs, clean the stables, or repair some tools, why not, there's never a lack of work. And then he'll be there for the autumn shearing, he'll pick up the wool, fill the sacks. This time, with Joaquin gone, maybe he'll have new responsibilities, if Mauro is willing, but maybe Mauro will choose Steban and there'll be nothing he can say to that, he's been gone so long, after all, they'll have made their plans without him. But he's sure they'll give him back his place, because of the work, the labor that wears you down before your time because no matter how boldly you go at it, there's always more than you'd counted on, and your hands are callused from the crowbar and the barbed wire, they're a wreck. In the winter they get so chapped they won't heal, no matter how much tallow you put on them; it feels like a knife blade every time you grip a shovel or a rope. At night the sons sleep with greasy rags wrapped around their hands, to try and heal them—in vain, because the next morning it starts all over again.

So, yes, the mother and the brothers will give him back his place, they'll be glad to, and more than enough work to go with it. But he doesn't care: he's bringing strength back with him. His hands will betray him if the others look, because the chapping has disappeared, and the open cracks across his palms have closed. All he did all this time was look after the old man, while the brothers were breaking their backs, he doesn't feel guilty, they don't have the smell of death clinging to their skin, or up their nostrils; it feels as if it will never go away.

He's coming back as strong as a man, with a treasure in the bag. But he was plenty mad at the old man for taking him for a ride like that, fooling him about what was inside, dangling so many things before his eyes. When Rafael opened the bag, once the granddad had kicked the bucket, he almost wept, even if anger immediately took over—the liar, the bastard, what did he think, that the boy would abandon him if he gave him nothing better to hope for? The old man had misjudged him, had really gotten him wrong. And yet now he wonders, because of the old man's lie, what would have happened if there hadn't been the bag? Would he have given up sooner? Rafael knows that as long as there was care to be given, he wouldn't have budged from there, bag or no bag. Of course it was better with the bag. But how can he imagine what he would have done if there had been no bag, when it was most definitely there, that damned satchel, how can you question something that didn't happen, rewrite history? He lowers his arms, gives some slack to Halley; the horse eases into a canter. Behind them, tied to one another, the horses surge forward; he didn't even need to pull on the rope. He turns around to look at them, their muscular bodies, the dust of the gallop, their nostrils flared with the thrill of the race. He lets them run flat out for a while, all four of them, he's intoxicated by their husky breathing and the pounding of hooves on the ground, by the rolling movement between his knees, and the horses on his left surging forward, Halley won't let himself be overtaken, he's sure of that, if he has to he'll go and corner them at the side of the trail. His heart is beating with pleasure, you'd think he's been deprived of it for years, the wild joy of eating up the space and being his own source of wind, his hair wild, he spreads his arms, lets go of the reins, and Halley gallops straight ahead.

And then without warning there it is just ahead of him, he is almost taken by surprise, he should have recognized it, of course, but maybe he wasn't expecting it anymore, and he is startled when he realizes what it is, and what it means; he's arrived, it's there before him. The road that leads to the estancia.

In his guts there's a burning sensation and it's not impatience, no, it's much more like fear—the way the mother will look at him, the brothers' words, so harsh, fear that it will all start again. So he brings the horses to a halt, the time it takes for his hands to stop trembling, the time to catch his breath, he feels he cannot breathe, a little more and he'll suffocate, everything's a blur. For a moment he thinks he should dismount, but out of pride he cannot arrive at the estancia on foot like some beggar, he has four horses with him, he owed them three, he's got one more now too, honestly of the four he has to ride one of them, for sure, he has to stay in the saddle, in the saddle with his back straight.

Between his knees he can feel Halley's shudder. The horse recognizes the road, too, and the little brother cannot tell whether he wants to keep going forward or bolt, because that would be one way out, too, spin around and leave, now, right away, before anyone has time to see them or hear them or get a whiff of them. The chestnut awaits his orders, his ears flicking from left to right, and nothing filters through, regarding what he'd prefer, it's impossible to tell, he's leaving it up to Rafael. Who is looking out toward the *mesetas*, the ground they covered far beyond the forests and the lakes, and life wasn't easy there either, and he became disenchanted with freedom, it's too great a burden, freedom, when it's nothing but a void, to do what. Ahead of him a reassuring routine is holding out its arms, reassuring and tough, a bed and meals all ready, livestock to raise, meat and wool, all reasons to get up in the morning— he saw how dismal it was those long weeks when he had nothing to do but look after the old man, when all the significance of the day lay in a dressing to change or some maggots to remove.

And yet he can't resign himself to it, to keep moving toward the gray buildings, he's held back by some indefinable instinct reminding him of the dark hours, the violence, the insults, the exhaustion, it's only a few yards from there that all that happened, has he forgotten so easily? If he could say that the mother or the brothers had given him anything approaching warmth or affection, he'd go there at once. But he can't even be sure of that, and now that he thinks about it, not a single tear comes to his eye, nor does his heart relent, it's as hard and dry as the rock he's been walking on for days, this rock that has worn and cracked the horses' hooves. Turn around. He hesitates. He's been thinking about it without realizing ever since he left the cave, he has a premonition that he won't be as lucky the second time around. No doubt deep down he already knows his salvation lies in leaving the estancia behind for good, a matter of minutes for him to make up his mind, a sad figure among the horses, no one looking at him, no one waiting.

Except the dog. Suddenly Three springs up when he sees him, races down the lane yapping frenetically, first to give the signal, but there is also a smell that makes him hesitate and lift his legs higher as he charges, like a question mark, this smell coming on the wind now and that he'd recognize among a million others, he's been waiting so long, and he almost comes to a halt, then bounds forward faster than ever, and it's not his hind legs driving him but his heart and his chest, pounding, elated.

As the dog comes up to them and looks at the little brother with eyes overflowing and a joy that catches in his throat in plaintive cries, Rafael bursts into tears. He didn't want to get off his horse, didn't want to come back to the estancia, all things considered, it was as if the prison door had been open and now he was going back inside of his own free will, a stupid, useless loyalty, because nothing would change, the bag would not transform the mother or the brothers and his own life would remain the same. He really had to seize the opportunity, quickly, while the horses were quiet, motionless. He knew he'd been spotted, because of the barking; from where he stood, he could make out a figure, unmoving, the mother no doubt, who must be looking at him. Had she already realized it was him, coming home? She should have moved, started running. Shouted his name. But she just stopped, to watch and listen. And then she turned to someone who was coming, it had to be Mauro, standing so tall above her. He too was looking down the lane. In that moment the little brother was sure of it, he mustn't go there, unless he was resigned to continue with life the way it had always been, and expect nothing, and if one day he had to point a finger, well, he'd have only himself to blame, because he'd had his chance, it was there in his hands, all he had to do was pull on the reins, swing the horses round, he was about to do it, in his mind he was already gone.

That is when the dog came up with his love-struck eyes, and in a rush the memory of his cuddles and closeness came back to Rafael, the way the dog would lie curled up next to him when he was recovering from a thrashing, and whimper as if he too had been beaten, and when the little brother reached for his coat to cry into, he would bump his brow against the boy's, and place his nose against his cheek and his tears.

And so in spite of his conviction that he should turn around and flee at a gallop, in spite of his certainty that nothing good could ever come of the estancia, Rafael jumped off his horse to take the dog in his arms.

MAURO

The mother calls him and, alarmed, he comes; the mother never calls. She says nothing, but she is looking out at the lane and now he follows her gaze, he sees those figures at the end of the road but cannot make them out, they are still too far away. His first reflex is to reach for a stick. He doesn't think it could be the little brother, he gave up on him days ago. When he glances questioningly at the mother, he senses that she too has no idea who's stopped there, and he scratches his head, wonders if he should fetch his rifle. He doesn't understand why the dog raced off down the path and is barking like that, as if he were ready for a celebration, not at all his usual throaty and angry growls, so Mauro narrows his eyes and scans the horizon, and the sun behind the figures of the man and the horses hinders his view, despite his hand held up to shade his eyes. All he knows is that they are coming toward the estancia. Three is with them, hopping and leaping, filthy creature not even capable of guarding his home.

When they get even closer, Mauro picks up his rifle and starts walking toward them, slightly ahead of the mother, a dozen yards or so—then she tells him to stop where he is. *Don't move, let them come.* He keeps his eye on the man's movements, his hands, any possible weapons. Doesn't see anything. And then he is the first to recognize him, the boy out there, and he nearly stumbles.

The little brother.

It is strange how at that very moment, just when Mauro

should have let out a big sigh, let go of all the tension he's been feeling for days and weeks, to succumb to relief at last, it is just the opposite that happens. A lump of hatred sticks in his throat, he doesn't even know why, instinctively, something uncontrollable, and it occurs to him that he could go ahead and fire, he could swear to the mother afterward that he didn't recognize him, that he thought . . . A bandit, a criminal. The steppe is full of them. But he doesn't move. He watches them coming, close together like a clan entering forbidden territory, vaguely anxious, and Three is running in and out of Halley's legs, if he wanted to hide from Mauro then that's just what he'd do, when Mauro's been feeding that mangy dog since Rafael left, look how it betrays him first chance it gets.

Now Steban has joined them, next to the mother, and now she, too, has seen, Mauro heard her come up behind him. *Christ's blood.* She stepped closer to him. No one rushes forward, though, neither the newcomers who are walking slowly, sniffing the humans who are waiting for them, nor the mother and the two sons watching them approach as if they were strangers, there is no haste on either side, maybe they are thinking of what to say. Mauro turns his head and asks the mother:

"What's that horse?"

She gives a shrug and he looks at the bay, too tall for a criollo, it's the only one he's interested in, he knows the others, the little brother and the horses, so what. And even when Rafael is right there before them Mauro is looking at the bay, straight ahead of him, staring hard at him, he only looks at his brother afterward, says nothing, even if he immediately noticed the change in the boy's thin face, and the bitter set to his mouth. He says nothing, because that's all he needs to know, there it is, the little brother has come back, he's not exactly thrilled but what's done is done, and he's standing in the mother's way, she's behind him, pushing him a little, she doesn't say a word, either, there are no embraces, it's as if they'd parted the night before and it's all perfectly normal, because they don't know any other way to behave, and basically there's no love between any of them.

The little brother rides up with the horses to Mauro, the mother, and Steban, stops, relaxes the reins and puts his hands on the pommel, braces himself in the saddle. He doesn't dismount, he forces them to raise their eyes to look at him, they're astonished he doesn't get off, and the tall twin would like nothing better than to grab him and pull him out of the saddle and teach him some manners, but the mother doesn't budge and he won't do it without her consent. Because it's up to her to speak first, not him, Mauro, not even Rafael who they thought was dead and has now returned, their gazes riveted on him, and he looks only at the mother, his dark eyes joyless, unkindly—is this really what he expected? At that moment the little brother hesitates and Mauro feels a fierce joy to see him like that, disconcerted, he's surely thinking he was wrong to come back, wrong to believe the mother would forgive him, or maybe even be happy to see him, what else, while we're at it? Because he thinks he's indispensable? The tall twin snickers to himself. The mother's eyes, shining with anger, are answer enough for him. He goes on watching the kid fidgeting in the saddle, then turning around to reach behind him for the satchel, suddenly perking up, and Mauro frowns because he doesn't recognize that bag—and yet he has a prodigious memory for things, and he's absolutely sure he's never seen that bag. Rafael has a sudden joyous air about him, he takes the three of them in with his gaze, the mother, Steban, and Mauro, he holds out his arm, freezes. So he wants to play, the little bastard, let their mouths water from wondering what might be in that fucking bag so that he can break into a smile, amused, like some kid who has brought them a nice surprise, sure of the impact it will have, oh, it had just better be worth it, keeping them in suspense like this, or else, mate, or else.

And all the while Mauro is seething with impatience and hostility, while Rafael is jovial, almost feverish, they both open their mouths to speak, of course they're so different, Mauro full of fury and Rafael practically shaking with cheer, and the words are welling in their throats, they're about to speak, when without warning the mother cuts them off, before they have time to say a word, she says, looking at the little brother:

"So you're not dead after all."

He could hug her, the mother, for interrupting Rafael, making his face fall with that mean little greeting of hers, crushing his unbearable cheerfulness and excitement, the victor's return with that smug expression on his ugly little insolent face. You need these decisive statements to put things in their place, and she must have sensed it, too, that she had to react, that the little brother was still the little brother, in his place, not even daring to breathe—he comes after the mother and the older brothers, just ahead of the dogs. Mauro feels like laughing, clapping his hands. He narrows his eyes and merely watches Rafael as he climbs off his horse now, as if stunned, and puts the bag at his feet and bends down to undo the buckles, and there is no more joy or eagerness in his fingers as they tug at the straps, even though the other three have their gazes riveted on him and the flap on the bag, still closed. Mauro has a sharp intuition that there is something waiting for them inside the bag, otherwise the little brother wouldn't be so focused, unfastening the straps, and he promises himself he won't cry out, he bites his lips in advance to keep silent, for fear of spoiling everything, irreparably. But it is Rafael himself, as he is opening the bag, who hesitates, and yet he knows what's in there, and the other three step closer, their curiosity aroused, the mother first, and she lets out a cry.

"Good heavens, where'd you steal that from?"

Mauro has seen what the bag contains, too, and he feels a twinge of lust in his guts, he looks at his brother, ready to cut his throat if the mother tells him to, suffocating with a visceral hatred, why did the little brother find this bag and not him, it should have been him, with a slash of his knife he can change the story, and the temptation is burning so badly that he stumbles. The mother thinks he wants to take the bag, and with a dark look she holds out her arm to stop him. He steps back, shaking his head. Very quickly Rafael says:

"I didn't steal it. There was this old man I found on the steppe while I was looking for the horses. After he died I came back with his criollo and the satchel, it's the truth, I swear."

The mother wipes her brow, sweat pearling as if she suddenly had sunstroke.

"What do you mean?"

"I tried to make him better, with plants, right, but he had a bad wound. I couldn't save him."

"And this bag was his?"

"Yes."

"And what else? What did he tell you?"

"Nothing. He didn't talk much."

Mauro interrupts, his voice deep and trembling: "Who was this guy?"

"I don't know. I just found him."

The four of them exchange glances, Steban with his empty gaze, the little brother tensely waiting, the mother and Mauro incredulous. The old lady has to lean over the bag again and murmur, "I can't believe it . . . "

She kneels down, and there is a gleam in her eyes, a strange shining. She holds out her hand, hesitant, moves it closer. And then she touches the bag, but first she holds back for a long while, and Mauro can feel a tingling in his arms, the same she must be feeling, maybe she's thinking there's a trap somewhere, anyway that's the sort of thing he would think, wary as he is, and he feels uneasy, for Christ's sake, let her go ahead and put her hands in there, so we'll know.

Then as if she had heard him, all at once the mother grabs fistfuls and fistfuls of bills and stares at them, breathless. She stays like that, not moving, the bills crumpling in her hands, waiting perhaps to be struck by lightning. But nothing happens. She looks at the sons, petrified, like a statue, and still nothing happens; after a few moments she lowers her head, evaluates the contents of the bag with a quick glance. Places her palm over her heart.

"God almighty. There must be millions. Gotta be, millions."

And no one laughs, or even smiles, other than Rafael, who says, "We're rich."

They stand there dumbfounded, the mother and the brothers, and the little brother waits, grows weary, takes the bills from the old lady's hand and puts them back in the bag and closes it again. As he is about to put it on his shoulder, she rushes over to him.

"Leave it. I'll take it. You look after the horses. Mauro, Steban, give him a hand."

"Are you glad, Ma? Does the bag make you happy?"

She looks up from her bowl of soup, frowning.

"Shut up."

He plays for a few seconds at drawing images in the broth, then persists.

"But it's a good thing, no, that I brought it home?"

This time it's Mauro who speaks before the mother, and he looks sternly at the little brother, as if he's done something stupid.

"Shut up, she said."

The next morning when they get up the mother is already in the kitchen. On the table she has placed a wallet that is full of money from the bag, hardly anything, compared to what must be left. The sons eat their breakfast, trying not to look or seem bothered by the money there in front of them, and yet they wouldn't hesitate to pounce on it if the mother should say, *Whoever grabs it first, it's his.* But of course they know she'll never say that. Mauro pushes back his empty coffee mug until it is level with the wallet, while the others look on, their gazes sharp. He cuts two thick slices of bread, takes the butter, the smoked meat. Concentrates on what he is doing. Not one look at the money: he scorns it. He's pretending. Deep down he is longing to slap his fat hand onto it, because of what he could do with it. Alcohol and women. He's been thinking about it all night long.

There is no trace of the bag. Mauro looks all around, discreetly, in vain. The mother has hidden it, she must have a good reason to do so. She is sitting at the table, too, waiting for them to finish. Then she clears the dishes and the bread, wipes the table with a rag. Usually at this point the sons get up to go out and begin work, but this morning not one of them moves, because of the money, it's not there by chance, at an equal distance from the three of them, it's like a bad game. Mauro gazes at the mother, who is watching them, scratching her chin. Either she's hesitating, or she's still wondering who to entrust the wallet to—no, of course not, she knows damn well, and she pushes it over to him, the eldest, and his blood begins to simmer deep inside, yes, he's got it. He pays no attention to Steban and Rafael, who are eyeing him greedily. He puts his hands on the table, close together, and concentrates, not to pounce on the money. He gives the mother a questioning look, and she says:

"Go and get Joaquin. You've got enough there to pay for him twice over."

The fox to mind the geese, that's what the little brother has brought them with that bag, unintentionally, but if he'd known, if he'd just used his head, he would surely have thrown the money out in the middle of the steppe. Mauro bursts out laughing as his horse breaks into a gallop. But there it is, the little brother is such an idiot, it never occurred to him that the first thing the mother would do would be to send for the lost twin, and for sure, it's hard to believe he didn't realize, and yet.

When the tall twin thinks of the expressions on their faces, Steban and Rafael, the moment they understood. How they looked at each other, the mute reproach in the half-wit's eyes, he got it right away, he must already be trembling in the barn. Maybe he even managed to put three words together to shout at the little brother, something like *You . . . you're just a shit . . .* and Mauro can imagine his hesitant voice and he laughs some more, he'll wet himself from laughing if he's not careful, what a day, what a magnificent day, move, move it, old nag—and he spurs the horse, it's not galloping fast enough for him.

JOAQUIN

His initial reaction, on seeing his brother waiting outside Emiliano's house, was to prepare himself for the worst. He immediately thought of the mother. An accident, maybe. Was she dead, or just injured? Out on the plain he urged his horse on. Something crumbled inside him, left him with a sort of guilt, that he wasn't there, that he couldn't help; because if Mauro had come all this way it must be serious. But he drew closer and the tall twin there at the end of the road didn't seem feverish, and Joaquin relaxed, his heart began to beat more calmly, and he looked for another reason. The brothers, must be. And yet that didn't concern him, he weighed the possibility in his mind, with neither emotion nor dismay. Yes, maybe it was because of them. He even felt a sort of morbid excitement, and he wanted to know which one of them it was, and how. An animal; an implement slipping. A fall.

He rides up to him. Mauro smiles.

And a few seconds earlier Joaquin had prepared himself for the worst, he really had. But not for this.

All three of them sitting around the table. Emiliano, the tall twin, and Joaquin himself. Not a sound. A few seconds ago, Joaquin delicately took the pouch placed before the old man and slid it back over to Mauro. And said, "No."

When the older brother had explained it to them—and he didn't say much, just that the mother had done a deal, and sent him to fetch Joaquin—Emiliano gave him the choice, to stay or to go, and the old man would respect it, either he'd take the money, or he wouldn't. Nothing obliged him, one way or the other. So now it was up to Joaquin to decide.

Joaquin thinks back on these recent weeks he's spent with Eduardo, Fabricio, and Arcangel. How can he explain it to Mauro, why the wound of missing the estancia healed so quickly, he doesn't know. Whatever he says he'll sound like a traitor, he doesn't dare look at his twin's face, he avoids his gaze, and yet they'll have to talk about it, he'll have to justify himself, make Mauro understand. The world back there is no longer his world, the mother yelling, her expression telling them she's never satisfied, the way she makes them bear a burden that isn't theirs, the routine of tension and violence. All these new mornings he has woken up without bitterness, no caustic remarks greeting him, to tell him that he's too late, too slow, that there's too much work. In the beginning he was expecting it, thought it was just a matter of time until the men would grab him and swear at him because he wasn't working hard enough, or to their liking, but the days went by and nothing changed. Only now has he understood. That cramped little life the mother imposes on him and his brothers: they don't know a thing, don't have any rights. In a few weeks he has learned more than in what will soon be nineteen years, and it has been a shock to his slow, heavy brain, his lazy reason, he recalls the sparks in his head when he discovered all these new things, and he had to understand, register, adapt as quick as he could, it was enough to make him cry like a baby—that wasn't how they tended the sheep, back at the mother's. At the time, it's true, it gave him a fright, he began to wonder if he wasn't a half-wit, too, all these years making fun of Steban and never imagining that he, too—but no, no, he managed, he forced himself, and nowadays he is just like anyone else, no one would notice any difference. And now Mauro has come to try and tear this boy away from his brand new life, has come with only one promise, to take him back and start over same as always, and he, Joaquin, would have to be out of his mind, so he said it very softly, not to offend him, he gave the wallet back to his brother and that was when he murmured, "No."

Emiliano coughs and pats him on the shoulder. Joaquin knows he has to get up and go out, and Mauro, too, because that's all there is to it. The presence of the old man reassures him, without him there it is quite possible the tall twin would try and persuade him or even force him, tie him to the end of a rope and take him trotting behind his horse back to the mother whether he likes it or not, turning a deaf ear to his protests, dragging him through the dust if he has to, even if Joaquin falls to his knees begging not to go. So he takes his time, hesitates as he walks through the door, does not want to get Mauro's back up, does not want to have to change his mind if he sees his pale face, and Emiliano can sense how uneasy and afraid he is, this young man he calls the kid, and he nods his head and orders him, so it will all be clear and he won't change his mind:

"Ride back with him."

First he had to convince Mauro not to chase him away, because when he got back on his horse, the tall twin put his hand on his whip and growled, sounding like an animal for a few seconds, until the words finally came out:

"Don't come near me! Go away!"

For a while they ride together in a disorderly way, cutting each other off with their criollos, and one time Joaquin just barely misses the leather strap, which cracks on his horse's neck, and then he shouts out because he wants this to stop, his horse is bad-tempered and now it is rolling its eyes and snapping its powerful jaws, beside itself, too, springing forward, steady, steady, Joaquin cries again. When the next crack of the whip comes he holds out his arm and it encircles his muscles with a hissing sound, but at least he's got it, and he yanks hard on it to try and unsettle Mauro, who is immovable and begins to laugh, a deep, ferocious laugh, the two brothers stare at each other, waiting for the other to speak. After a moment Joaquin unwinds the leather, it has stung his skin in long spirals, he drops it, watches the tall twin roll it up and fasten it to the saddle. There is still this silence between them, but it gradually changes in substance, there is something sad about it, something irrevocable. Joaquin knows he has won, not in the way of a fight, but Mauro understands that his brother will not be going home, so he frowns, thoughtful, then spreads his arms and shouts, "And what am I going to tell the mother?"

Joaquin sighs, looks in the direction of the town. *Why don't we go for a drink?*

They ride, side by side, and Mauro slumps beneath his tainted joy, his features set, perhaps it's the same melancholy his brother is feeling on this strange day, the last they'll spend together, that's for sure, that's what Joaquin decided just now at Emiliano's house, there was no discussing it. The criollos trot in time. The muffled sound of their hooves on the dirt road, of stones resonating when rock breaks through the surface: this distracts them and they don't speak, they keep an eye out on the road, the way they always do, for holes or cracks or traps. The summer drought has brought out the snakes, when they sense the riders coming they wriggle across the steppe in search of thickets and rocks for refuge, and the gray and yellow earth vibrates to the horses' hooves, quivers with scurrying reptiles; sometimes one of them stands upright, caught in flight, turns to face the riders because there is no time left, the horses are upon it. The criollos try to sidestep, lift their hooves, crush the creature out of awkwardness. They're not afraid of bites, they are native sons, used to enduring and surviving.

When they enter San León, Joaquin leads his brother

through the streets. It's easy for him, now. He points things out, comments. That's where you get the best empanadas; here they have terrific beer, and serve it with meatballs made with grilled mutton fat. And over there, that's where they hanged the Negroes three weeks ago, and he's almost disappointed that they've been removed, he wanted to show them to Mauro. They probably stank too much, and the residents complained. To act important, he tells Mauro the story. He laughs when he tells him that Gomez and his wife decided it was better to leave town, filled with shame, taking the little black baby with them—or abandoning it after a few hours by the side of the road, no one will ever know. No one gives a damn. They're gone, that's it. Mauro listens, looks, silently, taking everything in. Joaquin feels strong.

"I'll buy you a drink," he says, as if the town belonged to him.

At the bar, Mauro takes out the wallet the mother gave him.

"This is a gift from her. It's all her fault."

They look at the money and laugh. It would take them weeks to drink up that amount, and Joaquin peels off a few bills, puts the rest back inside, pockets the bills, then says with a laugh, while Mauro stares at him, puzzled:

"Trust me. You won't regret it."

He's already thinking about the brunette from last time, he's elated at the thought of going back to that street lit by two pale lanterns, and he gulps his first beers down all in one, joyful, agitated. Mauro imitates him and before long he has surpassed him, emptying his glasses as if he had a hole inside him, and nothing can quench his thirst. Joaquin teases him, rolls cigarettes, drinks some more. When they're good and drunk, the tall twin asks, almost cheerfully:

"Why don't you want to come back?"

"To have to live without this?"

"You come often?"

"We come down every Sunday."

"To go to mass, huh?"

Joaquin bursts out laughing. *Yeah. To go to mass.* Mauro blows on his cigarette smoke.

"Good lord."

"You could leave, too."

The tall twin opens one eye a bit wider and frowns.

"What'd you say?"

"Just stay here. I'm sure Emiliano could find you some work."

Mauro's reply is an inaudible grunt, then he laughs to himself, and Joaquin is not sure he's understood, so he says again:

"You don't have to go back to the estancia."

"Come off it."

"No, I'm serious. Don't you like the idea of all this?"

He helps himself to some of the *parillada*, wipes his hands on his trousers. The taste of braised beef fills his mouth, and the spices, and the delicious tortillas. It's true, why should life be anything other than working six days, and on the seventh, eating all the grilled and marinated meat and fat you want, guzzling beers while you listen to music, touching a girl. He explains this to Mauro, his voice slurring, and Mauro laughs too loudly, calls for more beer, and slowly shakes his head.

"I can't leave the mother."

"She'll manage."

"With those two idiots?"

"It's not your problem."

"I can't."

"Pass your glass."

As the hours go by they are reeling, swaying on their chairs, chattering senselessly and aimlessly, they don't even know why they are talking anymore, nor what they hope to convince themselves of. The night chill falls upon their shoulders, they don't care, they're burning up with booze. There is a pile of empty plates on the table, of overturned glasses they lift to their lips to make sure they're empty. All around them there is conversation, laughter, exclamations. Hands raised, calling for drink. Joaquin looks at all these people, they're no better than Mauro and him, drunk and tired, and tomorrow he'll have to be in the saddle at dawn, but dawn has already come, like a dark night, it's already tomorrow and he staggers, shakes the tall twin, who has collapsed facedown on the table.

"Gotta go, gotta go to the girls, or it'll be too late."

But Mauro doesn't react, he's snoring away, and Joaquin drags him along until he falls; it's pointless.

"Shit."

After several fruitless attempts, he lays him down against the wall. Slaps his face. Asks for a glass of water, splashes it in his face, but Mauro goes on sleeping and slumps further down, his arms around his head to be left alone, cut off from the world, from the noise, an enormous, soft mass, spread there on the floor, refusing to be budged with all his strength, and Joaquin can tell that soon enough there'll be no time left for the girls, he gets annoyed, stamps his feet. Starts shouting, until the proprietor stops him because he's pissing off the men at the tables nearby, they'd like to finish drinking in peace, and that big guy on the floor can just stay there, the joint isn't about to close.

So from the wallet Joaquin takes what he'll need to pay the girl, and shoves the rest of the money into Mauro's pocket, deep inside so it won't get stolen, he hopes, so he'll take something back to the mother, the price for Joaquin, minus one night of drinking, and he runs through the streets, unsteady, supporting himself against the walls of the houses, his mouth open, he's barely less drunk but just enough to know where he's headed, he laughs, his heart pounding, and his legs carry him like a giant, famished, like a man, anyway, and never mind if he's on his own.

RAFAEL

When Mauro returns the following morning without Joaquin, a blast of cold air blows over the estancia. Already the mother was worried when her eldest son didn't show up the night before—a curse upon her if he has disappeared now too, and that's what she screams as she goes out of the house, just as he's dismounting from his horse, a stream of acrimony flowing from her mouth, her nose, until the moment when she stares at Mauro and suddenly realizes he is alone. She falls silent. They are all silent. The little brother can tell that the twin is not in his normal state, his eyes are watering, he's dragging his leg, and this strange way he has of walking knock-kneed as he comes toward them and collapses on the stoop. Head down, his voice toneless.

"Didn't want to come back."

The mother freezes. Cannot believe what her ears are telling her.

"You didn't find him?"

"I found him. But he doesn't want to."

"Doesn't want to come back."

"Right. He said no."

"You've been drinking."

"So what? I know what I'm saying."

The mother turns to him; Rafael and Steban stand behind her, stunned, she waves to them to go. But they don't move and she gets annoyed: *Get out of here!* The little brother crosses his arms over his chest; he has the right to know. They

aren't children anymore, either of them, nor are they flies you
brush away with the back of your hand when they bother you,
and besides, it's his money, his bills that were supposed to buy
back Joaquin, so he stays there, and he's the one who says,
"Where's the money?"

Mauro tosses the wallet onto the ground; Rafael picks it up.
And says, once he's had a quick look: "There's some missing."

"Yeah."

"You gonna tell me what you did with it?"

"Don't get on my nerves."

"It's not your money."

"You want me to show you how it's not my money?"

The mother steps in, her tone abrupt. *Mauro.* In the silence
that follows, everyone turns to look at her, even Steban, who
hasn't moved, they look at her as if it were her treasure, and
she decides everything. The little brother raises an eyebrow,
makes an effort not to react. In the end, he simply shouldn't
have given it to her when he got home. And maybe she will
mutter that it's true, they have to take him into account too,
Mauro has to give back the money, because in a way it belongs
to Rafael, the money, in a way it's thanks to him, we can't
ignore the fact, can't just spit on him like that, shouldn't he be
entitled to a special cut, after all—but she doesn't say anything
like that, nothing at all, and truth is the money isn't his anymore, he can tell, when she grunts that she's going to think
about it, and orders Mauro to follow her.

That is how everything changed, where the satchel was concerned; that is how the little brother was swindled, by the
mother and the brother, and no doubt it's no coincidence if
Mauro has been making fun of him all his life, it's not that he
too is a half-wit, but he does believe everything people tell him,
even a sheep could tie him up in knots. Because it's obvious,
when the mother comes back out, she's got it all worked out.

Regarding the money that Mauro took, Rafael can forget about it, they settled the matter between them inside the house, he can tell from the mother's bloodshot eyes that she must have been weeping with rage to know that the money was gone. Now it's over. Now, they have to be careful—and she lectures them, her voice low, a little circle with her and the three sons in a huddle outside the house, she's practically whispering, they mustn't let on all at once that they have so much. Steban interrupts her.

"But w-what?"

And when the mother looks at him, of course he is startled, how could he forget, he apologizes: *Ah. Yes,* and the mother continues. People in town would think it was odd. They'd come snooping, ferreting around with their filthy gazes, asking questions the sons would end up answering, clueless oafs that they are. Might as well get things clear right from the start, she says, listen to me, there was never any old man—and as she hammers out her words she looks the little brother straight in the eye and adds, *I'm talking to you, Rafael, do you understand, from now on you never saw any old man. The money was already here, hidden in the house, it's mine, got that? Otherwise they'll take it from us.* And Rafael, lost:

"But I found it out there when I was looking for the horses."

"You didn't go out there. You never went anywhere."

"But—"

Mauro suddenly cuts him off, grabs his arm.

"You pretend nothing happened, get it, blockhead? You never left the house. The mother found the money hidden in the barn, must be the father who hid it there before he left."

And the mother nods. *That's right.*

"Oh, I s-see," says Steban in turn, stunned.

"So what are we actually going to do with it?" asks the little brother.

"Don't go mixing everything up," says the twin. "We'll talk about it tomorrow."

The mother stands up.

"Yes, tomorrow. The main thing is not to attract attention, we'll use it when we go to wool or livestock markets, a bit more, a bit less, no one will notice. Off you go."

The four of them scatter, and Rafael replays the discussion in his mind, staring at his hands as if they carried some sort of answer, on the one hand who he thought he was, the runaway horses, the wounded old man, the cave, the money, and on the other, what the mother just said, no horses, no old man, no bag. And slowly he opens and closes this right hand that doesn't match, he turns it over, examines it, does the same with the left, silently articulates once again, the criollos, the old man, the bag, no horses, no old man, no money, and obviously the two don't go together, he waves his hands, and in the end, disconcerted, lets them hang down at his sides. That is when he realizes he's been had, that the mother and Mauro have ganged up against him. And he doesn't like it.

Breakfast like any other day. On the table the same things to eat and drink as every morning. And yet nothing is the same, and the sons' hands are trembling, feverishly, their eyes are shining, searching in vain for a new wallet set down there before them, or for the bag on the floor. The mother serves them, not speaking, impassive: just to look at her the little brother would swear nothing had ever happened, neither his return two days ago nor the money that is seeping into them and making their heads spin. She is so perfect in her dour role that Rafael hesitates: what if he dreamt the whole thing? What if the mother was right, the day before, when she said that there hadn't been any old man or any bag. And he looks again, and turns around to glance behind him, but everything has vanished and the floor is empty, and the mother grabs him.

"What do you think you're looking for?"

"But the—" And he catches himself just in time, when he sees Mauro's dark look.

One second more and he'd have been in for it; he rubs his forehead. He gets up all of a sudden to go and check out the window, and freezes. But look. The bay is grazing in the paddock outside, proof that . . . and he feels the relief in his throat, he's not crazy after all, in spite of what he's been told to think. It all goes whirling through his mind in that moment—the money, the new life, and the nagging anxiety that's been lodged inside him since Mauro's return releases its grip, and the impression that things are not going the way they should, it's all swept away, all that's left is his happiness that Joaquin didn't come back, and a certain excitement, wondering how the mother will spend what's in the bag, what he'll ask for for himself, how they will live. There they are, the three sons, perhaps they are sharing the same expectations, looking up at the old lady, and she is waiting, too, but for something else, and Rafael has no patience, in his voice that has not yet changed he utters the first words of the day.

"What are we doing, Ma?"

Oh, the brief moment of silence. Maybe she herself was surprised by his question, because she drew her brows together in a questioning look, not for long, and the little brother cannot understand what is going on in her head, or only slightly, something to do with yesterday, and caution, to be sure, yes, he remembers, don't talk loud. But they will go to San León, won't they? To buy clothes and cigarettes. At least have a beer. He dreamt about it that night and, still droopy, he says—just in case the mother is having a slow start to the morning:

"We going to town?"

And at first she glares at him incredulously, then with anger, and it rumbles inside her, he can almost hear it. He senses he's made a mistake, but too late, because the mother suddenly snaps her dish towel against the back of his chair and he jumps, if she'd slapped him with it, it would have been no different. "How in the name of Christ is it possible to give birth to such stupid kids."

He huddles on his chair, stupefied, then angry. He glances over at his brothers, who give him a mean look, what an idiot to get the old lady in a bad temper first thing in the morning, even if they too are dying to know. The little brother shrugs, then looks down at the floor as the mother's shrill voice singles him out, with Steban.

"You two bring the shorthorns back here to see which ones are pregnant. Mauro, you get the paddock ready. And you two, watch out for the bull."

Now the tall twin protests.

"But—"

"I don't want to hear. From you or the others. Get going."

So one by one they do as they are told—it's the tall twin who obeys first, his allegiance to the old lady is unfailing, even when he's seething with anger, even when he gives the impression that there are claws holding him to his chair, he is that reluctant to get up and go out, but Rafael also complies, the mother has her reasons, she doesn't make mistakes, she's much smarter than the three of them put together, and an obscure force compels him to obey orders without thinking. And yet he's so angry at her, and he doesn't understand the way she does things! He could laugh and cry by turns, and when he walks past her to leave the room, he looks at her the way the others did, questioning, sullen. It's only once he's outside that it takes hold of him all of a sudden, inexplicably. He begins to laugh. Look at the fine way he was taken in when he came back and handed the bag over to her, really he ought to be hopping mad, but he isn't, he'd rather laugh about it; if only he'd known.

They saddle the horses, not saying a word, there is only Rafael's laughter escaping him in spite of himself. Mauro gathers the pickets and the sledgehammer and his jaw is clenched, but he doesn't yell at Rafael to shut up, doesn't rush over to hit him; it's not for any lack of anger, but something is holding him back, he clearly doesn't understand why the little brother is laughing like this, it almost worries him, his gaze is unfocused. Eventually he walks off, banging the handle of the tool against the gate. Steban is getting impatient.

"Y-you ready?"

"I'm coming. Where are the shorthorns?"

His brother doesn't reply, he's already in the saddle, waiting. It is only once they have gone through the gate of the estancia that he motions with his chin to the east. The criollos walk side by side, spirited, not bothered by the dust. Steban looks behind him, as if someone might overhear, but there is so much wind today that even the dogs have decided not to follow them. Rafael sees Steban concentrate for a moment before he manages to say:

"Wh-where is it?"

"What?"

"Bag. The bag."

"Oh. The money? She must have put it somewhere safe so it won't get stolen."

"For . . . for her."

The little brother gives a snort of laughter. *What the hell.* He cannot stand Steban's sorry look, staring at him from his horse with a crooked smile.

"You lost. Everything."

And it does something to him to hear it, even though he knows that Steban is right, but to be seen as the idiot of the family yet again is deeply unsettling, particularly when it's Steban who has taken the liberty of telling him, so he holds his chin up and says, practically hissing:

"What did you think, that I had no idea she'd do that? I did it on purpose. I couldn't care less about the money."

And the half-wit bursts out laughing on hearing his words. This raises Rafael's hackles, so much so he'd gladly smash his face in for laughing like that at him, and he's the one who never calls Steban a half-wit, but now he feels he has every right to, just look at him with his mouth wide open on his teeth already going to rot, and the noisy way he's mocking him, Rafael hates him at that moment, it's all he can do not to hit him, so he shouts, *Shit! It's my money! I have the right to take what I need, don't I? You understand that? Don't you think so, too?*

He knows it's pointless braying like this in front of Steban; now the boy is clapping his hands and saying, *Think so. Think so.* But it feels good to take it out on him, the only one on the estancia he's not afraid of, the only one he can shake or insult without fearing he'll get a hiding in return, because where the rest is concerned—solidarity, trust—forget it, there's no one he can count on. So the little brother splutters with anger and spite, for as long as he can give vent, settling pointless scores, shouting his lungs out with abuse, and when finally he grows hoarse, he pays no attention to Steban, whose face has grown stern, and he thinks about the money, bitterly, how this morning all four of them should have been woken up laughing and celebrating their luck. Right down to the mother who hasn't changed a thing, shoving them out the door the way she does every day, the cattle won't wait, what do they care if the little brother came home with a bag full of money, will that tend their needs, put water in their troughs?

"There," says Steban.

The massive shapes, their dark red, roan coats, on the plain up ahead of them. Rafael forces himself to set aside his bitter thoughts, he gauges the distance, the small but scattered herd.

"We should have brought a dog."

Steban shrugs. They ride over to the herd, blending into the landscape with the cattle, who hardly notice them; they locate the dominant cow thanks to the bell around her neck, a mature female with a brown coat. Steban holds up his hand.

"Me."

"Go ahead. I'll wait here. Watch out for the bull: he's over there on the left."

The half-wit glances at the huge male to ascertain whether he'll let him, then he places his horse behind the leading cow. Lets out a resounding *Yep*, driving her in the direction to go by guiding his criollo. Rafael stays further back, making sure the others gradually begin to follow, hustling the stragglers, channeling the young cattle that try to escape from the side. Halley pivots on his haunches, leaps forward, stops short, avoids a head butt, and starts again, the opposite way; to feel him tensing between his knees, muscles taut and eye rolling into the white, the little brother can tell that the horse has been missing this activity, work is written in his genes, along with his agility and resistance to fatigue. Rafael himself rediscovers sensations he had already forgotten, deep in his saddle, as Halley carries him, his eyes are almost closed, and it's as if he were flying, whirling, uncontrollably. When at last the herd begins to move in unison, the horse settles at the rear. From there he has a view of the entire group as well as the bull, walking apart, slightly to the rear, they have to let him go at his own pace not to get him rattled. The slightest quiver along a calf's spine and Halley gallops over to check, make sure, reposition; Rafael hardly has to urge him forward. Steban joins him. They drive the cattle, silently, glad of the simplicity of the task. Until the older boy slaps his hand on his saddle and looks at the little brother.

"This. I want a new one."

Rafael looks at his brother, astonished. Then glances at the horse, and it's true, the old leather is so worn down in places that it's battered, coming apart, full of stains and splits. Neither one of them remembers where it came from. All their gear was there, from before their birth, handed down from the grandfathers, or previous keepers, and the only thing they are sure of is that when they started learning their trade none of them ever sat their ass on anything new. *There's a sheen on that tack you'll find nowhere else,* grunts the mother with a shrug when they complain that a girth has snapped, and they spend hours taking the pieces of leather apart to sew them crudely back together, just enough to keep the saddle going for another year or two. And every year, every two years, it starts all over again. One day there'll be an accident, and the mother won't be able to say they didn't warn her. But now . . .

"Yes," murmurs Rafael, "that's a thought. I'd like a new one, too."

"Ah ha."

"We'll go buy them at Antonio's."

"Black."

"I don't know yet."

"Brown. For the . . . for the horse."

"Maybe. I'll see."

They goad the herd, laughing suddenly, waving their arms in circles. They'll change the bridles, too, while they're at it, and the bits, the mouthpieces are rusty. Horses all dressed up in new clothes! The very thought seems impossible. And hats to go with it, if the criollos can strut around with their shiny saddles, their riders mustn't spoil the picture. They can smell the well-oiled leather tingling their nostrils.

From the middle of the herd a calf escapes, but they don't notice. It is only when they hear a cow mooing that they realize, give a start, and rush off after it, laughing.

"It's mine!" shouts Steban.

"I'll get there before you!"

"No. You, stay there!" and the older boy points at the herd, already worried about the fugitive, hesitant and lowing.

The bull at the edge of the group has turned around and is breathing hard, sniffing the air. Rabioso—it's not for nothing that the mother gave him that name, given all his fury and strength and irascible power, and Rafael knows he has to keep the group calm to mollify the male and stop him at all costs from scratching the ground with his forelegs and shaking his head in readiness to charge. So he brings Halley to a halt, grumbles, heads off in the opposite direction, shouting at the horse so he'll gallop flat out. It's not a long way, a hundred, two hundred yards, but they cover it in a roll of thunder. Vaguely alarmed, the cows watch him coming toward them, and he steers clear of the herd not to panic them, riding in an arc so he can go around behind them and drive forward again. At that moment it seems like they'll never stop. The slightest error and they'll crash together to the ground, Rafael and Halley— at that speed, at least one of them will be hurt, it happens all the time, broken legs, and shattered horses that have to be shot. But this horse never stumbles or slips, he's a monster, born in the steppe, he knows the treachery of stone, and on his back the little brother knows neither fear nor hesitation, not a single foot wrong, the chestnut flies across the expanse of plain. Eyes narrowed against the dust, Rafael slackens the reins, opens his arms. No one can see them, neither the horse with his neck low in a wild gallop nor the little brother with his hands reaching for the sky like a laughing madman, otherwise there would be shouts and prayers, which they would not hear, screams to try and bring them back, but they know none of it, they're deaf and blind, captives of an immense joy that hurtles them forward, banishing reason and all the weight of the world.

MAURO

Two days later, Mauro pens the bull on its own. They've sorted the cows, on the one side those the male always covers, on the other, the ones he neglects, although a few of them continue to moo and come forward, looks like they're still really horny, those she-devils. As if the bull were the only one who knew exactly which ones are pregnant and which ones are still barren, which ones he can service and which ones he can ignore, he's got it all worked out. Mauro looks at the herd and does the math: if all goes well, next year there'll be thirty or more little *rabiosos.* Which translates, a few seasons down the line, into food for two hundred and fifty meat-eaters for one year; or if they sell them earlier, enough to buy one hundred new sheep, or completely rebuild the second barn, which is about to collapse.

Mauro closes the gate and in a rage hurls the stick he has been holding.

There is a thousand times that amount in the bag the mother has hidden somewhere, perhaps even more.

But the money has vanished, and the mother hasn't mentioned it again. Two days he's waited for this to change, for the old lady to get her wits about her. A dull anger has been building inside him, and it grows stronger as he thinks of Joaquin out there, Joaquin who got away from this godforsaken place, who with his meager salary lives so much better than he does, because he, Mauro, doesn't even have the means to treat himself to a beer, not a beer nor anything else, not even the tools he and those other two morons have been asking for, the better to slave away at their daily chores.

"Ma, we've had a thought. We'd like new saddles."
"Because the ones we've got, honestly."
"They're dangerous."
"And you know it, we've been telling you for years."
"Just some new saddles."
"And bridles."
"Yes, and bridles."
The mother looks at them, all three of them, since they all agreed on it.
"And how are we supposed to pay for all that?"
"Well . . . with the money."
"Money? What money?"

Mauro stands rigid by the motionless bull and clenches his fists. The mother hid the bag and they don't know where. Oh, for things like this, she's no madwoman, the old lady, she did it during the night when they were all asleep, you can be sure of that. She even confessed as much, laughing: *Sure, sure, in the middle of the night, you were snoring like angels.* Initially they didn't believe her, even if it astonished them to hear her laughing like that—when was the last time they had seen the mother act the least bit cheerful? The little brother said later that he'd never seen her like that. Maybe before, when the father was still around—but the older boys frowned, the father, really? Not that they can recall. On the contrary.
"Why'd you hide it, Ma?"
When she spirited the cash away, two days ago, and they grew alarmed—especially Mauro—the little brother opened his eyes wide, incredulous, and Steban, well, Steban still can't swear he understands what's going on—she hunted for the words to explain it to them, hunted for a long time, because it's

not her strong point, speaking, she had to think carefully, or come up with a lie. But the mother is not that gifted for this second option either, so she said, abruptly, "So it won't get stolen. And so it doesn't get spent just any old way."

They can protest and rant and even rail all they like, she doesn't care. She does things her way, she's shut herself away with her treasure, and Mauro doesn't get it, so he yelled, "And how are we going to spend it, if you won't even let us have the saddles we'd be using ten hours a day?"

"We'll see. It's not lost, don't worry."

"When can we buy something?"

"We'll see, I said."

"Ma, what's the point of having this money if you go and hide it?"

"We know we have it. If we need it, it's there."

"But we need it!"

"No, not like that. Mustn't waste it."

He nearly choked with rage that day, and he looked at the two brothers who were standing there dumbstruck next to him, why couldn't they help him out, with their innocent expressions, why didn't they say something, then finally Rafael reacted.

"But saddles would be useful. And there'll be so much money left over, even after that!"

"Not all that much. Not all that much."

And then the little brother squealed, as if she had dishonored him: *There is! There was a ton of money!* Naturally. That was why Mauro said, gratingly, "Did you count it, Ma, before you hid it?"

A shrug. He insisted.

"You wouldn't have hidden it without counting. Not you."

She conceded the fact. *Could be.* Grudgingly. But he didn't see things that way, didn't want her to stop now that she had started, didn't want her to take them for fools yet again, there was no other way to put it, that's what he told her when she looked them right in the eye and asserted she didn't know how much there was, yes, it was a good amount, but not as much as all that, exactly how much she'd forgotten, they had to believe her—a likely story. So Mauro gave them all a start when he began to yell, but it was eating him up inside and he might have wrung the old lady's neck if she hadn't replied on the spot, because he'd had enough of waiting and hoping, it was too new, too tempting, what was it to her to give them a figure, it wouldn't be taking anything out of the bag, it wouldn't kill her. So the mother gave in: staring at the floor, she mumbled something inaudible, her hands curled into her apron, and Mauro had to yell again, chanting each syllable: *I didn't catch that.*

She spoke again, a little more loudly. This time he paid close attention, and he heard, and the other two did as well, and they opened their mouths even wider, if such a thing were possible.

"Jesus Christ," said the little brother, and the mother slapped him.

Mauro was stunned. *Wow. That's a packet. We can buy all the saddles and bridles we want.* He saw the two younger boys next to him, counting in silence, trying to figure the number of zeros. But they didn't have enough fingers and they got muddled, started over, got the math wrong, and Mauro wasn't really all that sure himself, to be honest, and he was sorry Joaquin wasn't with them, he'd more of a head for numbers than they had and he would have written the sum out in the dust on the ground before they rubbed it out with the soles of their boots so there'd be no trace. Rafael, with his hand on his cheek, looked up at him as if he were bound to know, so the older brother put on a calculating expression and nodded his head, gravely, crossing his arms over his chest, because he too was nevertheless measuring the extent of the treasure, mutely, and the mother was, too, and the little brother looked at them one after the other with this prayer in his eyes, he wanted so badly to be able to comprehend what this sum represented, a sum so enormous that it made the older ones fall silent. As they still refused to say anything, Mauro guessed from the little brother's wrinkled brow that he was trying again, biting his lips from the effort, pressing his fingers discreetly to count and count again, eventually giving up, shoulders drooping, yes, it must be a huge amount all the same, to judge by the looks on their faces, the mother and Mauro, and with a knowing air the little brother said: "Ah, I see. That much, huh."

But now it's been days and Mauro's patience has run out, he doesn't want the mother to think he's forgotten about it, or accepted the situation, the next time he goes to Emiliano's he'll be the one taking Joaquin and paying for the beer and the girls, and next time could be tomorrow, time is short.

He has not gotten over the loss of his twin. Particularly as their first parting, the one owing to the mother and her poker, could have been fixed, in his opinion, because they bore no blame in the matter, either one of them. They would have seized the old lady by the waist before going into the bar, had they known, they're not to blame, no, not at all, no one would ever have bet a peso that the night would end like that. But the second parting had left the older brother with a bitter taste in his mouth, and he's been stuck with it, deep in his throat ever since, the insipid, metallic bile of the imbecile who didn't dare to leave, who didn't want to play the role of a traitor, and who looked at his brother walking away and was dying to go with him—*madre*, the old lady is going to pay for it, for everything that is collapsing inside him, eating away at him. There are evenings when he withdraws in the emptiness of the room and feels an abyss opening inside him, and it wouldn't take much for him to plunge into it altogether, all of him, overcome by unprecedented, violent terrors. So to keep from going under he seeks something to cling to—bestial work that stifles all emotion, the vibrant pain of his exhausted body, the hope of making a little cash so he can meet Joaquin for a night out—a few pesos, he begs, when the mother could be bathing in a tub full of bills, ever since the little brother came back with the bag, a few pesos, what would that cost her?

And like an animal, who mourns for two days when it loses an old companion, then rejoins the herd and finds a new one, Mauro has gradually drawn closer to his remaining brothers. Of course he hasn't stopped despising them, with all the force of his hatred, but without saying a word they have sealed a strange alliance behind the old lady's back, they are bonded by the feeling that they've been swindled, by their anger at not seeing the money again, neither Mauro nor the little brother, who fully expected some part of it to be his due, nor even Steban, who nods his head to everything they say at night, hiding in one of the rooms. Incomprehension has yielded to a cold, consuming rage, but for all that none of them have dared confront the mother. And even Mauro is restrained by a sort of fearful respect, a mixture of recognition and caution—and the certainty that if he resorted to force, the old lady wouldn't give in any more readily, stubborn as she is and, as he's found out, incredibly greedy. When he reproaches her, she shouts and defends herself; and maybe deep down he senses she is more frightened than miserly—with her features that have grown more dark and deep and hollowed out than in the days when it was a struggle to pay what she owed on time, but Mauro doesn't care, he wants some money, and he shouts and yells about it more and more often. Just let her sit down and complain that she's tired, and he'll bark, *I don't give a damn!* Or that she's got aches and pains: then he will laugh out loud.

"If we had money, you could see a doctor. Seems a bit stupid, don't it, Ma."

She never reacts to his jokes, which aren't jokes, because

he's not in a laughing mood, his tolerance has been undermined, he wants to shake her up but doesn't know how to go about it, his mind is full of a treasure that's spilling over and preventing him from thinking, and he feels the bitterness into his very gums when he has to speak, he hates her for standing up to him, for sticking to her guns. Because the money will stay right where it is until she decides to get it out, is what she said, and Mauro knows just what this means: he'll never see the color of it, in spite of his determination to show her she's wrong, to convince her the bag is worth no more hidden than it would be lost for good.

So he looks up at her from under his brows, and spies on her every moment he can, seeks in every flicker of her eyes where she might have put the satchel to bed. One day when he's talking about it yet again, vehemently, and she glances over at the barn, he's convinced she's just given herself away, and he drags Rafael and Steban along with him and they spend the night digging through the hay. In vain. Tired and exasperated, as dawn breaks he curses her, thinks up plots that will go nowhere, while the other two listen and vigorously nod their heads without doing a thing. Yet his hope goes on tormenting him, indestructibly, and every morning he launches a new attack, interrogating the mother and driving her crazy with his insinuations, and she yells and insults him in turn, all the trouble she's taken to raise him, to raise all of them, honestly.

Rafael says he is sure the money is in her room, and that now she too sleeps on it, to reassure herself. One morning he deliberately cuts his finger, runs back to the house to treat it, and slips into the room with its closed shutters. He opens the wardrobe, hunts around, bends down to peer under the bed. Probes the mattress and checks the slats of the floorboards, but he finds nothing, holding one hand cupped under his bleeding finger all the while; finally he has to wipe his finger on his trousers. When he goes back out, frowning, he looks at his brothers and shakes his head, almost imperceptibly.

"Fuck," spits Mauro.

Behind him, the mother says, *What's the matter?*

"Nothing. Nothing's ever the matter around here."

Thoughts, dreams come to Mauro, all tinged with violence. Squeezing his hands around the mother's neck until she confesses, until she capitulates, spluttering the hiding place, her eyes popping out and her tongue turning blue, and when he has heard he goes on squeezing, to teach her a lesson, and because he doesn't need her anymore. Yes, in his dreams.

In reality, he's hopping mad at the little brother, who was the cause of it all, coming home like that and saying life was about to change—well, you can say that again, it's changed, you can't see it but underneath there's this huge transformation, the spite and frustration the sons relay to each other and exchange, just whose fault is it, the mother who hid the bag, or Rafael who came home with it, spreading the poison over the estancia, or even Steban and Mauro, the former through his fearful immobility, the latter because he shoots his mouth off but is none the more active for all that. But if he did take action . . . Christ, the carnage, because nothing would stop him then, and the house would become a cemetery, bodies spread all over the place, even those of the dogs, no, honestly, he'd better get a hold of himself, he trembles with fury, it mustn't get out, that's what he says to Steban and Rafael, and the little brother frowns.

"If we kill her, it's up to me to do it," he says.

Mauro lets out a nasty guffaw.

"You? And why should it be you?"

"It's my money. I'm the one she robbed."

"She didn't take it from you, you gave it to her."

"She didn't ask me. Did you hear me say even once that I was giving it to her?"

The two brothers think for a moment.

"That's true," says the twin.

The little brother nods, insistent.

"I just wanted to show it to her."

"But if we get it, you'll have to share with us."

"Yes. We'll share, of course. That's what I meant to do."

In the stables the sons go on plotting and murmuring, their blood boiling. As for the mother, they don't even call her the mother anymore. They say, "she." In that *she* there is all the defiance and rage on earth.

So Mauro decides. One evening he explains to the brothers—he doesn't ask, he imposes, this is how it will be. He says: *We stop working. She doesn't want to listen, doesn't want to know. So we show her.*

"I agree," says the little brother.

And Steban nods his head. *Yes.*

They look at each other, their eyes black, their faces hard. Mauro doesn't recall them ever being so determined and unanimous, so he looks at them again carefully to ensure their pact is firmly in their minds, then he clenches his jaws, what a pair of idiots, if for once he manages to get something out of them, and he holds out his hand.

"Let's slap hands on it."

Just as they're about to put their three hands together, a cow moos out in the pen and the dogs leap up, barking. Rafael twists around to see what's going on, and misses Steban's and Mauro's hands, which slap together just the two of them, so the little brother apologizes and fumbles to slap their hands in turn, but it's too late, he's botched it, Mauro is choking with rage and gives him an almighty punch, fist closed so it will hurt, damned idiot Rafael, useless, worthless bringer of bad luck, they're not out of the woods yet.

THE MOTHER

Oh how she hates and despises them, little beggars who don't understand a thing, look at them still sitting outside the barn against the wall in the afternoon, same as this morning, when Mauro came to tell her they wouldn't lift another finger until she gave them the money. She's begotten a filthy race—to see the three of them bored and wandering around in circles and sitting back down again, rather than giving in after a good fit of anger. At least that's one meal to the good, since she didn't make lunch, what did they expect; maybe they thought she was going to feed them to be idle? But it's meager consolation, and while the mother may have plenty to do around the house, the farmyard, and the kitchen garden, she also knows the cattle won't be fed or looked after, and all it will take is a premature birth or an injury or a fight and she'll lose a steer or a lamb. So that lot sitting there on their asses waiting for time to go by: she truly hopes they will die of hunger.

And give up this harebrained scheme of theirs.

Because shearing season has begun.

But with all that's happened, and the little brother's return, and the confusion on the estancia, she's running late. The ewes should already be here. And now these idiots balking and staring at her from afar with their arms crossed, if she tells them to go and fetch the sheep, they'll laugh in her face, they'll want something in exchange, set their conditions. Only a few weeks ago she could have ordered them out to the pastures with one shout. Nowadays by granting herself the right to hide the money she has lost every other right: those of demanding, deciding, and commanding. But she knows she is right, and she won't give in.

Because she is the only one who knows.

This money is tainted.

It didn't take her long to make the connection with what she'd heard in town. The breeder who was robbed, up there in the pampas, and the bandit who managed to get away from everything—rifle shots, traps, the militia. Only to end up in the clutches of her youngest kid, leaving him the money, but the money wasn't his to begin with, so if she'd really wanted to do a good deed she should have given it back—what is to her a godsend of a treasure—give it back? Jesus Christ, did you hear what you said, woman: *Give it back?*

Maybe, to thank her, the rich man would have given her a roll of bills. One roll, when there are a thousand. And give up all the rest?

Even when she was gambling she'd never had the opportunity to get her hands on an amount like that. She's so unused to the idea that every evening she scribbles figures on the table before she cleans it, putting lines between the zeros so she can scan the thousands and the hundreds, and of course it's lunacy to have hidden it all, an absurd decision she's sinking into ever deeper, the sort of choice an unhinged person would make, she trembles at the thought of it, while she scrubs hard at the polished surface to erase all trace of her arithmetic. And yet she didn't hide the bag just on a whim, and she'll stand by her decision whatever it takes. Don't reveal a thing. Wait however long it takes until everyone has forgotten the story about the rich breeder, so that no suspicion will fall on her, the mother, that she might have stolen the bag from the corpse and, consequently, from the breeder, she wouldn't like to bet on her chances of survival at that point. But how many years will she have to be patient, until she's no longer afraid? They'll all be dead first. And deep down, knowing the money is hidden away where no one can find it reassures her a little.

So the mother goes on lying to herself, making up stories she herself does not believe, as if she were incapable of finding out how to cope, a solution, as if it were a moral issue troubling her. Since when, honestly? On evenings when she's had too much to drink and her hands curl around the void, she pictures herself rushing down to San León with the bag in the cart to go play the game of a lifetime. She wouldn't bet it all, obviously. But she'd play for high stakes. She'd win, because chance, too, only favors the rich, and when the wheel turned she'd lose, she'd bounce back, lose again. If she had to add more, she'd add more. Once. Twice. Ten times, all night long. She's telling herself fairy tales if she thinks she wouldn't bet everything: she would gamble every last centavo. Until she'd lost everything, because if the only purpose was to win, she's already won.

What remaining spark of conscience informs her that the temptation will be too great if she sits down at the gambling table, what unkindly lucidity amid her obstinacy in keeping the money hidden in darkest gloom and deepest memory? She wishes she could forget it sometimes, she forces herself to, and when the image of the bag comes knocking at her brain, she crosses it out with a thick line, to erase it once and for all. She knows she could lose everything; and besides, she swore she would never put her hand on a pack of cards ever again. The only way she can preserve her treasure is to act as if. A magician—in reverse.

Just in case, if we need it, you never know, ah, big deal: she hears the furious sons shouting in her head. They don't get it, not at all, they are blind to the fact that as long as the money is hidden here, it exists. Of course it's useless, but at least no one will take it away from them. Whereas if they spend it . . .

They'll have had it, and all of a sudden there'll be nothing left, like a spell dissolving after midnight, nothing but a nice memory in the dust, and a great deal of regret. This is something only she can sense and foresee. Her three sons have so little common sense, wanting to fork it all out at any cost—they get that from their father, who'd have let himself be stripped down to his last peso for a drink.

Already they've been working sluggishly as of late, the lazy-bones, dragging their feet and showing little spirit in handling the pitchfork or the ax; and less and less as the days go by. Until this morning, and them sitting down. The only thing she's seen them do with any stubborn application lately is follow her around. Not one instant where she's been alone at her task. Whether it was hanging up the laundry or feeding the hens, there was always one of them there to help her, even if it only meant carrying the basket or throwing the potato peels out, something they never do, have never done, would never do if—and the way she sees it, their strange solicitude is nothing short of unbearable, she would gladly throw the garbage pails at their heads and yell at them to stop.

They've arranged to take turns, half-days each, and she comes upon them walking past each other with a little nod, passing the baton to one another and murmuring instructions. They are getting in her way. That's what she thinks. And if she gives in, they'll be there to see it. They will end up finding that bloody satchel, just by following her around. Even at night, now, there's always one of them lying outside her bedroom door. A sort of cautious status quo prohibits her from losing her temper. She wishes she could yell at them, heap insults on them while they watch her cooking the meat, or when she hears one of them lying down with a sigh outside her room, like a dog. But she holds herself back: something inside her knows that her silence is frustrating their incipient violence, and that as long as she doesn't protest, they will keep a certain distance, waiting to use force though she doesn't give them any reason to. Wait and see. Maybe they'll do it all the same, after all, and she can sense Mauro is on the verge, his big hands are trembling, the tall twin who cannot stand it when things don't go his way, he's not used to this, he's so accustomed to being of the same mind with her. So she watches him in particular, says nothing when he hits the younger boys, first of all because they wouldn't intervene if it was her getting beaten and basically, they'll just have to sort things out on their own, but above all she mustn't provoke them, no missteps, not a word out of place. And yet Mauro is getting closer, with his seething anger, just one more tantrum, one unchecked gesture, and a shower of reproaches in that voice that worries even her, if it comes to blows then all will be lost.

Sometimes Rafael is present at these strange confrontations, and he sways from one foot to the other and murmurs, *Little mother, little mother.* This shrunken vision of herself—wasn't she *the mother* not that long ago?—puzzles and constricts her, in her body and above all in her mind, and the words go round and round, little mother, because around here anything that is little is worthless. That's how she refers to a calf or a lamb that is born sickly and won't live long, or a tree that's dying, or even Rafael himself, with his scrawny arms, makes you wonder how he'll turn out when he grows up, if he grows up. But as for her! She doesn't belong to that race of weaklings.

Except that.

Maybe she should have said yes, for the saddles. Maybe she went too far there, she can tell. But to backpedal now is out of the question, they'd get the upper hand once and for all and they'd want more and more. Stubborn mules are what she's ended up with, but God knows she didn't stint on the rod, seems she should have used it even more, she was too soft. If they are gaining the upper hand like this it's because they don't fear her enough, and then of course there was always the bad

seed on the father's side, but she could have guarded against it, with a stricter upbringing; spoiled, she's spoiled them, they're like overripe fruit.

They're kids, who are after your money, with no hesitation, they're eating away at you day after day, particularly the eldest—the other two are just little ferrets on the lookout, keeping watch, from a distance, waiting for something to happen so they can come and beg for their share of the loot, but they'll never dare take the first evil step, she's sure of that—so the eldest, all muscles and nerves, this morning when she snapped the dishrag at his ears and he tore it from her with a flip of his hand. She knows that at that moment she lost big, like an old hunter without his gun confronting a puma on its hind legs, an old hunter who'll never frighten anyone again. Since then she has been trying to come up with a solution, but cannot find one. She thought of kicking Mauro out, but she can't bring herself to, even so, and yet she can see it in his gaze, that he is capable of cutting her to pieces to get her to tell him where the treasure is, if it were all to end like that it would be a pity, she'll take her chances, better to wait. She keeps a knife hidden in her blouse, just in case. To defend herself.

And when like lumbering children the younger boys pester her, she slaps them, they're like little wild animals, that way they have of putting their hands on her and waiting until she's beside herself, she can feel them there next to her, she can't take that constant contact anymore, so the moment she sends them flying with a slap—then they'll have won, not the money of course, but the fight, patience—power, in other words. She has to keep away from them all. She'll go mad, she's sure of it. But isn't that what they want? She laughs to herself. When she loses her mind she won't even remember where she's hidden the money. Aren't they clever, the bunch of them. Her finest revenge.

What are we going to do? was what they said.

Nothing. Just keep it. Possess it. So shut up.

*

And then, just when the mother thinks it's all ruined and those wretched boys will never go back to work, just when she's hesitating between letting the ewes rot under their wool and shooting one of her sons in the leg to show them that the fun has gone on long enough, something happens, something she no longer expected, it comes like a miracle to pull her out of the quicksand she'd been slowly sinking into. Truth is, she's not sure she has really understood, and when Mauro grabs Rafael by the shirt and yells, *You what?* she listens as closely as she can, with an innocent expression on her face, her fists already curled into a silent prayer. *Santa María, por favor.* And the little brother holds his ground.

I'm going, he says. He doesn't yield to Mauro's thunderous expression, and this suddenly affects the mother, she feels a knot in her stomach, and a luminous flash in her brain, don't say anything, don't get involved. Listen to Rafael when he replies, of course his voice is trembling, too shrill, a sort of cry, but he wriggles out of his older brother's grasp and holds his head high at the same time.

"I said I'm going."

And Mauro hovers over him once again and growls, *You're not going anywhere.*

The mother watches them, fascinated, the raw power on one side, and this little mule determined to go and fetch the ewes on the other, and it's impossible to tell who will win—if it were just a matter of strength it would be Mauro, indisputably. But something quite different is brewing in Rafael. The last few days she's noticed his pained gaze looking out over the plain, the way he holds his nose in the air, searching for the smell of the sheep he cannot see, as if he could sense them, locate them, lure them home. She can see he is disoriented, to be sitting like this for hours, for the first time, while the animals wander where he cannot keep watch over them,

perhaps they are in trouble, and the wool is thickening on their damp backs. It's the height of shearing season, and they haven't done a thing. Three more weeks and it will be too late, the Andean winds will bring the cold air over the steppe. No one will venture out to undress the ewes, with their bellies growing round with their unborn lambs. What's to be done, then? The mother has resigned herself to the loss of her summer wool. But as for Rafael, and his animals . . . Now he's turning his back on Mauro to go and fetch his horse and his dogs, and God only knows what will happen next.

The older brother lets out a roar.

His rifle on his shoulder, he is taking aim at his brother.

"Another step and I'll blow you to bits."

The mother freezes. They all do. In her head it all goes so fast. What if they end up killing each other. What if she's left without a single son, or just Steban, which is as good as none, just her and her money. But things haven't reached that stage and she won't think about it, imperceptibly she withdraws toward the house, instinctively, she too needs a weapon, a real one.

Then there's the half-wit. All three of them had forgotten about him but now he suddenly starts walking, she doesn't know whether he has any purpose in mind, and truth is at the time the mother thinks: so he still doesn't understand what is going on, look at him walking calmly along, if he picked up a pitchfork to go and clean the hutches she wouldn't be surprised. Mauro watches him out of the corner of his eye, doesn't even call out. They're used to Steban's aimless ways, he's never really there with them, he's responding to some thought that suddenly occurs to him, he'll stop in the middle of the road, too, when he no longer knows where he's going. He's like the dogs, here and then there. And the mother and brothers pay him no more attention than they would the dogs.

But this time she watches him, intrigued, and sees him go into the stable. And out of sight.

Mauro is focused on the little brother, who has not moved, and who is waiting, hands in his pockets. Something has to happen, but she wonders what, she's still too far from the house, Mauro and Rafael like statues, Steban whom they've forgotten about once again, in his strange transparency, until a bird flies overhead, perhaps, and Mauro's finger slips over the trigger, or a horse arrives. And then indeed, the mother staring at the two sons with the gun between them hears the sound of hooves, but she doesn't believe it, doesn't look away, as if she could freeze the scene as it is and nothing will happen—but if she looks away Mauro will kill the little brother, at most there is a flicker, a blinking of his distracted eyes when the sound of the criollos comes closer, and just when the twin turns to look, too, and only then, does she too turn her head to see what is going on.

Steban is in the saddle, holding Mauro's and Rafael's horses by the reins. The little brother reaches out to take Halley, and Mauro shouts again, "Shit, what are you doing?"

Rafael swings up onto the chestnut's back.

"We have to go. We can't leave the ewes like that."

"I'll blow your head off!"

"Gotta go, I said."

"Fuck, you gonna let her win? She'll think she's won, and she'll be damn right!"

"It's not because of her."

"It's because of us, then? You think you'll get your part of the sale, when she's flogged the wool?"

"No. It's for the sheep."

And the mother listens as they argue back and forth, and she knows the little brother means it when he talks about the sheep like that, that nothing will stop him, not even the rifle, and she sees Mauro's hands going white with anger, his chin trembling with rage, all it would take is one shiver for the shot to go off, and everything is motionless for a few very short instants, until Steban without warning urges his horse forward, the criollo takes a few steps, then turns its back on them to head down the path leading away from the estancia and out onto the plain.

"Fuck!!" roars Mauro again, his crazed eyes flickering from Rafael to Steban, and he doesn't know who to aim at now, who to watch, his own horse in the line of fire, waiting, snorting.

So he lowers his rifle, defeated. Turns back to the mother, who doesn't move an eyelash, she is almost absent from the world, but he hasn't forgotten her, and in a voice choked with fury he points first at her then at the little brother and says:

"You. The money from the wool will be mine. You hear? It's for me. And as for you, bitch, it's not over between us. I swear."

One second later he springs into the saddle, gallops past the two brothers, and leads them out onto the plain.

Rafael

Once again, he slams the gate shut, sliding the bolts, and there are so many sheep that they press up against the fence. Close to two thousand head, brought back for the shearing, the mother always says she's obliged to cut their fleece twice a year, with this breed and their wool that is long and thick in winter and short in summer, so that she won't end up with fleece of two different lengths that nobody wants. Truth is he knows it's to sell more wool, and even if what they give her for the thin summer wool is a pittance, at least it's that, even if a few ewes will lose their lives, if the mother gets it wrong and the weather turns cold in the days just after.

A sea of white sheep covering the earth. It took them several days to round them up, and the dogs show it, now that the work is over, they're dragging their feet, their tongues hanging out. They emptied out the pastures, circling, nudging, herding the sheep all the way to the long corridor that leads to the estancia, to drive them into this huge field. Two or three weeks: that's how long it takes to cut their fleece and roll it up in the sacks. Every day they take on a hundred sheep or so, squeezing them into smaller pens near the house, holding them between their knees, plying the scissors. Backs aching from bending over fifteen hours a day, and two years ago Mauro built a wooden hoist he fastens his belt to, to support his back and find some relief from the unbearable pain. At the end of the day he walks bent over like an old man, unable to stand straight until well into the evening; in the morning he starts again, one knee to the ground, waiting for his muscles to warm up, for his body to comply without forcing a grimace of pain. But he doesn't complain, every evening he shouts out the figure of the money that's been made and that will soon be in his hands, and he pounds his chest, looks at the others and shouts:

"It's mine! All mine!"

Steban keeps up almost the same rhythm, silent all day long, sweat on his brow, focused and impassive. The mother and the little brother bring in the sheep, bag the wool, sweep up. They tirelessly open and close the gates, at Mauro's urging or at a grunt from Steban, and sometimes Rafael gives a start when he's called back to order, when he cannot take his eyes off the fleece from the animals' bodies, it's as if they've been skinned alive, but naturally they don't bleed. He takes the wool the older brothers hand to him, strange curly shapes, empty sheep, like the sloughed-off snake skins he finds in the spring, hanging from the thorns of the *neneo* shrubs in the steppe. If he hadn't seen the ewes scrambling back to their feet and running off, stripped naked, he would swear they were still inside the wool.

To see the four of them like that, you could almost believe they'd been reconciled, thanks to the sheep; they're absorbed in the shearing, in the days hurtling by. But Rafael's no fool, and every glance he intercepts among them is charged with immense hatred; even if it took them three months to cut the wool, the anger would not dissipate, there would still be more than enough to raise a blade or a rifle, word of honor. Only Steban goes around with his blank expression, no fury, no nothing, oh, how Rafael envies him for being sheltered from everything—Mauro's spite, the mother's blackheartedness and spying and riling them up, the violence between them held firmly in check by the specter of the hidden money; they are devoured by greed. So, no, they haven't begun to get along, how could they, they just act as if they had, to get the job done together—the work obliges them, forces them to be near each other even when doing so makes their hackles rise, and the little brother tries to avoid contact with the mother as best he can when they shove the wool into the sacks together, he doesn't want her to touch him, he doesn't want her evil to rub off on him, or his brothers' evil.

The only caresses he'll accept are from the ewes, and he plunges his hands in their thick fleece to push them into the pen, circles their necks with his arms in more of an embrace than a shove, when it comes to encouraging the animals; they're afraid of the shearing, everyone knows that, and he fusses over the stunned sheep once Mauro and Steban have let them go again. He is nauseated by the sickly-sweet smell of skin that has been encased in wool for so long, but he cannot get enough of the warmth of their bodies, the damp softness that clings to his palms and which the ewes lick for the salt. In the evening he wanders around the pens, running his hands over their rough backs, stroking their attentive ears, and forgetting that he or his brothers kill one of these animals to eat it, every other day, it could be the very one he cuddled that morning, the one he reassured with a few softly spoken words.

Because for as long as the shearing goes on the mother keeps the brasero lit outside, tossing a few handfuls of dead wood onto it, covering the hearth with a sheet of metal in the evening at bedtime, stirring the embers first thing in the morning before she even prepares breakfast. The embers smolder, kindled by the wind, nestled in their iron belly. And the sons gobble down the sheep until their bellies hurt, fresh meat is a feast. Ribs, saddle, shoulder, leg—they eat it all, and when the carcass is sizzling its last on the grill, Rafael goes at it with his fingers, scraping and tugging at shreds, gnawing at bones, his mouth shiny, as if he had to stock up for the entire winter. The smell of it tickles his nose the moment he gets out of bed, and yet there is no disgust, no weariness in the way he watches the meat cooking, breathing in the air that is heavy with the sweet smell of roasting. It's as if he could eat it for years, decimating the herds, he's exalted by the feeling of wanting for nothing. This is the only time the mother does not restrain his brothers and him. When for once she does not put the lid back on the pot saying, *It's all gone*, even though in fact they know she will serve them leftovers the next day, along with a few extra vegetables to make it look like something different. Not that they've reached the point where they count every portion; but the mother can't help it. She's got scrimping and saving in her blood, you have to put some aside, spend less in days to come, whether it's money or stew it's all to the good.

"More," says Mauro.

The little brother hurries to finish and hold out his plate, too, not to miss his turn, and the mother bristles, surely she's wondering if they're doing it on purpose this year, to punish her, because they've never eaten this much, and if she wasn't holding herself back she'd shout, *enough!* For sure they've eaten eight chops each, and potatoes, and vegetables. She looks at Mauro, who looks back at her, then at Steban who is too busy gnawing at the tiniest little filament of meat still on the bone, and finally at Rafael, who watches her and the older brother at the same time. Not one of them bats an eyelid. And the mother says nothing, but he can tell how exasperated she is from her clenched jaw, her wrathful face. She stabs at a piece of meat and she puts it on the twin's plate, does the same for Steban and Rafael, and she cannot help but yell at them.

"Go ahead, stuff your faces. Eat! Choke for all I care!"

Mauro laughs and the little brother does likewise, what will they look like, bloated and dead, once they've devoured the entire herd—and the mother will laugh at their still-warm bodies, at their mouths dripping with grease. He holds up his chop, shoves almost all of it into his mouth, looks as if he is about to choke. Steban laughs, a peal of strange joyful cries which the twin brusquely interrupts.

"Shut up."

In the kitchen the coffeepot is whistling. The mother gathers the plates immediately, the little brother finishes his meat holding it in his fingers. She hands out the tin coffee mugs, pours the coffee, spilling some as always. And the strange thought occurs to Rafael as he watches her, how all of a sudden she's grown old, with her sad expression, not that she's truly declining or the work is wearing her down, but that she's bending all the same. You hardly notice it, maybe only he does because he's paying attention, his gaze accustomed to the animals and their weaknesses. Sometimes he thinks he's spread a more bitter poison than ever over the estancia, and they certainly didn't need it, with the way they already couldn't stand each other, not yet another venom, if only he'd known, and for sure the poison is eating away at the mother and turning her hair gray, maybe like him she has nights when her heart pounds, it's as if it's risen to her temples and it's trying to get out of her body by whatever means it can. So he watches her, trying to determine whether the evil he can sense all around her has already taken hold, he's good at sensing things like that, better than at remedying them, and more than once the mother catches him staring at her and barks, "What you looking at?"

But now they've decided not to talk to her anymore, or as little as possible, in order to keep a shred of dignity when they get back to work, and Rafael shrugs his shoulders as he finishes his coffee, scratches his cheek where an insect bit him, God only knows what sort of beast it was that gave him such a blister, it itches so bad, and he says he's going off to bed.

At night his dreams are full of faded sheep and veils of white wool, which keep him from truly resting, the work to be done leaves him tense, and he goes through the days like an automaton, already tired when he gets up. There are purple shadows under his eyes, and he stopped joking long ago, as he catches the ewes or fills the bags with wool, he's been defeated by exhaustion and the general mood, which keeps them in this gloomy state, it's overwhelming. He does not stint: this is life, and each of them does what he can, within his capabilities, as sore as the others when it's time to get up in the morning, his gaze just as empty. The days go by, crushingly routine. Sometimes the little brother says something that almost cheers them up: *We've done more than what's left to do.* They've passed the eight-hundred mark, then a thousand. Before long a thousand five hundred sheep—and his brothers nod, it's all grist to the mill, even the slightest bit of good news, during these exhausting weeks.

Next to them the mother keeps busy, yet a strange slowness has her in its grip, even as she rushes from stable to kitchen, setting a handful of wool down by the sink that she forgot to put in the sack. She washes, cooks, roasts, cleans, sorts the sheep. Rafael records everything, the way she speaks, swallowing her words, how often she grumbles, her hands over her face as if to hold her thoughts in place, and her eyes wide open after that, she too is immensely tired; one time she brings Mauro a sheep that's already been shorn.

"What am I supposed to do with this?" shouts the twin.

He kicks the ewe away and Rafael starts laughing, too loudly, as if to convince himself that there's something funny about the mother's distress, something to convince him that they are right to remain bitter and spiteful, struggling with her every inch of the way as she gets more exhausted than them, they'll wear her down, for sure, even if she's seen worse, but this time there's a greater anguish, which the little brother notices though he cannot name it, or does not dare to, both excited and terrified at the thought that the mother might leave them. Because she is drifting away. From them—but for a long time they've been no more to her than free labor; from the estancia, which she looks at without seeing; from the livestock, which she forgets about, even from the town, where she no longer goes, having given up first poker then booze, and the little brother would like to yell at her to go on back there and come home drunk in the middle of the night, at least back then she was alive and her voice had a snap to it, if this is what it means to go under, he'd rather not witness it, not see how it has come over her all of a sudden. As if you could see through her, as if she were shadow, like a ghost or a witch, he dreams that she is disappearing into the sand, and he wakes with his heart pounding with fear. He waits to hear her piling up the dishes or opening the door to the woodstove, then he feels better, she's still there, she hasn't set off down the path of flight, like the father, like Joaquin, or like he himself might do someday, and the thought vanishes at once from his mind, because he would never leave the sheep and the dogs, or his horse, or his arid land. But she would, the mother, wouldn't she—every night he wonders, and every night the nightmare returns.

Because he is so absorbed by the mother's sullenness, and for many other reasons, no doubt, when one morning the little brother finds the kitchen empty, as if deserted by the old lady, he is hardly surprised, and he strolls around the room as if she might be hiding behind the stove or the table, then says to Mauro when he walks in:

"She's not here."

And maybe it is the twin's astonishment that alarms him then, because he suddenly realizes this is the first time since he was born. The mother has always gotten up before them, breakfast ready, the smell of coffee when they walk in. But now. Only the smell of old fat, no one has opened the door at dawn to air the room, and the fire has gone out.

"Right," says Mauro.

And the little brother looks at him.

"Right, what?"

"Well. She decided not to get out of bed."

"But why not?"

"What do you think? She knows she won't get the money for the wool. So she doesn't give a damn whether we get our breakfast or not."

"But she's got the other money. The bag."

The older boy shrugs.

"It's never enough."

"What if she left?"

"She didn't leave. She's just acting stupid, that's all."

Rafael nods, not altogether convinced by what the older brother has said, because he's had this weird impression for days now, and he puts his nose against the glass pane in the door, to see whether there is any sign of footprints receding into the dust, but there is nothing he can see; maybe she swept behind her to fool them? His throat tightens a little, for no real reason, just that it's unlike other days and he likes that tiring routine—the meals, the animals, the wool, then another meal with the smell of meat and spices roasting, and the ewes, and their bleating which almost lulls him when he begins to feel too weary. Now he would like to turn back the clock, come again into the kitchen ten minutes ago, and find the mother bent over the stove, their mugs full, the reassuring odors of bodies and coffee. Standing a little off to one side, he bites his lips, a strange emotion twisting his guts.

"Stop whining!" barks Mauro, and the little brother, his eyes red, waves his hand and turns his back to him.

But is it even his fault, if he can't help it, if he knows that now it's happened, she too has left. The dreams came to warn him and he didn't believe them, too impossible, but oh, he should have, he would have kept an eye out, he would have peered into the darkness until morning, and suddenly he stiffens.

"Who slept outside her door last night?"

In the heavy silence of the room, he follows Mauro's gaze, and Steban opens his eyes wide.

"Didn't . . . didn't see."

"You fell asleep, huh," says the twin.

"No. No."

"Can you swear she's still in her room?"

But Steban doesn't answer, swaying his head from left to right in a sign of panic, and Mauro loses his temper.

"Hey, half-wit! I'm talkin' to you!"

"No . . ."

"No, what? Is she in there, or you can't say?"

"No . . ."

"I can't hear a fucking thing, can't you talk normal like other people?"

Just as the older brother stands up out of his chair in rage, Rafael leaps forward. *Stop, we're not gonna start arguing now, all right?*

"Did you fall asleep or not?" shouts the twin.

Steban bangs on the table and cries, "N . . . no!"

"Look at this jerk, the way he lies, just like the old lady!"

So Rafael steps in, puts a hand on his older brother's shoulder.

"But honestly, Mauro, what if she's not there?"

"You shut up too!"

The little brother recoils, swallows his protests. But he doesn't let go, he holds his hand out before him, in case the twin tries to hit him, and he continues his train of thought.

"Maybe she's hiding."

"Huh?" says Mauro. "Like the money, is that it? And then what?"

But suddenly he freezes. Looks at the little brother, who has opened his mouth, and they both look stunned. The same thought flashes through their minds.

"No," says the little brother, who refuses to believe it.

"Because maybe you don't think she could do such a thing?"

"No, she wouldn't do that."

"Fuck!" shouts Mauro, rushing out toward her bedroom. "She's gone! She left, with the money!"

Rafael speaks first, breaking the silence that has paralyzed them for long stretches of time. His voice is trembling and he looks at no one, does not specify which one of his brothers he is talking to, but obviously it's Mauro, because the big brother did not believe him when he said it was impossible, and now he has no choice, does he.

"You see she didn't do it."

The twin nods.

"Yup."

"That's . . . that's for sure," says Steban.

They scratch their heads. The little brother does likewise, and continues: "But hey, this doesn't look any better, huh."

"I don't think so, either," says Mauro.

"What are we going to do?"

"Chrissake, that's all you ever say."

"I'm just asking, is all."

The older brother shrugs, disconcerted.

"Well . . . we're gonna bury her, what else can we can do."

It is as if he has been watching the mother lying dead on the bed for a long time, and the room is so silent he could be alone. Even Mauro is silent, God knows what he's thinking, looking at that motionless shape with its mouth half open, hair spread across the pillow, this presence that is no longer there troubles them, weighs on them, and the little brother stares at the mother, looks for a tremor, and out loud he wonders:

"Are we really sure that . . . "

And at that moment he falters. It reminds him of too many

things, too recent. Instinctively he steps forward, tugs on the sheet to see if the mother moves, but only the cloth rustles in his fingers and he recoils, next to his brothers, all three of them in a circle around this strange coffin, looking at the old lady as if she were pretending, playing a joke on them. But they've been there so long already, after slamming the door against the wall, certain they would find the room empty; so long already, she would have opened her eyes, sat bolt upright, and they would have jumped. And besides. She'd never do that, anything mischievous. Argue, swindle, yell, okay. But nothing else, none of them remember her ever being the least bit jokey or playful, and the act she's putting on, lying on the bed, is no act, they can tell. And yet, murmurs the little brother as he looks at her face, already pale, her milky complexion, and yet there's no blood on her belly.

"What'd you say?" grunts Mauro.

"She's not hurt."

"Nope."

"How could she have died if she's not hurt?"

"Maybe she's hurt inside."

"Or maybe her heart stopped, like with the critters," murmurs Rafael, thinking out loud.

And he tilts his head to the side, and asks again: "But are we sure?"

"Of course!" says Mauro, getting annoyed; he walks over to the bed and shakes the mother; she bounces on the mattress. "Look!"

"Stop it!"

"But look! You can see she's not moving. She's as stiff as a post!"

"Stop it, I said!"

The older brother raises an eyebrow.

"You're an idiot. Okay, all we have to do is put a mirror in front of her mouth, that way at least we'll be sure, no need to wonder."

And the three of them lean close in, holding their breath, after Steban hands Mauro the mirror, refusing to do it himself, as if the mother might bite him, as if she actually could. They wait. Until the ache in their backs obliges them to stand up straight, and even then they stare together at the mirror there before them, tenaciously, as if their gazes could make the glass surface steam up all of a sudden.

"There's nothing," murmurs the little brother at last.

Steban presses his lips. *N-nothing.*

"Right," says Mauro. "So we'll bury her."

The Mother

From somewhere in her extinguished consciousness, lying on her bed, the mother listens to the sons, observing them from the top of the room, where she has perched like a curious bird, and she hears those strange words, *she is dead,* cannot understand that they refer to her, looks again, tries to protest when Mauro comes over to the bed and shakes her, scolding the little brother, it's not very pleasant, after all. She sees herself before them in her nightgown, and she doesn't like that either, what are they doing in her room, is this some sort of new trap they've come up with to make her tell them where she's hidden the money, then she suddenly wonders, what time is it? And she's still in bed, she's not dreaming, outside it's broad daylight, the light is pouring into the room despite the drawn curtains. A moment later the incongruity of the situation has left her, she doesn't think about it anymore, she is still watching the sons, who are saying all sorts of things as if she weren't there, her thick, stubborn sons, the best she could do, and she scolds herself, it's not her fault, if the father had been there too, to help raise them— alas, it was up to her alone.

Bury?

The mother pricks up her ears. That's Mauro who just spoke. And now he adds:

"We'll deal with that later. We've got work to do."

One by one the sons leave the room and she finds herself alone; she would like to call out, but nothing comes out of her inert mouth, and she turns this way and that, unsure. From up where she's hiding she can hear them in the kitchen, doling out the morning's chores, while Steban struggles to light the fire and brew some bad, lukewarm coffee, and it makes her laugh, they're not used to this. There'll be a fine scene at noontime. And as no one wants to do the job, Mauro appoints the little brother to make lunch, because at the shearing he won't be missed as much, and as he swallows the donkey's piss from his mug the little brother squeals:

"But I don't know how to cook!"

"We have no choice! Carve up the last of the sheep, we'll grill it, then all you have to do is get some eggs to make a tortilla."

"If you know how to cook, you do it!"

Mauro grabs him by the hair.

"Listen, snotty nose, who's gonna shear the sheep, if I start doing the women's work? You got anything better to suggest?"

This time Rafael clenches his teeth, not to respond, and the mother realizes he's in a peculiar state, and she wonders if it has to do with her, and it surprises her how she wishes she could put her hand on his head to reassure him, she's never done it before, but it's come over her all of a sudden and she raises her arm, as if, then lets it drop, something stops her.

Never mind. Don't worry. This morning, it's all the same to her.

And the four of them embark on a strange day, the three sons at the shearing and her in her bed and in the air at the same time never wondering how this could be, maybe once or twice she looks down and thinks, *Well, well*, and things go on as before. Rafael puts some potatoes on to cook, then joins the others, bringing sheep in, taking them out again. In the meantime he runs to the kitchen to check on things, break the eggs, do more cooking, how long, of course he has no idea, and the mother shakes her head, shouting, *Stop, stop*, he doesn't listen and she gives a shrug, after all, it won't kill them to eat something that's overcooked, and they'll add the salt and spices he forgot to use, too. Oh how sorry they must be that she's not there! She stretches and expands through the universe, feeling snug and peaceful, yawning now and again. She looks at the sons with curiosity. As if she's never really seen them.

The little brother is going to pass out if he keeps up at that pace, for sure, trying to do everything, cutting the chops, swatting the flies, going back to the sheep—they're alive, at least—tossing wool in the bags, dragging them panting over to the wall when they're full, blowing on the embers, putting the meat on the grill: how did the mother ever manage? Ah ha! she laughs, hearing his murmured thought, well, it took a lot out of me, didn't it.

At lunch, Mauro yells at him.

"It's disgusting, this food of yours."

"Told you so."

"You call this a tortilla? We're gonna choke on this stuff."

"Just tell Steban to do the cooking."

"Steban's helping me."

"Why should I have to do the cooking?"

"That's how it is."

And the mother remembers when her own mother said the same thing, *That's how it is*, whether you're a girl or the youngest, your fate is pretty much the same. With the years you get used to it, and you'd better, because among themselves men are no better than animals, don't go thinking, don't go hoping they might help those who are weaker than them, they're just waiting for a chance to hold those weaker heads underwater, the better to drown them for good. How many times, back in the days when there were still savages on the steppe, not that long ago, huh, twenty, twenty-five years, had she seen troops and families who'd abandoned their livestock and their old parents, or one old parent, anyway enough to arouse the Indians' hunger, while that would give them a few hours to get away, it was like a tacit agreement, one old man or one old woman to save the rest. And sometimes the Indians would kill all of them, when they were angry. Truth is, the sons don't know how lucky they are to have been born in these plains once Roca had swept them clean, a real warrior he was, expanding their farmland all the way to the edge of Patagonia by wiping out those tribes of barbarian foreigners.

Now the mother has to focus, because the sons have come back into the bedroom.

What a strange impression, to be borne away in a wooden box that Mauro has hastily nailed shut, it's like a coffin, couldn't they have found a more thoughtful means of conveyance, and with a great deal of curiosity and not the slightest emotion the mother wishes she could ask where they are headed, the four of them, where they are going to launch her on the water, in this strange boat they've built for her.

As they leave the house, she is bathed in light, in her box, sheltered from the wind like this she can smell the sweet air, and even if the sons stumble now and again, she won't go far in her four planks, she's almost pleased they're looking after her like this, so on we go. They're still thinking of burying her, and the mother raises an eyebrow to peer outside, they're on their way to the orchard, which surprises her, because the fruit was picked ages ago. It's annoying, in the end, that none of them will answer her, they don't even turn toward her, as if she didn't exist, couldn't speak, couldn't question. They can do whatever they like, get up to all sorts of tricks to get her to tell them where she's hidden the money, she knows damn well how they'll treat her afterwards, as if she were some trifle, and for Chrissake would Rafael stop drumming his fingers on the box, it's damn annoying.

"What the hell is that?"

In vain does she cry out at the sight of the pit, because they don't react. And when they slowly lower her into the hole they've dug at the edge of the orchard, she begins to worry, they know she hates the dark, at night she always keeps a candle stub lit. Then she calms down, she can still see the daylight, in her shallow ditch. She waits for the next stage. Opens her eyes in astonishment when Steban steps forward and tosses a few long grasses into the pit, and Mauro has his hands on his hips, while Rafael explains apologetically:

"Normally it should be flowers, but we don't have any flowers."

"It's dried grass," says the eldest, his voice full of reproach.

"We looked but we couldn't find anything else."

"Do you remember what we're supposed to sing?"

Steban shakes his head and the little brother spreads his arms. *No,* groans Mauro, *that's what the priest does.*

So what are we going to do?

"Sing, dammit."

"I've never been to a funeral."

"Sing any old thing, who cares. It's so there's some music."

So Rafael hums and the mother wishes she could block her ears, even though he's singing quietly—some sort of melody with no harmony, she recognizes snatches of the popular songs she used to hum in the kitchen; and as on top of it he doesn't know the words, he can only enhance the refrain with a few plaintive *la la las*—and the brothers stand stock-still as they listen. Then Mauro raises his hand.

"That's enough."

"Is that all?" asks the little brother.

"It'll do. And anyway, she can't hear you."

"F-f-fortunately," adds Steban.

"What do you mean I can't hear you?" shouts the mother, trying to sit up, until she realizes there is a lid on the box.

The sons do not weep, not even Rafael, whose eyes stung

briefly then stayed completely dry. The mother is glad of it: no milksops in her house. If she has put up with boys and given them a hard life, it was to turn them into men. Oh, she noticed that the little brother was upset, but she's not crazy, she could read his mind with disconcerting ease, he was thinking about the dog just then, not about her, the dog who would die one day and be buried in turn, and then he would cry, for Three, and now he's turned around and the mastiff has come to lick his hand. *Ungrateful brat*, thinks the mother.

But now she's considerably intrigued by this tiny ceremony, the three sons, and the three dogs as spectators, and she's still wondering, when Rafael shakes his head.

"We should've let people know."

Mauro grunts. "We don't want them sticking their noses into our business."

Who, they? Did someone find the money? Down in her hole the mother feels a tug of panic. And even more so when Mauro jumps down into the ditch and sets about nailing down the lid—how will she manage? Is this the only horrible solution the sons could find, did they really all agree to it?

"Hey!"

She can shout her lungs out, they go on acting as if they can't hear her. Just then she realizes that even if they have completely sealed her in the box, she can still see them, she is floating around them, and she bursts out laughing. She doesn't understand, but she doesn't care, and she jiggles her legs contentedly.

But when the first handfuls of earth hit the coffin lid with a dull thud, she begins to wail.

"What the hell are you doing!"

And then she falls silent. Outside, as the sons gradually cover the box, Rafael murmurs: "After this we won't see it anymore. There won't be any more hole."

"There'll be a dip in the land," says Mauro.

"The grass will grow again."

"What do you want, should we put a stone, maybe, to mark the spot."

"I don't know. I was just saying."

"With all the shit she gave us."

"I don't know."

"Come on. Let's get it over with."

The older brother shoves Steban and Rafael aside and picks up the shovel. He fills in the pit for good, with sweeping gestures, and doesn't stop until he's finished. Since they put the mother deep in the hole in her box, there is too much earth now, and it leaves a mound on the surface.

"There you go, that'll make you happy. You can see where it is."

Steban rakes the surface smooth and wipes the sweat from his brow, leaving a long brown streak. Then they wait in silence, shifting from one foot to the other in awkwardness. The mother is beginning to suffocate down there, and she shouts at them: "Go on, get going now. It'll be fine."

They don't dare leave her.

"Go on!" she screams, coughing.

"Were we sure . . . ?" hesitates the little brother, one last time.

Mauro, beside himself, shouts, "Of course, fuck it!"

Of course, echoes the mother from deep in her hole, it's time to go now, and leave her alone, she's out of breath. Let them go where they want, it's no longer up to her to say, let them leave her in peace in her warm, silent earth, she'd have done better to come here a lot sooner, had she known. And for once her prayer does some good, because above her Mauro is moving, she can tell from the vibrations in the earth, and he orders the other two, the way she wanted: "Get going."

Slowly, they rouse themselves to follow Mauro. Take a step, then two, then three. It is a strange, almost sweet parting, growing sadder and lighter as they move away, as if the mother's hands were opening to let them go, and yet how many times have they dreamt of it, and what a disappointment, what a gut-wrenching feeling, not the slightest joy, just fatigue right up to their eyeballs. They turn and look back.

"It's not how you thought it would be, huh," snickers the mother.

One last look, and Rafael sighs: "Didn't think it would be like this."

"Things'll be better tomorrow. We'll have forgotten," Mauro assures him.

The little brother makes a skeptical face. *Not so sure of that.*

"I know we will."

"Well, we'll find out tomorrow."

"That's right," says the mother, expiring at last. We'll find out tomorrow.

They all nod their heads, at least they agree on one thing, let this day be over with, they'll go to sleep, wipe it from their minds for a while, until morning, yes, then they'll see. For no particular reason the little brother raises his shoulders, just to give himself an air of composure. Then he says, "Okay, then."

The other two look at him.

"Then what," murmurs Mauro.

"Well. Amen."

This time, the mother can no longer hear them.

RAFAEL

The following morning he can scarcely believe the sky can be so blue, and for a moment he smiles, because it is going to be a fine day, for a moment, before reality hits him again, painfully, in a heavy silence, and he remembers and unintentionally utters: *The mother.*

But it wasn't a dream, even if he'd like to convince himself it was, as he goes to open the door to the bedroom, where the bed is still unmade, and then to sit at the table where once again nothing is ready. Rafael says nothing, without being asked he stirs the embers in the stove, and puts water on to boil. He won't replace the mother at the stove, that much is for sure; but for a few days, the time it takes for them to find their places, share out their roles. The time to finish the shearing.

And to clear the temptation from his thoughts.

But he is not the only one who has it, they have all succumbed to this feverishness. Mauro taps his fingers on the table, his attention drifting, and Steban eats, looking up at him from under his eyebrows, waiting for him to speak, the hypocrite, the mother still warm three feet under the ground and already they are thinking of nothing else, wondering where to start, dreaming they could read the old lady's mind for even just a second, hear her whispering from the hole, one word, just one word.

The little brother places his cheek against his palm and waits. After a while he says, "There are a hundred or so sheep left."

Mauro laughs.

"Go fly a kite, you and your sheep!"

He suddenly gets to his feet.

"What are you doing?" asks Rafael.

"I'm gonna find the money. It's here, I know it is. What do you say?"

"Fine, but, well, what about the sheep?"

"We don't need them anymore, damn it! Never again am I going to stuff myself with wool the way we've been doing, you hear me? There is a fortune somewhere in this house, and that's the only thing I care about."

He leans forward, blowing his acrid breath on the little brother, who pulls away.

"Where is it, do you think?"

"No idea. Uh, if it were me, I'd start in her room."

"I already looked there."

"You didn't have time to do it properly. You know what she's like, she won't have hidden it just like that. She could have dug in the earth with her fingernails to hide it, she could have stuffed it one bill at a time in some mouse hole, just to be sure we won't find it."

"And if it's not there?"

"We'll look elsewhere."

"Yeah. That's what we'll do. If we have to we'll take this house apart board by board, but I swear we'll find that money."

Steban holds his head in his hands.

"What if . . . what if we . . . I mean, n-never—"

"If we don't find it?"

"Y-yeah."

Mauro interrupts them with a thump of his fist on the table.

"Impossible. It's bound to be here somewhere."

But the little brother doesn't see it that way.

"What if she found some unimaginable hiding place."

"Stop bringing us bad luck, are you on our side or not?"

"Of course I am! But she wouldn't tell us a thing and we never found out a thing, so I figure that if she didn't want us to find it . . . "

"We'll find it all the same. We're not that stupid."

"How should we go about it?"

"I suggest we search one room at a time, all of us together. That way, if one of us finds it, he won't be tempted to keep it all to himself."

"Oh-k-kay," says Steban.

The little brother nods.

"Fine by me."

Then adds:

"So what do we do about the sheep?"

The dogs circle the huge herd, panicked at the sight of so many animals, and Rafael feels strange to be on his own leading the bleating herd, both exalted and uneasy. But he doesn't have far to go: he'll let them loose on the first plains they come to. When they herded them there a few weeks ago, they left the gates open all the way to the far reaches of the estate, ready for the return. The old ewes will know how to find their way through. He orders the dogs next to them, slightly to the rear, aware that as soon as they start to move, One, Two, and Three will hurry to the rear to contain the majority of the animals, the way they always do. Rafael hesitates to push the way the dogs do, or hem in the right-hand side, where the sheep could most easily scatter because of the crops. If only they would keep to the path without wandering here and there. If only they could reach the pastures the way they always do; but normally there are three of them to control two thousand head, one man for seven hundred sheep, and today, alone with the dogs, he's thinking through the way they must go, trying to predict the spots where the youngest will try and get away. Finally he opens the gate, shouts to get the herd moving. The dogs bark. Halley moves into the white tide.

For two long hours he drives them onto the steppe, whistling to the dogs a hundred times over, setting off at a gallop and snapping his whip to keep the sheep from running off. He's had his fill of hunting, and he won't chase them out on the plateaus; if they get lost, he'll give up on them. Tracking lost animals for days on end, walking all the way to the cold forests, he's done his bit. And made his way home: and what good came of it? If he ever finds an injured man in a cave again, he's almost certain he'd go the long way around not to see him again. And he's absolutely sure he would bury the bag of money and not take it home with him, that it was a poison that drove the mother and brothers crazy, the mother now dead and stone cold under the earth, and the brothers he has left behind at the estancia, hammers and pliers in hand, singing like enraged soldiers about to attack the room and shouting at him to get lost, him and his sheep and his wool and his bags. That's when he decided to take the animals back out onto the plains, just keeping the hundred and two unshorn ewes, despite Mauro's exhortations, swearing that he personally would never shear them, that Rafael would do better to take them out, too, and let them go with the others. But Rafael refused: he could not leave the creatures sticky with sweat under all that wool. While the older brothers take the house apart, he'll learn how to use the shears.

He'll shear the one hundred and two ewes.

All on his own if he has to.

On the first day he does six ewes. Next to him lies the pile of wool, an untidy accumulation of scraps. Not once did he manage to peel off the fleece the way Mauro does, in one go, revealing with the last snip of his scissors a second skin in the shape of the sheep. All Rafael got was clumps and scattered handfuls, which he shoves into the bags, pressing down hard so it won't show.

Six ewes. All of them hurt. Not badly, benign nicks and cuts, when they move and the shears are already open, hardly serious gashes, drops of blood. Rafael took the vinegar from the kitchen to disinfect the sheep before letting them go. Mauro merely spits on his fingers and wipes the scratches with his thumb, a quick, careless gesture, so sure is he that the animals will heal all on their own; but the little brother is not as sure of himself, and he wants to do things properly. He talks to himself in a low voice, conversing with the mother. He justifies himself when he hurts a sheep, makes excuses when the wool drops off in ridiculous little pieces a couple inches long, apologizes. Once it's hidden in the fleece of one thousand nine hundred properly shorn sheep, his harvest will be invisible, and he spreads it out, a little bit in each bag. He doesn't give up. Because he cannot just let these sheep go like that, they would die from the heat by the end of spring, sweating, harboring too many germs and parasites in their tangled curls. And once disease gets in among the ewes, it spreads through the entire herd, as if they were giving it to each other on purpose. Then the wool is no good, and their skin itches and burns, even when you daub them with cob to help the scarring.

Of course he couldn't let them go without shearing them first.

He nods to himself, tries to wedge the creature between his legs; she slips down. And yet she's doing her best, immobile, resigned, her head turned to the side, she doesn't look, doesn't judge. She waits. *Nearly there*, apologizes the little brother, in a sweat. Between two ewes he runs to the kitchen to keep an eye on the vegetables, adds wood to the brazier. He doesn't dare go into the mother's room. He can hear the hammering, Mauro's swearing. The floorboards cracking under the crowbars, as if the money might be hidden underneath. They threw the mattress out the window after slashing it to pieces with a knife. They must have emptied out the big wardrobe, spilled out the drawers; and the dressing table, the only piece of furniture she really cared for, will have been shattered and taken apart. He'd rather not see. By lunchtime, Mauro is foaming. Steban stands in his shadow, pale and withdrawn.

"Have you finished?" Rafael asks timidly.

"It's not in the bedroom," rages the tall twin. "We'll keep going elsewhere. We're going to search the kitchen."

"Oh, no!" protests the little brother. "We have to keep this room intact, we have to live somewhere, after all."

Mauro looks at him, nonplussed. Then agrees: "Fine. We'll search here last. And anyway, this is where we spend most of our time, she'd never put it here."

"And what about the barn? There are hundreds of possible hiding places there."

They wolf down their bad meal—*I hope you're gonna learn how to make something better, and fast*, complains Mauro— and rush out. Rafael listens to the brothers opening doors, their muffled shouts as they divide up the work. He washes the dishes, trying to hear what he can; the wind brings only incomprehensible sounds. Once he's wiped the table he goes off to do his three ewes.

In the evening Mauro tells Steban off: for not working fast enough, for not being methodical enough. The proof is that the half-wit doesn't remember where he's already searched in the barn, and where he hasn't; he's been rummaging with no logic, when he should have been working on a grid and not leaving one spot until he was sure he'd searched the whole area. The older twin is annoyed, he wanted to find the money right away, according to the dream he'd made for himself, and the little brother shakes his head in denial, what did they expect, maybe they both thought the mother had left it right out where they'd be able to see it, so they'd find it right away? He laughs at the thought, she was a clever old lady, and hell, they don't even know how clever.

"You think it's funny?"

When he sees how angry this makes Mauro, Rafael grovels, like a cat about to get attacked, ears flattened against his head and eyes half-closed as he waits for the blow. But the twin has his mind on other things and he gets up and paces back and forth, kicking the floor.

"We have to start all over," he says. "Tomorrow we'll get better organized."

"Besides," murmurs the little brother, almost inaudibly, "there's nothing left to eat."

"Well, we'll kill one of your hundred and two sheep. That way you'll have fewer of them to shear."

"It would be better if you took one of those I already did today, I think."

"What bloody difference does it make, one more or less? What the fuck do we care about a few pounds of wool, with the money that's waiting for us?"

"I'd just prefer it that way. That's all."

"Yeah," says the twin, "but at least if we kill her, she won't wiggle, and maybe you won't have as much trouble with your shears. Did you think about that?"

He bursts out laughing and slaps his hands on his knees, and it is that raucous laughter that Rafael knows only too well, the laughter goes with alcohol and brawling, and yet he was careful to hide the last of the whisky after the mother died; now it's weariness, waiting, tension. Timidly he murmurs:

"Don't do that."

"What, you think you're going to stop me?"

"Don't take one who still has her wool."

"And what if I feel like it?"

Mauro stands up to his full height, aware of how he intimidates the two of them, Steban and the little brother, and he pounds his chest. *Show me who's gonna tell me otherwise!* He bounds away from the table with a laugh, brandishing his knife, running toward the pens while the little brother cries out in protest, and Steban restrains him by his sleeve. *D-don't, he's g-gone c-c-crazy.*

In the light of the oil lamp, sniffling with anger, he shears the dead ewe, she is lying on his lap, and the blood runs onto his trousers and his pants and his shoes, but he doesn't stop, by the time he finishes cutting the wool the brothers are already asleep, and he stuffs the sacks. In the silence of the night he sweeps the stable and the stained floor, feeling strangely lonely next to the creature, her eyes are wide open, staring at the roof beams above them, and the lamp causes fleeting shadows to dance over the walls.

STEBAN

For his second day in Mauro's wake, Steban moves the stores of hay in the barn, lifting up the fodder and examining the ground attentively. All morning they've been picking things up and putting them back, digging and scraping, finding worn boards that they toss to one side, and the older brother's furious complaints make him tremble every time, and curse the mother to whom he addresses his prayers, if only she could hear him. Make her agree to help them at last. But probably she doesn't really want to, because all their searching is futile, they ferret through sheaves and cough with the dust and in the evening they leave the barn like exhausted miners, their faces black, their bodies stiff, and by the time they sit down at the table where the little brother serves them meat and vegetables, fatigue has triumphed over anger; shadows yawn beneath their eyes and they leave half their food on their plate.

And Steban is really beginning to wonder whether, all things considered, it wouldn't be better if the mother were still there, because life here with Mauro is turning sour, he loses his temper and jabs with his pitchfork, mindless of the fact that the half-wit is right there behind him, that would be too much, if he ends up crippling him, then there would be only two of them, the older brother tearing the house to bits and the little brother stubbornly shearing his sheep, and no one to tell them what is right and what is wrong, to put things back in order, for sure Steban's not the one who's going to do it. Mauro's fury upsets Steban, and he keeps as far away as possible in his corner of the barn, far from the pitchfork but also from the waves of hatred emanating from his older brother, leaving a chill down his spine. He is terrified by his older brother's power: what if he loses his mind for good, if they fall victim to his rage Steban doesn't rate the little brother's chances of survival very high, or his own for that matter; the little brother especially, Mauro has always despised him, an immediate, gut aversion, as if Rafael couldn't be his brother, given the fact that the father was already gone, and maybe that suspicion is at the origin of everything, the older brother's ignorance, his inability or unwillingness to count nine months, all he saw was the arrival of this squalling little baby, and his mother, exhausted.

If only he could find the words that would calm Mauro down. He'd have time enough to try, there with him in the barn. The irony of it is he can only open his mouth to stammer a few syllables, he's learned to spit out what's important and nothing more, and sometimes when he's alone he practices, but to no avail. Not a single whole sentence wants to come out of his constricted throat, and yet it's not the fault of his throat, he knows that, neither his throat nor his vocal cords nor his teeth, just his damned head which never got over the terrible fright of that night with the father, so terrible he's never told anyone about it—but then, who would he tell?

So, night before last, when they found the mother dead, he felt a very distant relief, a sort of rush in his guts, of tension finally being released, for the first time she could do no harm, never again would there be any danger of her taking him away too in the middle of the night, going home with the horse's coat stained with blood, just a little there on his flank, where Steban's legs would have been dangling. It is a huge comfort to realize this, and to know for certain that she's buried in the ground and will never come out, after those hours of terror, yes, right to the end he thought he could see a tiny spark of life in her inert body, right up to the moment they left the orchard he thought the mother might rise up all of a sudden, call out, bang on the lid of the coffin. And everything would have been lost, they would have dug her out again and the fear would have started all over again. Whereas now.

But Mauro's violence is beyond anything he expected, and he wrings his hands in silence while the older brother, coming away empty-handed yet again, bangs the walls of the barn and screams, "Where is it? Where is it?"

All the twin's strength has gone into destruction, and the building is in ruins—the hay scattered everywhere, boards torn away, stores tossed to the ground. A vision of devastation, in which Steban is participating only out of cowardice, to escape a beating, but he's used to it, his entire life has been a long apprenticeship of transparency and domination, down to the very name the older brother has given him: the half-wit, which offers him a certain peace and to which he submits without protest, so now he leaves the barn behind.

The building looks as if a storm had swept through it, and they would just leave it like that, a monumental waste, were it not for the little brother.

Because Steban knows that after supper the little brother will come and pick up the hay and stack it all again neatly, he'll drive in a few nails to put the boards back in place, he'll pick up the overturned churns and sweep the floor. He won't leave the barn until it's back the way it should be, a strange sprite repairing the damage his older brother has wrought, and never mind if Mauro smashes it all up again tomorrow, he'll do it again, he'll spend his life at it if he has to. Steban cannot understand what motivates the little brother to mend and restore so tirelessly, he's vaguely fascinated by this determined struggle to keep the estancia going, and the way he said, at supper:

"I did twelve ewes today."

"So what," said Mauro, "you want a medal?"

"And I only hurt five of them."

The twin gives his nasty laugh. "That's still five too many.
And your potatoes are still raw inside."

Rafael lowers his head.

"It's better than yesterday."

"It's still disgusting."

"Didn't stop you eating."

"Go on provoking me, you'll see."

"And you didn't turn your nose up at the chops, did you."

"You really are out to annoy me."

"I'm just saying, it might not be great, how I cook, but in
the end you don't seem to mind."

"Like I have a choice, for fuck's sake!"

This time Rafael doesn't respond, and Steban begins to
breathe more easily inside, slowly, feeling the specter of the
quarrel move away, and it's strange how as he observes the pair
of them—the older brother getting more and more worked up,
and the little brother snappy, digging his teeth in where he
can—Steban feels sure that something is about to overflow,
when neither one will back down, both convinced they are
right, just a simple little thing, for sure, some petty little quarrel. Something will trigger it. Of course, since it's him, the half-
wit, who is having these thoughts, no one would pay him any
attention if he actually spoke his mind, and yet he perceives
things that others overlook without understanding, stubborn
impressions, vibrations in the air, when he puts it like that it
seems ridiculous, but he's used to being taken for a fool, he
keeps quiet, he observes. The rising tension. The disappointment that is poisoning Mauro, and the little brother running all
over the place trying to do everything and forget nothing, neither the ewes nor the horses nor the dogs nor the hens, nor the
vegetable garden, nor the house that the older brothers will
soon be attacking, since the money must be there, they should
know she wouldn't hide it in the barn, they'd already searched
there once before. Steban, to be honest, doesn't even know

why he too is hunting for the bag, because he knows full well that if they find it he won't get a thing. He wouldn't know what to do with the money, he would use it unwisely, or so Mauro would say when he confiscates his share. So what's the point, he searches half-heartedly, more a question of moving furniture and items around than impatiently going through them, he doesn't think, doesn't even wonder where the mother might have hidden the money, he just waves his arms around so Mauro won't suspect him of giving up, as they turn the loft in the barn upside down, already sure that the treasure isn't there.

On the third day he has to bandage Rafael: the shears, too big, are giving him blisters on his thumb and middle finger. The little brother had rolled a scrap of cloth around his hand to protect it, but it keeps sliding off and he has to put it back whenever it falls, and spends most of his time struggling with his rag-bound fingers.

Summer ends and departs and they do not really notice, one morning they go out and for the first time they shiver. Steban looks up and realizes the birds have gone, abandoning their nests and refuges, and the twisted branches of the *coihues*. That morning he recalls that since the change of moon the sun has been less kind and the wind hasn't dropped, blowing a chill air day and night, obliging them to turn up their collars and keep the fire going all the time. The brazier went out so they seek shelter by the stove in the house, and Rafael says, smugly: *I told you we'd have to keep the kitchen tidy, otherwise where would we go now?*

For the first time Mauro is consumed with doubt: they've been searching for the treasure for six days now, and they've ended up going through their own bedrooms, you never know, could the mother have been that devious, to hide the money right under their noses, sneaking in soundlessly as they slept, laughing to herself about her despicable scheme. They tore up the floorboards, ripped out the walls. Apart from the kitchen, the house looks as if a tornado had barreled through it, a home ravaged by an insane fury. When he walks through it at night to go back to his bedroom, Steban gazes in silence at the ax-gutted walls, how they open a prospect all the way to the end of the corridor. Boards have been piled here and there, studded with upturned nails, and Mauro punctured his foot on one of them the night before. The little brother looked after him the way he does the ewes, using vinegar, tearing up one of the mother's old shirts for a makeshift bandage.

"I'll have to mix some plants so it won't get infected," he said.

The twin grimaced.

"Yeah, same plants you used for the old man you tried to save?"

The little brother shrugs. *Have it your way.*

He too seems to have given up. He no longer repairs the older brother's destruction, but Steban sees him piling up the cracked boards, pulling out the twisted nails, and he knows he's being patient, it is just a question of time, eventually Mauro will have to admit defeat. In the meantime Rafael is getting better and better at shearing, he comes home in the evening as proud as a peacock and he tells them about his day, in spite of the twin's sarcastic remarks, either he's decided he doesn't care, or else he doesn't hear him through all his own chatter and babble, he's so absorbed by the progress he's made, by his sheep, truth is it doesn't matter if Mauro despises him, and the dogs sit behind him, their ears pricking forward when they hear their names.

In his mute lucidity Steban observes the tired, happy kid, the position he is gradually assuming, not the mother's, obviously, because Mauro wouldn't allow that, but a sort of cheerful omnipresence, he's there ready to give opinions or advice on everything, ignoring the older brother's interruptions, and gradually he wears him down, by keeping up his incessant prattling, exhausting the others with constant chatter. Where did this come from, Steban wonders, shuddering—the mother's death, perhaps, because this mood came over him the day after the funeral, such as it was, there in the orchard, and he feels an icy chill in his veins thinking of the mother's weight upon them, and Mauro who has that same hardness about him, that same coldness, they mustn't let it poison them all over again, the little brother must not stop talking: silently, he encourages him.

May he go on hugging his horse and his dogs. Spreading this strange cheer over the steppe, when, to be honest, there is nothing to be cheerful about, it doesn't matter, it's all to the good, he too would so love to have that happy glow in his eyes when he looks out over the estancia and the plains, and the evening sun. Without the mother there to complain and yell the next day's instructions, these late afternoons when they sit on the stoop outside the house with mugs of maté in their hands could seem infinitely sad, and Steban has to admit that this is the very situation he feared, because he saw it coming; but now there is the little brother's prattling, this vast thing inside him that is surfacing, bursting forth, inexhaustible, it wouldn't take much for Steban himself to be infected with laughter and ready to seize his portion of joyfulness, were it not for Mauro's black eyes reminding him that happiness goes against nature, that it is too ephemeral, and they have no right to it.

He is stark raving mad now, is Mauro, probing the hollows in the roof beams and the abandoned birds' nests stuck in the rafters. Earlier that afternoon he broke the tiles to climb up on the roof, and the little brother protested from below.

"So I can have a better look," the twin shouted back.

"Well, for sure if there's no more roof, we'll all be having a better look."

"So what? What do we care about this house, nothing good ever happened here."

"I care about it."

"Well then. You can fix it."

And he ferrets and roots around, and Steban observes him too; he stayed down in the attic because he felt dizzy, and he shudders at the blaspheming, every time a splinter wedges under the brother's nails and he has to remove it with his teeth. What unbelievable illusion has led him to think the money could be there, rolled up in wads between the slats or wedged in against the shingles, what sort of image of the mother does he have, to think she could climb up and hide the money in such a vulnerable place, just under the roof tiles, all it would take would be a puff of wind or a leak in the old roof. And now he's groping everywhere with his hands, unflinching, careless, like a dormouse scampering along the roof. There's something pathetic, almost moving, about his determination, it's completely futile and he knows it, when fate has decided to turn its back on you, and Steban wonders why the older brother hasn't realized this himself.

From down below it all seems so laughable; the light around Mauro is so dark.

"H-how many more?"

The little brother counts in his head, looking at Steban who is pointing at the ewes, and after a few seconds he says, "Twenty-three."

"Oh. That's . . . that's good."

"Yes. And by the time I finish you two will have torn the house down."

"Now what do we do?"

Rafael spreads his arms in front of the barren, gutted house. A ruin, a real reason for tears, but in the little brother's voice there is none of that, no sorrow, no pity: anger. He turns to the older brother.

"I said, now what?"

Initially Mauro doesn't react, he is dazed, undone by the mother's craftiness, how after all these frenzied days she has bent him to her will, she is a shadow above him, suddenly annihilating him. He doesn't even hear. Steban can sense the bottomless void in his gaze, the absence of any solution, the raving thoughts that surface when there is nothing left, and which the older brother expressed just before: what if the mother got back up on the night of her death, and took the money with her in her coffin to die with it? He was on the verge of going and digging her up again, if he hadn't been so exhausted just then no doubt he would have, his eyes bloodshot, the muscles in his arms throbbing from so much digging and shoveling. There is a sizzling in his brain. Everything is saturated.

And then come the words.

"Pathetic bastard."

And the moment the little brother says it, Mauro's lips curl back over his teeth in a furious grimace, at that very moment Steban knows he was right, seven days, they have lasted seven days, and now the moment has arrived, there's no more postponing it, it's there and it's Rafael who has just announced the end.

RAFAEL

Rafael confronts the tall twin and thinks of these last few days—the shorn sheep, the dismantled house, how the order of things has vanished. He was sure Mauro would not find the money. Of course he had moments of doubt, seeing how the older brother was prepared to dig up the thousands of hectares of the estancia by hand if he had to; but all of a sudden he could sense it was going wrong, and that in the brother's mind everything was getting completely muddled, fatigue and rage combined to bring him to a halt at last, yes, let it be over with, this frenetic quest for money, and then there is Rafael himself with his sheep, too, his one hundred and two ewes that now number only ninety-nine because they took three of them for food, and the third one was well-fattened, to last several days, he chopped it up and put half of it in salt, otherwise what would be the point, to let the meat go off.

And the money they haven't found: so much the better, basically. Because who knows what they would have done if they'd come upon it in the middle of the farmyard, not even well hidden, if they'd come home drunk with exhaustion and anger and just stumbled on the bag, to the point of no longer believing, no longer knowing what to do with it. There has already been so much misfortune since the money first appeared on the estancia. Really, Mauro mustn't find it, he would want to keep the lion's share, because when it comes to sharing . . . don't even think of it. He would steal this treasure with its legacy of blood, and with no remorse, convinced as he is that he deserves it more than the others, that he ought to be the sole heir, and who gives a damn if the mother never earned it in the first place. If it had to cost them their lives, Steban and the little brother, Mauro would not hesitate for one moment. What better opportunity to get rid of the half-wit and the leech, as he sometimes calls him. And maybe Steban would have been in luck, if he'd sworn allegiance forever, becoming a sort of doormat for the old brother to wipe his feet on in the evening, a stooge, less than nothing. But Rafael had been damned from the outset, with the old hatred lingering since his birth, the place he occupied as if he had taken the others' shares, imposing his guilty presence on the mother, who by then was on her own; so the money he brought back was a way of repairing the wrong he had done, however involuntarily, not that he ever could altogether, because nothing could erase those fourteen years of wretchedness, but it might have been a start—yet in the end he's the one who has destroyed everything. As he stands there across from Mauro he can see the vengeance in his eyes, in his silence, his need to find a culprit, and Rafael is the perfect one. Who knows how far the older brother would take him today if he could drag him from his horse at a gallop? Who knows if he wouldn't go and bury him alive next to the mother.

And yet it was happiness Rafael dreamt of when he brought them that leather satchel, a strange happiness for sure, which killed the old man and then the mother, that didn't manage to bring Joaquin back, and now it is dragging the three of them down in its destructive momentum, and there's no telling where it will stop—knock down the house, and then what? Set it on fire? Kill all the animals, one after the other, for no reason, just to destroy this life of poverty? All across the steppe, two thousand sheep with their throats cut. And the cows. And the horses. It seems so long ago, the time when his only thought on getting up in the morning was to saddle Halley and go and count the steers. Years ago, it must be.

Or only a few weeks.

Such a monumental waste, a monumental sacrifice, starting with the mother, the way she rushed to hide the money, even if it meant having to deal with the three of them, all of it for nothing—unless want and deprivation had become a source of tiny pleasure to her, but he finds that hard to believe, like a rodent stashing nuts away all season while slowly starving, has anyone ever seen the likes of it? So the mother went crazy, that's all. And as for her sons, look at how she destroyed them, with their gazes as empty as on the last hour of the last day, when it is all over.

So Rafael says, as if reading Steban's thoughts:

"That's it, huh."

But he's not thinking about the end of the world, because that strange lucidity is the half-wit's alone: he's referring to the shearing, and the race to find the money. That's why he doesn't ask the question. He already knows the answer. And he says it to say something, because Mauro is still digesting the two words he just said: *Pathetic bastard.* And inside he's boiling, digging a deep fire, you can almost see the red in the older brother's eyes, his jaws clenched so tight they could break. All three of them know that the line has been crossed, the line that was drawn in the future seven days ago.

Steban is the first to move. A movement so slight that the little brother is not sure Mauro saw it, Mauro with that crazed expression that hasn't left him and his mouth open in silence, as if he were rehearsing some improbable tirade, as if he had to go deep in his throat for the flames that could burn him alive, or the noose to hang him. And what Steban is commanding in his almost imperceptible blink of the eyes is flight. The herd. Rafael has his back to the pen but he knows that the ninety-nine ewes are there behind him, and he doesn't understand, the sign is too faint, he wants to shout at Steban: "What did you say?"

But there is no time. All of a sudden Mauro turns around and rushes back to the house, slamming the freak surviving door in the midst of the wooden frame, of no use now with the walls destroyed, to go into a room you can step over the wall, and Steban and Rafael see him run behind the beams, stop for only a second, turn around again. Stamping his feet, the half-wit points again to the sheep and screams.

"G-go!"

When he reaches the fence the little brother shouts at the top of his lungs.

"Go do what?"

And suddenly his heart seems to fail him, because he sees Mauro standing framed by the blasted house and there is something on his body like a protuberance, a malformation, a long bone growing, of course he went to get his rifle—and in that very moment Rafael knows that Mauro is going to use it, that this is no longer a time for threats or intimidation, that Steban is shouting in vain to stop him, then falls silent when the weapon slams into his ribs with the twin's roar billowing out onto the plain, and Steban makes himself as small as he can, on his knees, weeping, his hands on his head, as if that could protect him if Mauro fires.

But Mauro couldn't care less about the half-wit. It's Rafael he's after, and he strides toward him bellowing his name, to give him an idea of what is to come:

"Rafael!!"

Even the dogs have come running. In a flash the little brother understands what Steban was trying to say. He jumps over the fence, into the middle of the herd, and crouches down among them, almost invisible. He runs his hands along their spines, hoping to reassure them, the sheep are startled, go back to grazing the short grass, and Rafael encourages them in a hushed voice: *Good girl, fine girl, lovely girl.* He weaves his way through the rough fleece, moving away from the edge, where

Mauro has come, almost running, the hunter thrilling to the prospect of blood, his rifle on his shoulder, his laugh terrifying.

"You think your critters are gonna save you, little shit?"

A second later he fires. A few yards from Rafael a ewe collapses. All around him is panic. The sheep start running, fleeing, they knock him over, bleating as if they were being flayed alive, a terrifying chorus in the dust, and he follows them, bent double, seeking the shelter of a body, a belly, legs, for a few moments, the time it takes Mauro to reload and fire again.

When the second ewe falls the herd has already clustered in a corner of the pen, and for an instant they freeze in fright. They climb on each other in a desperate attempt to get away from the danger, they have formed a huge mass, stumbling together, rolling on the ground, trampling each other, crying pitifully. Rafael, on his knees, looks at the dead ewes, the color on their wool, a brilliant, festive red, spreading, staining. His eyes are wide open, and in spite of his stupor he can feel the stinging tears, the infinite distress of having kept them behind to shear them, taking them unknowingly to the slaughterhouse; if only he had let them go with the others.

But there is no time for his bitter thoughts: Mauro has again taken aim. With the next shot the little brother feels shards of rock pebbling his legs: he clings instinctively to a creature's back and it drags him screaming with the herd to the other side of the pen. He sees Mauro leap over the fence, still laughing, take aim, fell a fourth ewe, then another one is lying on the ground, shaking violently, so Rafael shouts: "You bastard, you could at least hit them good!"

And he cannot tear his gaze from the sheep's convulsions, his ears are ringing with the dying creature's screams, and the screams of ninety-four other sheep clambering on the fence in hopes of an escape, he cannot tell them apart and he puts his hands over his ears not to hear the sound that penetrates and wounds him inside; then he dries his tears and makes another dash.

Mauro is getting closer. Squinting, Rafael gauges he must be twenty yards away, twenty-five at best. The sheep are scattering as if they have understood that the boy is the target, and he scatters with them, trying to stay with those that are still clustering together, this shield of panicked creatures, the clicking of the rifle, yet another one down, two, maybe ten, and the red stains growing on their flanks, their breath stopped, their eyes staring at nothing, straight ahead.

The next shot hits a ewe that is right next to Rafael and throws her against him, he loses his balance and they fall together, he is crushed by her weight, pinned, and he struggles to get out from under, grabbing her with both hands, blood on his arms and seeping through his shirt, for a moment he thinks it's his own blood, and then the ewe tips toward him and he sees her wounds and the life gone, he sits up with a cry, and Mauro is there, a few yards away.

It's crazy how in this moment when he is paralyzed by fear he has time to think of so many things, the mother, the brothers, the horses, the time to tell himself that life is unfair, the older brother with his rifle and he, Rafael, with only a dead sheep to defend himself, he doesn't let go, and when Mauro fires again, he can feel the bullet penetrate the animal's body as he squeezes it against his stomach, right in the front, his shield, his armor. He stumbles again with the shock. He is holding the heavy body with one hand, catches himself with the other, recoils, crawling. Mauro bursts out laughing, walks over to him.

"I'm gonna fill that sheep with loads of little holes! And when there's nothing left but space, the bullet will be for you. Sound good?"

Point-blank. Rafael sees the barrel pointed at him, perhaps six feet away, a barrel that seems to yawn like the gaping mouth of a monster, and for a fraction of a second he thinks Mauro won't do it, not this close, not an execution. In the instant that follows he knows for sure that the older brother will not stop.

This time, the sheep's body thuds against him when the bullet enters, and he wonders if it hasn't gone through, the shock wave shakes him right to his heart, he instinctively gasps for air. Suddenly he can't hear anymore, just a strange buzzing, and the panicked bleating behind him has vanished; he turns his head slightly and it hurts, but the sheep are still there, he can see their mouths open in mute complaint, why don't they cry out, and then he looks again at the ewe he is holding, the blood flowing on his hands and the torn flesh, and still his tears and terror.

And even if it does no good, he lifts the inert body up over his chest, burying his face in the creature's still-warm fleece, like a last caress, they could have been one, and been saved, if life had turned out different, and he will never let go of his sheep, above him Mauro is taking aim, he doesn't want to look, his arms tighten around the animal, he hears only the clicking of the rifle, and the falling of bodies.

It's the dog he sees first when he opens his eyes. How much time has gone by, he couldn't say. It's hard to come back to the world, because his face is swollen; don't move, and his head pounding, it takes him a while, to get used to the light, regain consciousness, somewhat—and that is when the dog appears in his left eye, since the other eye won't open.

Rafael holds out his arm, not far, too painful. Three comes closer.

"No," says Steban's voice, somewhere.

The dog stops, uncertain. Then the little brother moves a finger, just one finger in a sign of prayer, and the dog springs forward, comes to sniff his hand and lick it, and still right up against him, the blood on the dead ewe.

S teban, standing in his stirrups, pats the bay's neck and turns around, giving the younger brother a strange smile, and a nod of his head, while Rafael responds with the same incredulous smile, and a wave, they are both at the threshold of a new world they did not go looking for, the steppe there before them; Halley snorts, Steban opens his palms to the sky.

"So that's it."

"Are you sure that—"

"I'm sure."

And the older boy's voice and his delighted peal of laughter, the timbre gradually returning and the words taking shape since the day before, there's still some way to go, he says, but it's there, he knows it, rasping and joyful, he cannot get enough of uttering and articulating the crazy words that flood out all on their own. Two weeks, he gives himself two weeks to start chattering just like Rafael, and the little brother shrugs and gives a laugh.

"You don't want anything else."

Steban strokes the saddlebags.

"I've got everything I need."

"Well, then."

He says he has taken the big horse, the old man's bay, so that the estancia will be rid of its history. So that every trace will disappear. So they'll have a chance to erase the ugliness of these days of blood, to start over—the little brother at the estancia and Steban riding off toward the cordillera of the Andes, he won't come back, his life isn't here anymore. He feels only the faintest twinge in his guts. Gaucho or shepherd, someone's always in need of one; he's dying to urge the criollo into a gallop, to go faster, to start over in a place where no one has ever called him a half-wit. In a place where his words will come back at last.

The day before, when he ran in turn to get his rifle then came breathless to shoot Mauro in the back, not a second too soon, these were his first words. Erase. And go away.

If anyone asks, the little brother will say that Steban is keeping the herds in the west.

They buried the twin next to the mother, not too close so they won't yell at each other under the ground, but near enough to make it look as if there is only one big grave. No one ever comes to the estancia, of course. But you never know.

They didn't toss in any sprigs of grass, didn't sing. They didn't wait.

Rafael, still dazed from the fight and the slaughter in the pen. Steban quickly covered the grave with earth.

Then he said, "I have to leave."

"They'll never find out you did it," murmurs the little brother, staring straight ahead.

"We can never be sure."

"In any case you don't want to stay."

"That's it."

They are both silent for a long time. Deep inside Rafael feels an extreme weariness; for a start, his aching body, shattered by fear, his muscles still tense as if they had to prepare to flee again; and then this little thing that is sad, but not entirely, this strange impression that things are turning out as they should, and somewhere inside a faint sense of relief is suddenly making its way in, a chink, a breach in the density of all these previous months, with his search and the old man and his strange return, and the days unraveling: it's all over.

"Shall we?" asks Steban.

Ahead of them, the road leading out of the estancia. Rafael gives a quiet laugh.

"Not a race, okay? That'd be cheating, I'm aching all over."

"Okay, sure."

Steban sends the dogs back, a sharp order. They trot back to the house, sit in a row, whimpering plaintively. As soon as they horses have set off at a gallop they'll get up and pace aimlessly at the edge of the terrace, watching the figures heading into the distance, worried and complaining, trotting up to the main fence which they know they have no right to cross on their own.

The two brothers spur their criollos, riding side by side, at a rhythmic, pleasant pace, and Steban looks at the little brother.

"Will you be all right on your own on the estancia?"

Rafael raises his thumb in reply and the older boy nods.

"I'll take on seasonal hands!" says Rafael. "And besides, I'll only be keeping the sheep."

"Don't sell the steers to Ignacio. He's a fucking thief."

"Not a chance."

"You remember what we said about Mauro?"

"That he went west with you. That's all I know."

"That's it."

Steban gives his horse its head, because Rafael has increased the pace; he catches up with Halley and cries, "You just can't help it, can you?"

The little brother snorts and lets the chestnut run flat out, surging into the wind and the dust. In a few strides he has reached the rocky trail, and Steban moves to one side behind him because of the flying pebbles, and clicks his tongue to encourage the bay. The horses are again side by side. For the first time in weeks Rafael lets out a shout of joy, reaches forward to fill his hands with the horse's mane, and leans close to his neck. He does not see his brother taking hold of Halley's bit and raising his arm, hampering the horse so he nearly comes to a halt, and the little brother slips slightly from his forward position while Steban overtakes him and spurs his criollo into the lead, his fist raised.

"*Ay!*" shouts Rafael, catching up with a flick of the reins, driving Halley like a madman. "*Ay! Ay!*"

The chestnut explodes under the saddle, projecting his forelegs as if he wanted to make the road vanish beneath his stride. The little brother weighs nothing on the horse's back, knees spread wide not to hamper his movement; Halley's eyes are riveted on the bay, on his massive rump as they draw closer already. When they pull alongside him Halley finds his own pace, you'd think he's tiring the other horse on purpose, just to keep him shoulder level, eyes rolling into the white and lips curled back, and he drives harder, the big bay criollo has his ears flattened, lengthens his stride, Rafael gives a shout, to be sure Halley keeps up. For a moment they continue at their devilish pace, the brothers laughing, the horses furious, and the trail blurs, vanishes, the little brother can hear the horse's rapid breathing and he wipes from his face the damp splatter from the horse's nostrils, dilated with effort, mouth open on white froth, the sound of hooves resonating into Rafael's guts, shaking him more than he likes.

In the distance the trail vanishes into the steppe.

Rafael straightens imperceptibly, slows. Steban does likewise, calming the bay in turn, he knows it well, the beginning of the plain, its dangerous potholes, its sharp pebbles. Again they gallop abreast, the hoarse breathing of the sweating criollos, necks outstretched, Rafael with one hand on his hat that's too big, to keep it from flying off in a gust of wind.

Gradually he reins Halley in. In any case, they'd have found nothing to say, truth is, might as well avoid the awkwardness for both their sakes. Struggling with his horse, who does not want to yield any ground, he watches as the bay's shoulder pulls a stride ahead, then his flank, then his rump. He knows that Steban understands. The gap grows wider and he slows to a canter while the older brother pulls away into the distance. Halley drops down to a trot, stops at last. They watch. Listen to the sound of hooves on the earth. The vibrations growing fainter, and the dust. The little brother narrows his eyes. Just as he is about to head back in the other direction, Steban turns in the saddle and waves. So he too raises his arm in a sweeping gesture and cries, *Que te vaya bien, Steban, adios!* Of course the older boy can no longer hear him but he shouts anyway, and the shout goes with him, flies over the plain, coils around the wind, and then there is nothing left but silence and emptiness, and when even the dust has settled on the steppe, Rafael lowers his arm, puts his hand on the horse's mane and looks at the estancia behind him, and murmurs:

"Well then. That's it."

At the fence the dogs are waiting for him, long and rawboned, tongues hanging, flanks throbbing wildly from their frenetic chase, and the boy laughs at their distraught expressions. *I wasn't gonna go and leave you.* So they continue on their way at a walk, all five together, the horse, the dogs, the boy, and Rafael counts them as if to convince himself, still five, like before, never mind if they're not the same five, this is his clan, and he repeats it to himself: "Five."

After lunch he rummages in the shed, finds some unbroken tiles, and repairs the roof. Even if daylight is still pouring through the open walls, this gives a reassuring impression of shelter. He nails extra thicknesses of boards together to stop up the holes where the constant wind is getting in, it will be like this until springtime, cold air running over his skin, assailing him the moment he steps outside. So he has to keep it warm inside, stuff rags around the old windows, get ready for winter the way the animals do with their thick fur, their stores of food in nests and burrows, and Rafael feels so close to them, he wishes he could shut himself away and sleep, only the time hasn't come yet, yet, and he hasn't finished.

With the dogs he takes eighty ewes back out onto the steppe, a tiny herd compared to the nineteen hundred head he let go after the mother's death; he has to goad them because the few animals that stayed behind in the pen, that he had neither the time nor the courage to shear, are constantly calling, even though he gave them some fodder to fool them, but the group turns this way and that, hesitates, worries, and Rafael shudders as he thinks of the previous day's carnage, can the ewes still smell the blood on his hands? He doesn't want to touch them, frighten them. During the night he and Steban carved up the fourteen sheep that Mauro had killed, in fine strips, the way the mother used to do them, then thick chunks when they ran out of time, and Rafael said, *Never mind, they'll make good hams.* Because there was too much, they had to use the manger in the stable to store the chunks in layers of salt, and now he lifts the boards protecting them from insects, checks, sniffs, puts the boards down again. It will take him months to eat all that. For now, the smell of meat disgusts him, and he leaves the shed feeling vaguely nauseous.

At home he looks after the dogs, treats a gash Two made in his paw. He tends the fire and brings in a few logs for the night, makes himself a lukewarm coffee and goes to drink it sitting in the doorway, staring into space, then focusing again and again on the empty horizon before him, but Steban has not come back, he never thought he would, anyway. In the spot where he disappeared a few hours ago the sun is slowly setting, infusing the landscape with a light that shows already that it will not last, and the orange plain, flaring with an incandescent glow, is preparing for night, protecting its hares and its birds, causing the wind to drop—an ephemeral respite, although every time, one would like to believe it is eternal.

And the boy says, "Right."

He leaves his mug on the ground and picks up the shovel. Looks at the window of his room behind him. Of course the mother had no idea he wasn't asleep, that night, and that from where he was, he could see her digging under the moon.

Why Mauro was so sure the money was in the house, Rafael has no idea, but that was just what the mother had counted on, it would be the first place they would search, the most obvious, the stupidest—and she'd got it right there too, that they were stupid, that they would go for what was easiest and never think beyond that. And why did he never say anything, he still wonders.

Because they didn't deserve it? Because everything had already been so ruined that if there was one tiny thing to be saved, he would be the one to do it, and no one could say that he had destroyed their life right to the end. Or else he no longer knew, already, was merely content to respect what the mother wanted: for them not to find the money, for hatred and envy to fade with time, dissolve on their own the way sorrow and injury do, that way there could be a new beginning.

The estancia, their life and their grave, he used to say; and now two brothers were gone away and the third freshly buried next to the mother, the estancia trapped them, withheld its riches, drove them out.

Rafael grabs the shovel and starts digging at the foot of the *calafate*. He doesn't have far to go, but he notices that the mother was careful to turn the soil over, cover it with her dried grasses, to make it look normal once she'd buried the treasure.

An invisible hiding place. Perfect, had it not been for his insomnia, the agitation that makes sleep impossible.

Sealed inside a metal chest, there is the bag. Rafael loosens the straps. The bills are intact.

He has sat down outside the house and emptied the satchel out between his knees. He picks up the wads of bills one by one and removes the bands holding them together. Then he takes them in his hands, examines them, the color, the transparency. The smell—there is no smell. He thinks about the sheep in the pasture, the steers he will try to sell next week to Valdo, who has the neighboring estancia, so that he won't have to go into town. Where the wool is concerned he knows the circuit. The sheds are full of fruit, potatoes, and meat. The contented feeling of being ready for winter reassures him.

So again he looks at the bills and slowly, holding his arms up high, he tosses them into the plain, far, as far as he can, slips of paper all around him, as if he were planting them in the steppe. A circular movement he repeats twenty, fifty times, again and again, until there is nothing left in the bag. The wind has dropped but the bills are still there, however, fluttering, as if a magnet were holding them to him. Never mind: he will wait. Wrapped in a blanket he lies down on the ground next to them. He has all night. He knows the gusts will come back at dawn.

Yes, all night: he watches the bills trapped in the short grass, sees them vibrating in puffs of air, moving a few inches as if they were alive, as if they were animals that want to run away and cannot, and sometimes he closes his eyes, half asleep, and when he opens them again the money is still there. The hours are endless. He feels as if he has been lying there for days, and the sun will no longer rise; he feels as if he has slept thousands of times and the money will still never go away. His cheek on the empty leather bag, his eyelids close in spite of himself, while his eyes still struggle to stay open.

The sky turning gray, announcing dawn. It is cold. Rafael pulls the blanket up to his chin.

With daylight the wind rises. Swells, slowly. The boy thinks, *At last.*

The first bill blows away, and of course it is not really the first bill, because they all begin to flutter suddenly, stirred by the air. In the beginning they look like frenetic insects, larvae unable to jettison their cocoons, fidgeting and turning every which way until gradually they break free, and the wind makes a strange noise as it strikes them, like crumpled wings, butter-flies crashing against windowpanes and struggling to fly away again. All at once everything changes: the grass that was restraining them gives way to eddies of air, lets them go, rolls of paper somersault on the ground and on the pebbles, and from his face Rafael wipes the strands of hair that are making it hard to see. One by one the bills escape, mingling in flight with the twigs and dried leaves, and before long it becomes impossible to tell them apart, the leaves and the money, impos-sible to know which ones will blow even further, which ones will soon be torn, caught on thorns in thickets and on the sharp edges of stones, and Rafael, lying on his side, watches as the misfortune he brought evaporates, becomes ephemeral, laughable.

By the time it is fully daylight the bills have disappeared, borne away by the southwest wind, and the boy, freezing in his blanket, blows on his hands to warm them, feeling light and joyful, if that was all it took, but Mauro would never have let him scatter the money this way, and nothing could have turned out any different, not even the mother's madness, Rafael had to keep quiet and let her die, keep quiet and wait for things to happen, even in death and blood, for everything to be erased so that it could go back to how it was before, but before no longer exists, he knows that very well, too.

Far off in the sky, beyond the grayness, the light is reborn, a low-angled glow that does not warm the earth, and a raptor cries; he cannot see it. He pictures the money sweeping along the plains, caught on the *neneos*, drowned in puddles of water; he projects it into the sky, maybe it'll catch up with Steban, and fly so high above him that he doesn't even realize, doesn't understand, and all he'll say is: *What a nasty wind today.*

Now at last Rafael begins to laugh, and the laughter swells inside him and spills over, freeing his throat and his belly, so alive and so bountiful that he shakes the earth, and in the fierce cry he sends out into the world everything begins again and everything is forgotten, from the day the horses ran away, to the evening Mauro beat him up, to the night when he should not have been born—but since what is done is done, he will have to live with it, and he laughs again, lying with his arms spread wide, singing at the top of his voice.

The sun rises on the horizon all at once.

Behind the boy the dogs wait, motionless.

And the boy looks at them, and at the sky, and like the sun he too rises, dusts the dirt from his trousers, gives a stretch, and says, "Right."

ABOUT THE AUTHOR

Sandrine Collette was born in Paris in 1970. She divides her time between Nanterre, where she teaches philosophy and literature, and Burgundy, where she has a horse stud. She is the author of numerous novels. *Nothing but Dust*, winner of the Landerneau Prize for crime fiction, is her English language debut.